FIRE MAGIC

& Ice Cream

CASUAL
MAGIC
BOOK ONE

LAUREN CONNOLLY

FIRE MAGIC & ICE CREAM

LAUREN CONNOLLY

CITY OWL
PRESS

FIRE MAGIC & ICE CREAM
Casual Magic, Book 1

CITY OWL PRESS
www.cityowlpress.com

Cover Design by MiblArt. All stock photos licensed appropriately.

Edited by Yelena Casale.

For information on subsidiary rights, please contact the publisher at info@cityowlpress.com.

Print Edition ISBN: 978-1-64898-149-4

Digital Edition ISBN: 978-1-64898-150-0

Printed in the United States of America

Also by Lauren Connolly

Casual Magic:

Fire Magic & Ice Cream

Earth Magic & Hot Water

***

Forget the Past:

Rescue Me

Read Me

Resist Me

Praise for Lauren Connolly

"Cleverly crafted, sweet and spicy, *Fire Magic & Ice Cream* is wittily written and explores all the emotions! With very imaginative world building, the elementals' that live alongside humans all have certain 'gifts'. Ms. Connolly has crafted a plethora of characters that are unusual, endearing, and full of loyalty." — *InD'tale Magazine*

"If you are looking for a fun, delightful, and super steamy romance that's a quick read, look no further! *Fire Magic & Ice Cream* brings it all in one charming package." — *Kat Turner, author of the Coven Daughters series*

"The relationship between Dash and Paige, in *Rescue Me*, will bring the warm-fuzzies, as both step out of their comfort zones to give it a chance, and boy is their chemistry sizzling. A page turner from start to finish, the reader will be reluctant to put it down!" — *InD'tale Magazine*

"If you're looking for a fun, low stakes, lighthearted, magical, and steamy read for the summer you HAVE to read *Fire Magic & Ice Cream*! This book was so much fun and I breezed right through it. I loved Quinn and how she had to learn to control her magic and the cinnamon roll ice Viking man August who balanced her out. Their chemistry was on point, and the way they navigated their relationship was so adorable." — *E.E. Hornburg, author of the Cursed Queens series*

"*Read Me* is a perfect sunshine-and-grump tale that is an absolutely delightful addition to the Forget the Past series! Readers will feel the gamut of emotions throughout this tale, from laughing out loud to reaching for tissues, and it will be worth every second. If one loves a second-chance-at-doing-life-right tale, this book is definitely one to add to the must-read pile! Unputdownable from start to finish!" — *InD'tale Magazine*

"All of Lauren Connolly's books that I've read this year put a smile on my face. This book was what I needed after a long and hard day. Her books are my mental cinnamon rolls. Thank you for being a 'Dash' of joy in my life." — *Meg Fitz, author of Best Laid Plans*

"Once again, Ms. Connolly has written a tale full of heart, fun, and adorable animals with *Resist Me*. Pig, the adorable rescue pit bull will bring smiles to reader's faces, and the ending will leave one wanting even more! Utterly delightful from start to finish!" — *InD'tale Magazine*

To the romance authors who write fiery women. The Byrne sisters are alive because of you.

Content warning: This book contains sex scenes that involve fire, non-life-threatening injuries, and harassing comments from a stranger.

Prologue

The Gods of the Elements exist in a realm no mortals may enter. They were born of Mother Universe and given control of an adorable little planet called Earth.

Some may say those living on Earth got a raw deal.

Like any big family, the Gods of the Elements host a range of personalities.

Goddess of Earth. *The earth*, not Earth, as her siblings constantly insist on clarifying. All things green that sprout from the dirt are under her dominion. She's the oldest of the bunch, prone to nurturing and mothering her younger siblings. Don't be surprised if you hear her called a bossy bitch on occasion. No need to be offended on her behalf; she wears the title with pride.

Goddess of Iron. If she could dig a hole in the ground and stay there, she would. Commander of all metals and stones, she is an inventor, an artist, and the epitome of an introvert. Everyone's business is their own, so keep the hell out of hers.

God of Water. All the oceans of the world shift and flow under the control of his hand, but why bother with controlling anything when letting loose is so much more fun? If a party is occurring, he is at the center of it, soaking in every ounce of celebration and giving back tenfold.

God of Ice. Master of all things cold and frozen and twin brother to Water, though he doesn't often admit it. Where his brother flows, he stands firm, responsible, structured, and uninterested in shenanigans. In fact, if an outsider had to guess who his twin most likely was, the vote would be for the Goddess of Iron. The two of them might get along, if either took the time to venture out of their comfort zones to invite the other out for a drink.

Deity of Wind. With a flick of their wrist, a tornado could barrel across a town, or a small kite could be lifted into the air. Their emotions are ever changing. They rarely conform to a shape, much less a gender. They are mischievous, always planning pranks meant to knock their elder siblings down a peg or two, but at the same time bring smiles even to the faces of Iron and Ice.

Goddess of Fire. Heat and flames dance to her tune, and she is not one for slow ballads. She is passion, excitement, lust, and fury. As the baby of the family, she learned to make herself heard, even if it meant burning everything to the ground in the process.

No doubt these siblings have tales to tell, but their adventures are not for mortal eyes or ears. Instead, let us meet their offspring. The descendants of the Gods of the Elements.

The Elementals.

Chapter One

QUINN

My body is on fire and not in a good way.

"Door!" I screech, sprinting through the kitchen, my bare feet squeaking on the tiles.

Luckily, Cat doesn't hesitate. She jumps from her stool and whips open the sliding glass door.

I knew there was a reason she was my favorite sister.

The sun beats down, high in the blue Phoenix sky. Anyone else might find the intense rays uncomfortably warm. But most other people don't run around wrapped in a toga of flaming bedsheets.

Fortunately for me, a swimming pool sits a couple of frantic leaps out the back door. The water shimmers, its calm surface cool and inviting.

I wreck the tranquil scene with a self-serving cannonball.

Safely in the water, I hold my breath and stay immersed. The cool, gentle cradle helps soothe my racing pulse and clear my panicked mind. When I can think again, the only thing that keeps me from groaning in mortification is the fact that I would drown myself in the process.

I can only deal with one life-threatening event each day.

My lungs ache, demanding I stop pouting and give them some well-deserved oxygen. With a strong kick of my legs, I break the surface and breathe in deep.

"Hey, Fireball. You have an accident?"

Immediately, I miss the almost meditative silence of being underwater. Harley, my older sister, grins at me from her poolside lounge chair.

I do my best to affect a casual air, which is an impressive feat for someone treading water while clutching the charred remains of a bedsheet to cover her naked body.

"I wouldn't call it an *accident*. Merely a failed experiment," I say.

That does her in. Harley collapses back on the cushions, cackling like an evil villain. I imagine the red-gold curls spiraling down to her shoulders are Medusa's snakes.

As Harley shakes in mirth, the sunlight glistens on her gloriously tanned skin. She's one of those elusive redheads whose melanin decided to work right. The only reason someone might mistake *me* for tan is because I have so many freckles that they blend into a solid brown blur at a distance.

Big sisters suck.

Cat, who followed after my mad dash from the house, settles at the edge of the pool, dipping her feet in and offering me a sympathetic smile.

Baby sisters are much preferred.

Once Harley calms down enough to talk, she gifts me with a smirk. "Guess those flame-retardant sheets didn't work out like you were hoping."

"Not exactly." The blackened edges float wistfully in the water around me.

Not for the first time, I curse the means in which my Elemental gift chose to show itself.

Dad had told the three of us, once we were old enough to understand, that the Byrnes descended from one of the rare family lines who could trace their origins back to the ancient Elemental Gods.

Our ancestor being the Goddess of Fire.

"One day, your powers will reveal themselves."

"When?" Harley, the oldest and most demanding of us, asked.

"I'm not sure. But the magic is normally tied up with a strong emotion. And it

will likely be different for each one of you. None of you need to worry though. I will help you. I'll teach you how to control the fire, like my mother taught me."

Dad kept to his word, helping Harley when she was thirteen and her fear of a rattlesnake ended up setting the whole front yard on fire. And again, when Cat was eleven and her anger melted the tires off the bike of a bully who was mocking her best friend.

Fear. Anger. Those were emotions my dad could incite in them enough to practice. He was mostly successful. I'd say, ninety percent of the time, my sisters were in complete control of their abilities.

But when I was fourteen and the sight of a teenage heartthrob singing about basketball on my TV had the couch underneath me going up in flames, we ran into a problem.

No way in hell was I going to try getting aroused when my dad was anywhere in the vicinity.

I insisted on practicing by myself.

Unfortunately, that meant no one was waiting to douse the heat if it got out of hand.

Fourteen years later, and I'm still setting furniture on fire.

"It's not fair!" My feet settle on the pool floor, my body having floated to the shallow end. "I can't even touch myself unless I'm in the shower."

"You could always hook up with a Squid," Cat supplies, her voice gentle.

If it were Harley who had made the suggestion, I would've snapped back. Instead, I groan in defeat.

"All the Squids are cocky bastards. *You* can barely stand to be around them, and you're one of the most chill people in the world. Last time you ran into one you melted his shoes to the ground."

Cat blushes at the reminder. Most people are shocked when they see a girl so sweet lose her temper. But I love it. She's glorious when she's in a rage.

"I'm not saying talk to them. Just...sleep with one."

The plan might appear good in theory, but reality is often a disappointing bitch. A Squid helped me pop my cherry.

Even in my brain, that sounds gross.

Correction: a Water Elemental was my first. And what a disappointing event that was.

Twenty-two and desperate, I caved. When the guy was finally naked, he spread his arms wide and raised a set of thick eyebrows, as if to say, *You're welcome*. Suffice it to say, I didn't have to battle my fire too badly during that drunken escapade. Whenever a little flame popped up, he'd just douse it with a wave of his fingers.

So I know what a dick feels like inside me, but I would've thought a Water Elemental would be better at getting a girl wet.

A repeat held no appeal, and I was back to practicing on my own.

And failing miserably at it.

"Forget Squids. Quinn runs so hot, she needs an Ice Elemental," Harley declares as she rubs on a generous coating of tanning oil.

I snort in response. "Sure. I'll go out and find one of those. And I bet he'll be riding a unicorn on his way home from tea with Bigfoot."

None of us have ever met a descendant of the God of Ice. Dad said they were rumored to have died off over a century ago. Elementals in general are rare. Phoenix is home to well over a million people, and there are maybe fifty of us magic wielders among that number. Possibly more, but it's not like we put our powers on display. That's a good way to get yourself dissected in some government lab.

No thank you.

We keep our abilities to ourselves and fit in with the humans as best we can.

Harley twirls a curl around her middle finger. "I fucked a guy with big feet. And I'm talking *mythically* large. Plus he had more hair than an entire waxing parlor could handle."

"Are you trying to tell us that you not only met Bigfoot, but that you also slept with him?" Cat asks, flicking water at our big sister.

Harley fiddles her own fingers, evaporating the droplets before they land on her sun-drenched skin. "I'm just saying you never know what's out there. Maybe you need to take a sex pilgrimage north. Search the wild, frozen tundra to find yourself an Icie."

"An Icie?" I tug the mostly disintegrated sheet around my legs as I head for the pool stairs. "Is that what we're calling them?"

At some point, someone made up nicknames for each of the

Elemental descendant groups. Squids, Petal Pushers, Airheads, Stoners, and Pyros. They aren't the most flattering, but we all seem to have embraced them.

Harley shrugs. "Nah. I can think of something better. Give me a minute."

As I climb out of the water, dripping and barely covered by my singed bedding, a rush of jealousy overwhelms me at the sight of Harley, so relaxed and carefree on her lounge chair, and Cat, calm and rational while making gentle waves with her feet. Both of them are able to explore their sexuality, sleep with whoever they want, without worrying that they might barbecue their partners or turn their bedrooms into ashes.

"Why are you here? This is Cat's and my house. Ever think we might like our privacy?" I know I sound spiteful, but I'm strung tight and looking for a fight.

My big sister lies back on her chair with a smug smile. "My apartment doesn't have a pool. Plus, I like to be around when you turn into a fiery comet of lust."

"Why? So you can mock me?"

A flicker of something wicked flashes behind Harley's hazel eyes. "No, though that is a fun bonus." She holds a hand up to stop my angry growl. "I'm here because I know a perfect way to cool you down."

Chapter Two

QUINN

"This is a horrible idea."

I shouldn't have gotten out of the car, but I realized where we were too late. Harley already pressed the button to lock the doors.

"It's my idea, which means it's genius. This is exactly what you need, Fireball." Harley saunters across the steaming parking lot.

With another mighty tug, I try heaving open the car door. My effort is futile.

Cat hovers, dancing from foot to foot. "You told me you wanted to try this place."

Sometimes, I wish my little sister had more evil in her, like Harley. Then I could give her a proper glare for outing my secret longing.

"I said I *wanted* to try it, but that I *can't*. It's too much of a risk."

"Stop being so dramatic. It's not like you're walking into an ammo store, about to set off all the gunpowder," Harley growls at me, already at the front door. "It's an ice cream shop, for goddess's sake."

I know exactly what it is. Land of Ice Cream and Snow. The newest addition to the strip mall where I get my biweekly pedicures. Every time I hobble out of Tulip's Nails with my fresh coat of polish, the acid smell of acrylics clears from my nose, and I get hit with the most delicious scent imaginable.

Waffle cones.

Even though it's torture, I tend to take a roundabout route to my car, just so I can glance in the windows. Not that I ever see much. The interior is dimmer than the blazing Arizona sun.

The easy solution would be to walk into the shop, but I've never done it. Not once.

"I can't go in there!" I lean back on the car, arms crossed.

"Why not?" Harley glares, fists on her hips.

"You know why! The second I step through that door, I'll melt their entire stock. I'm a menace!"

"Oh Quinn. You're not a menace." The distress in Cat's voice almost makes me take the description back. Just to keep from upsetting her.

Harley stalks across the parking lot, coming to stand in front of me. "Listen here, little miss firecracker. You might not be able to control your powers yet, but I can. You start to spark, I'll shut you down. Now get your apple bottom in gear because I'm practically orgasming from the smell of that place, and I'm not about to rush through eating because you're pouting in the car."

We meet scowl for scowl, but I give up first. Probably because this ice cream shop has been taunting me for months.

"You really think you can keep my heat in check?"

My big sister loses her annoyance at my hesitant question, replacing her glower with a saucy grin. "Hell yeah, I can. Could help you out other times, too, if you weren't such a prude."

"Gross! I don't care how kinky your job is. We are *not* that kind of family."

She rolls her eyes. "I'm not asking to be in the room with you like some poorly written porno. I could sit outside your door, read a magazine or something, and make sure you don't burn the house down." Harley tilts her head as she looks me over. "Are you super loud or something?"

"Gah!" I cover my ears and sprint for the front of the shop. "Stay the hell away from me and my sexytimes!"

Through the earmuffs I've created with my hands, I pick up my sisters' laughter. Ignoring them, I take the step I've been holding back from ever since Land of Ice Cream and Snow flipped on their *Open* sign.

I grab the handle and slide in through the front door.

What greets me steals all words from my throat. My nose was already full of sweet scents when I stepped inside, but before my eyes can scan the room, my entire body focuses on the feel of the place.

Cold.

The sensation skitters over my skin, prickling tiny goose bumps and eliciting a shiver.

A shiver.

Shivers and goose bumps aren't for people like me with a constant fire sitting just below the surface of my skin. But here, in this ice cream shop, I experience the sensation of being chilly for the first time in my life.

The bell chiming over my head alerts me to my sisters' arrival.

I whirl around to clutch Harley's shoulders. "This is amazing! I didn't think you could control the fire this much!" I'm so moved that I rise on my toes to press a kiss to her cheek.

She stares at me with eyebrows scrunched together and her lips pursed in a confused smile. "What?"

"Oh my gosh. I've never...this place is so cool!" Cat's exclamation as she dodges around us breaks into my out-of-character thank-you.

Moving past my first experience with the sensation of cold, I finally take in my surroundings. No wonder I was never able to spy much from outside the window.

Most ice cream parlors are all bright colors and delicate furniture. Cute little shops that bring to mind quirky sprinkles or fragile ice sculptures.

Land of Ice Cream and Snow crushes the idea of delicacy under the heel of its heavy boot. This place resembles the homestead of some rugged mountain man or the headquarters of a Viking clan. Solid wooden furniture stretches the length of each wall, and the floor is dark oak. Lights hang from the ceiling, giving off a low glow—small areas of warmth in the stark terrain of the shop. I'm not even sure *shop* is the right word.

More like cabin. A cabin that sells ice cream.

A handful of people sit, talking and eating. I expect, if we came a couple of hours later, after dinnertime, this place would be overrun with sugar-hungry customers. A granite slab serves as a counter in the back of the shop, next to it the one familiar item all ice cream parlors possess—a glass container to view the offered flavors.

I take a single step before realizing the danger behind the counter.

A man.

But not just a man. This man is...well...a *man*.

I think I've found the Viking who pillaged and plundered and built this cabin of a shop with his bare hands. A black T-shirt stretches over shoulders wide enough for me to perch on one side and Cat on the other. His strong, ivory face belongs in a superhero movie. Sculpted cheekbones, square jaw, and enough golden stubble to leave a delicious burn on the inside of my thighs.

Oh shit.

The wonderful cold sensation drifts away as my inner fire senses a rising lust. Heat trails just underneath my skin, pulsing with a life of its own.

"I was right. This is a horrible idea."

But as I turn back toward the door, Harley wraps an arm around my waist. To onlookers, the embrace probably appears friendly and innocent. But in truth, her hold is stronger than steel as she drags me to my doom.

"Focus on the ice cream. Ignore the beautiful man."

"Ignore him? By gouging out my eyes?" I mutter, fighting an onslaught of lust and panic.

The ice cream god steps forward, his frosty gaze locked on the three of us. I watch with fascination as he slips a blue apron, the same shade of his eyes, over his head. The muscles in his biceps flex as he reaches to tie the strings behind his back.

At the display of his glorious muscles, I brace myself for another surge of heat. Instead, my fire remains stoked. The embers are there, teasing me, but they don't burst forth, causing mass chaos.

I guess Harley is as good as her word.

"How can I help you?" The ice cream god's words rumble out like tires across gravel as he watches us.

Not us, I realize. *Me.*

Being the middle child, I've often silently longed for a little bit more attention. But right now, I'm considering hiding behind my curvy older sister or picking up Cat to use as a human shield. All in the name of self-preservation.

As if sensing my cowardly plans, Harley gives me a shove forward, so I end up stumbling into the granite counter. My hands land flat on the surface to steady myself.

Cold shocks through my palms, racing over my skin, practically extinguishing my fire, if not my lust. To my utter embarrassment, my nipples tighten with a shiver, and my bralette does nothing to hide the reaction.

When ice cream god's eyes drop to my chest, I'm torn between crossing my arms over my boobs and attempting another escape or ripping my shirt off and asking if he has a bed in the back room.

I settle on the happy medium of staring up at his gorgeous face and losing the ability to form a coherent sentence.

Maybe, if he were a creepy perv, I'd be able to collect myself. Unfortunately, ice cream god almost immediately removes his stare from my overly excited nipples to look me in the eye again.

"Do you know what flavor you'd like?"

I begin to thaw with a shake of my head. The Viking man turns his back. Steady again, I drag my hands off the frigid counter, rubbing my palms on the sides of my jean shorts.

Not that I mind the cold. In fact, I find the sensation fascinating.

I'm never cold. I was beginning to think I'd have to be dropped in glacial waters or launched into space to truly experience such a low temperature.

But apparently, I just needed my big sister to crave ice cream. Despite her borderline bitchiness earlier, I throw a grateful smile over my shoulder.

In classic Harley fashion, she pokes me in the back. "Stop ogling the man candy and figure out what you want."

Feeling less generous, I stick my tongue out at her and then glance forward, attempting to kick my brain into gear so I can remember what flavors I like.

But I'm thrown off track again when I find a mini wooden spoon in my face.

"Flavor of the day: blueberry pie." Grumbly voiced ice cream god holds out the offering.

On pure instinct, I reach for the spoon. The tip of my finger brushes the edge of his thumb.

At the brief contact with the gorgeous man, I fully expect the utensil to burst into flames, forcing me to pretend I'm a street magician and my sisters are my camera crew and that everything has a weird but still plausible explanation.

But instead of heat, there's another trickle of coolness.

Harley is going to be exhausted after tamping me down. She'll probably pass out in the car on the way home.

Ice cream god continues to watch me, and I realize I'm just standing, holding the sample, and staring at his expansive chest. To my amazement, the sample hasn't melted. However it's headed in that direction with one and then two drips falling from the spoon onto the counter.

Desperate not to reveal my detrimental effect on frozen treats, I shove the flavor of the day into my mouth.

When I smelled waffle cones outside the shop, I kept my composure. When I set sights on the mountain of sexy behind the counter, I had a brief internal freak-out, but overall, I held it together. When cold visited my nerve endings for the first time, I kept my reactions on lock.

But this? It's too much.

"Oh, fuck me," I groan, not caring if there are children around, being corrupted by my involuntary reaction. In my opinion, no one under eighteen should be allowed in this shop. This ice cream is too sinful for young innocents.

I want to fashion a man out of this ice cream, marry him, and then devour him for as long as we both shall live.

The Viking ice cream man clears his throat in a glorious deep rumble as he crosses his arms over his chest, all the while watching me. The pressure of his eyes sits cool and heavy like the chilled treat currently melting on my tongue.

Would he taste just as delicious?

Chapter Three

AUGUST

"Oh, fuck me," she moans.

Yes, I want to say. *Anytime, anywhere.*

The gorgeous redhead gazes up at me as if I'm somehow fascinating to her.

Little does she know, I've caught myself staring at her multiple times before this. Every other Tuesday. Maybe it's pathetic that I know her schedule, but she's the one who keeps showing up at the same time, staring in the tinted front window of my shop with an adorable pout.

The last few times, I've been halfway around the counter, ready to open the door and invite her in. But she always disappears before I get the chance.

Not today though.

Today, my mystery girl was dragged into the shop by two other women. The three of them show off how beauty can come in many shapes. The curly haired one has an Amazon's height, soft curves, and an energy that fills the room. Her opposite stands a few paces behind, pixie-short hair and small all around with a shy smile. But it's only the woman in front of me, average height with a hint of an hourglass figure, who holds my attention.

First, my eyes catch on her complexion. The riot of freckles covering her face is a rare treat. Like I took powdered cocoa and sifted it over pale cream. That, paired with her flaming hair, draws me in, tempting me.

The image could've been enough, but her touch has my blood pounding in my ears.

Warm. The heat of her skin still tingles in the tip of my thumb where it brushed hers.

My life is constant cold and ice, but she's all heat.

And I'm staring.

I clear my throat again, which I seem to have to do a lot around this woman. "So, the special then?"

She blinks up at me and then gives a slow shake of her head.

"You didn't like it?" From the lusty tone she used, I thought my new creation might be a success.

"I did..." She trails off, flicking her eyes toward the glass container where the rest of my daily flavors are housed.

"I am about to light a literal fire under your ass, Quinn. Stop undressing the man with your eyes and tell him what flavor you want." This from the taller of the woman's companions.

Quinn. I like it. Odd but not completely out of the ordinary.

"Asshole," Quinn mutters just loud enough for me to hear, and that's when I realize her pale skin has turned remarkably rosy. But instead of ducking her head and skittering away in embarrassment, she meets my stare with a newly determined air. "I'd like chocolate."

"Plain?" Disappointment trickles through me. Not that chocolate isn't delicious, especially *my* chocolate. It's just that I've spent time crafting creative flavors. I want her to try something I made. I want to hear her mutter more expletives when she samples my hard work.

Again, Quinn shakes her head. "No. I'd like more to it. Just...could chocolate be a component?"

The way she asks, as if I'm the final word on the matter, swells pride in my chest. Not many people appreciate the amount of effort I put into my craft. This woman allowing me to choose for her is like deferring to a sommelier about a wine selection at a restaurant. Leave the choice up to the person with the best palate.

"I have a raspberry and dark chocolate."

"Yes. That. Please." Quinn leans forward, her hands on the counter, almost as if she expects me to be hiding the treat behind my back.

I can't help grinning at her eagerness. "In a cone?"

The smile that started to form on her soft mouth dims. "I probably shouldn't. I'll just make a mess of it." Though her words say no, her eyes rest on the stack of waffle cones I have ready, next to less exciting cups.

Again, I take the lead. "So what? With something as good as this, it's okay to get a little sticky."

Her face flushes red again, and I can guess the dirty place her mind went. At least, I know where mine is.

Before she talks herself out of it, I grab a cone and fill it with two generous scoops. As I pass the dessert over, I intentionally brush her hot skin, savoring the searing sensation.

If I had my way, I'd just lean on the counter and enjoy the sight of her licking my cone.

I mean, the ice cream cone.

Although, if she offered to lick my cone, I'd usher everyone out of the shop and close down for the day. No doubt in my mind that Quinn's mouth would be worth it.

Instead, I let the sight of her go, shifting my focus to her companions. Caramel peanut butter swirl for the taller and strawberry cheesecake for the shorter. Both of them are attractive in their own right, but my eyes continue to wander back to Quinn.

And what a sight she makes. She wasn't exaggerating when she said she was worried about getting messy. Despite her eager licks, drips of raspberry and chocolate escape the edge of the cone to trail over her hand to her wrist. Catching sight of the sweet streams, she ventures further with her tongue, lapping up the little spills.

I've never seen anything more erotic than Quinn licking melted ice cream off her skin. Momentarily, I consider if it would be weird for me to offer to help.

Yeah, that would definitely be weird.

What if I asked her to suck it off me instead?

Nope. Still weird. Don't do that.

Instead, I act like a rational person and grab a handful of napkins, walking out from behind the counter to offer them to her.

Her plump lips tilt in a self-deprecating smirk. "Told you I'd make a mess." She accepts one of the napkins, wrapping it around the base of the cone. "But it's no use. I run hot."

My brain briefly short-circuits, all thoughts flickering out, except for the single image of her fiery body pressed tight against mine.

"How much do we owe you?" one of the other women asks. I think the tall one, but I'd have to stop staring at Quinn to find out.

And what's more, to give her an answer, I'd need to attempt some sort of math, which my mind isn't capable of handling at the moment. So with what little brainpower I have remaining, I manage to mutter a single phrase, "On the house."

Most of the population would be overjoyed or at least mildly excited to find out they're getting something without having to pay.

Quinn, apparently, exists in the minority.

She glares up at me, all traces of embarrassment gone. "That's ridiculous. If you want to run a successful business, you can't just give your product away for free."

I stifle a smile, instead peering down at her like I'm mildly curious. "Isn't that what everyone does?"

Quinn rolls her hazel eyes, and I catch a glint of golden flecks in her irises. "Don't be an ass..." She peers at my chest, as if searching for something. "What's your name?"

Ah, name tag. Guess I forgot to pin mine on in my hurry to serve them. Normally, I'm not the one working the front counter, but since it got slow, I gave Marisol a break.

"August."

"August." She doesn't say anything else for a minute but then shakes her head. "Don't be an ass, August. If you give ice cream away all willy-nilly, you'll eventually go out of business. And where would that leave us?" Quinn throws out a hand to encompass her companions, who are standing back a few steps, watching the two of us with interested expressions. "Ice cream–less! Sans ice cream!"

I choose not to point out that Phoenix has plenty of other ice cream shops. I don't want Quinn to cover herself in melted ice cream anywhere else.

Still, I continue playing devil's advocate. "It's a marketing technique.

Giving people a free cone every so often establishes a rapport. Makes them want to come back again."

I want *her* to come back again.

Quinn glares at me as she drags her tongue over the back of her hand where another stray drip of raspberry has escaped.

Suddenly, my pants feel tight, and I consider ducking back behind the counter to obscure anything happening from my waist down.

"If it's marketing, then where is your advertising? And what exactly is the deal? How does it work out that me and my sisters get free ice cream?"

Her sisters—that makes sense.

"Redhead Day." I'm pulling this out of my ass, but each time I don't agree with her, a flare of heat stains the tops of her cheeks. I can't seem to stop myself.

"Redhead Day," she growls.

I nod and double down. "Redhead Day. Redheads get free ice cream."

The shorter of her sisters giggles behind her hand, eyes dancing as she watches us. The older one smirks and throws me a wink that seems more conspiratorial than suggestive.

"That's ridiculous. I refuse. Harley, pay the man." Quinn looks to the taller of the two.

Harley shakes her head and gives a dramatic lick of her cone. "It's Redhead Day."

An adorable scowl wrinkles the freckled space in between Quinn's brows. "Bullshit! I call bullshit!" She stalks away from me, up to the counter, rummaging around in the back pocket of her shorts.

The jean material hugs a tight, round ass, and I'm sure each cheek would be a lovely handful. As I openly stare, she slides her fingers back out, clutching a twenty. Before I can stop her, Quinn leans far over the counter, reaching out to place the bill on top of the cash register, all the while balancing her still-dripping cone in the other hand.

I press a fist into my mouth, barely stifling a groan. The sight of her like that—bent over the counter, ass in the air, toned legs spread wide enough to maintain her balance—is practically pornographic. My mind memorizes the image, storing it away for later, probably for tonight when I'm alone in my bed.

"There. Service provided and payment given. Fair exchange."

Harley snorts, and the small sister grimaces my way. "Sorry, she can't help it. Quinn's an accountant."

An *accountant*? The word brings to mind a guy with sensible glasses, a starched white button-up, and a calculator. Not a gorgeously freckled, flaming-haired beauty dressed in denim cutoffs and a thin white T-shirt that does little to hide the lacy bra she's wearing underneath.

Quinn stands up from the counter, returning to licking her treat as she takes a step toward the door.

I scratch the stubble on my chin as I search for some way to keep her from walking out of my shop and never coming back.

"If you're so concerned with my profits, maybe you could take a look at my books."

My tossed-out comment gets her attention.

"Some of us don't work for free." Quinn trails her eyes over my body, her gaze heavy as a physical caress.

Delicious chills skitter over my skin, like the hint of snow beginning to fall.

"I wouldn't expect you to. I'm talking about hiring you."

An eyebrow curves high on her forehead. "You don't know me."

Stepping in close, I cross my arms over my chest to keep from reaching for her. "We can change that."

Quinn considers me, licking her cone all the while.

Why am I asking to hire her when what I really want is to fuck her?

A visible shiver quivers through her, and I remember why.

Women like Quinn aren't for me. I can look, but I can't touch.

Again, she reaches her clean hand into her pocket, this time one of the front ones. But instead of pulling out money, she comes up with a black business card.

"All right then, Mr. August. When you're ready to start taking your finances seriously, call me."

I pluck the card from her grasp, denying myself another brush of her skin.

Quinn saunters out of the shop, her sisters on her heels. The smaller one offers a friendly wave over her shoulder, and Harley gives me a thumbs-up, both gestures happening behind their sister's back.

Seems I have a couple of allies.

Once all three are gone, I study the card.

Quinn Byrne

Freelance Accountant

Then her contact information. I should rip the card up and toss it in the trash. Keep the memory of this exchange but not hope for anything more.

Problem is, the card burns hot in my hand, and for someone who lives a life as cold as mine, I can't find it in me to give up even a hint of heat.

Chapter Four

AUGUST

"I swear, Damien promised to pick me up. Next time, I'll just take his car. I'm so sorry."

"Stop apologizing, Marisol. It's no big deal."

I throw a reassuring smile toward the passenger seat, attempting to soothe my employee. She gives me a doe-eyed smile and fiddles with one of her loose black curls.

Damien warned me his sister could get a little dramatic at times, but I figure everything has an added importance when you're sixteen. Plus, he's the one who flaked on giving her a ride home at the end of her shift.

Luckily, I scheduled her through closing, so we both finished working at the same time.

The house Marisol lives in with her older brother is only a fifteen-minute drive from my shop, and when we turn onto their street, I catch sight of a few extra cars pulled into their driveway and parked along the sidewalk.

Glancing over, I receive an eye roll from Marisol.

"Game day," she mutters, as if annoyed, but I catch an excited glimmer in her eye.

I park behind a blue Subaru and shut down the engine.

"You're coming inside?" Marisol's voice has developed a high-pitched quality to it. Almost like she's nervous.

"Yeah. Thought I'd say hi to everyone. And maybe watch the game."

She tilts her head. "Do you even know what sport they're watching?"

I rack my brain. "Uh...football?"

Marisol giggles and shakes her head, a riot of curls bouncing around her face. I'm not surprised Damien has been complaining about random guys showing up, expecting to take his little sister out on a date. She's a cutie.

"It's soccer." Her humor dims as she nibbles on her lip. "They'll probably all be too distracted to talk."

I shrug. "Still, I'll walk you in."

Her copper skin goes dark with a blush before she scuttles out of the car.

As we navigate the rocky yard, loud shouts echo from inside the low-roofed stucco house. The dramatic difference in architecture between homes in Phoenix and Alaska, where I left a little less than a year ago, still fascinates me.

Different climates, different needs.

Marisol pulls open the front door, charging in ahead of me. Off to the right is a room full to the bursting with men and women vibrating energy, attention focused on a huge flat screen mounted to the wall.

"I'm home!" Marisol calls out, walking past the crowd.

Damien, dark hair flopping over his eyes, pops up from his chair, confusion wrinkling his thick brows. "Sis?" He weaves through the spectators. "How'd you get home? You were supposed to text me when your shift was over."

Her blush returns full force as she backs toward the hallway that leads to her bedroom. "I did. You didn't answer, so August gave me a ride."

Damien catches sight of me then, sending a nod my way before focusing back on his sister. He slides his phone from his back pocket, swiping his thumb across the screen. "I don't have any texts from you."

Marisol throws up her hands with a theatrical flourish that comes naturally to a teenage girl. "So it's my fault you have a crappy phone? Sounds like *you're* the one with a problem. And I don't appreciate getting interrogated the second I walk in the door!" She twirls on her heel and storms away from us.

A door slams, and Damien snorts as he turns to face me. "That little sneak didn't text me."

I scratch my jaw. "You sure? She seemed pretty embarrassed when she had to ask me for a ride."

Damien scoffs and waves for me to follow him into the kitchen.

The house isn't huge; it's a comfortable size for two people even if one of them is a teenager. Damien does well for himself, selling real estate around Phoenix, but I'm more impressed that he's basically become a father for Marisol. A few years ago, their parents decided they were tired of staying in one city and left to travel the world. I don't know if Marisol was invited to go with them, but either way, she moved in with Damien. Now he's the one who makes sure she is safe, is fed, and shows up at school come fall.

He pops the top off a beer and hands it to me. "She's gotten the lead in the school play twice now. Probably get a scholarship to some art school—her acting chops are that good. But she knows I see right through her." Damien opens a fresh beer for himself, clinks the neck of his bottle to mine, and downs half of it in one swallow.

"What do you see then?" I sip mine at a more sedate pace.

"She's got a crush on you."

Good thing I wasn't gulping my drink down like him or else I would've spat a lot more out when I choked. The spray should've coated Damien, but he's too fast. With a wave of his hand, the droplets halt midair. The liquid hangs there, glittering golden in the kitchen light, until another dismissive gesture sends the wasted beer into the sink.

Water Elementals only get wet if they want to.

When I'm done coughing beer out of my throat, I glare at my friend. "Stop being ridiculous."

Damien smirks as my cousin, Sammy, saunters into the room. Well, technically, Sammy is my second cousin, but growing up as an only child, I'll take any family I can get.

"What's this goldfish trying to sell you, Auggie?" Sammy pulls open the fridge to grab a beer for himself.

If there's one thing that can be relied upon, it's that Damien always has a fully stocked fridge.

"Nothing," I mutter, too embarrassed by the idea of what he just said to repeat it.

But Damien, I'm starting to discover, tends toward brutal honesty. "Just pointing out that my sister's in love with his icy ass."

I expect Sammy to laugh and deny the claim.

Instead, my cousin nods. "Oh, yeah. She's got it bad for you."

"Shut up." To think I moved here because I wanted to see what it was like to have siblings. Didn't realize I'd have to deal with this much immaturity.

The two of them laugh at my expense.

I take revenge the only way I know how. When they go to take swallows from their bottles, I let go of some of my pent-up energy from earlier. The power prickles over my skin, just a light touch but enough to chill the air around me. With an extra bit of concentration, I'm able to direct the icy force into a focused shot. Specifically, two focused shots.

"What the fuck?" Sammy tries to take a drink multiple times, shaking the bottle as if that'll help the beer flow.

Damien peers into his, only to come up glaring at me. "Not cool, man."

Now I'm the one smirking. I take a sip of my delicious, non-frozen beer. Since I'm the only Ice Elemental in the room, I now have full control over their alcohol. Makes me glad my human grandpa fell for my grandma, a woman from the God of Ice's line. Gramps's sister married a man from the God of Water's line, which is how I ended up with Sammy in my family tree. I guess the two humans both wanted some magic in their love lives.

"Fucking icicle up your ass," my cousin scoffs.

"Careful," I warn. "There's a lot more beer in the fridge that could use a super freeze."

Damien stares at me, horror on his face. "You wouldn't."

"I might. Or I might be nice and unfreeze your beers if you both stop talking about inappropriate teenage crushes. And if you answer a question for me."

Sammy nods readily, expectantly holding his drink out. Damien tilts his head, reminding me of his sister, but then relents with a begrudging nod.

I pull the frost back, leaving just enough to ensure their beers are chilled. Because I'm nice like that.

"So what's this question, Auggie?" My cousin uses the nickname to annoy me, but I kind of like it. Mainly because I've never had anyone around willing to nickname me when I was growing up, other than my parents.

"You've both been with humans, right? Slept with them?"

The two men share a confused look before returning their attention to me.

"You mean, like, this week?" Sammy asks.

"Are you asking for an exact number? 'Cause that's going to take me a minute." Damien starts mouthing names to himself as he holds up fingers, counting them off.

"No, for fuck's sake. I just meant...hell, never mind." I drag a hand through my hair as I swallow a hefty gulp of beer, trying to calm the simmer of lust in my chest that appeared this afternoon.

"Are you saying you've never had sex with a human before?" Sammy stares at me as if I just told him I was dying of an incurable illness.

"I have, but it's never...ended well." Standing in the kitchen with two men who have likely slept with more women than I've met in my life, the few sexual experiences I've had suddenly seem even less noteworthy.

"What do you mean?" Damien at least keeps a neutral tone, holding off on the outright mockery.

"My powers are arousal-induced."

They both wince simultaneously, and I know for sure I'm not going to find a kindred spirit in either of them.

"That's some bad luck, man." Sammy taps his beer against mine. "What happens exactly? You get off and start shooting frozen cum?"

Damien snorts into his beer, and I glare at my cousin.

Absolutely no filter.

"No, thank the gods. I just get cold—like arctic cold—and spend most of the time worried I'm going to hurt them."

Sex is supposed to be hot and heavy, leaving people sweating.

I leave them shivering.

"You just need more practice. I used to flood a room when I got pissed off. Now the air barely feels humid. It's all about control." Damien grips my shoulder, grinning up at me with an apology in his eyes.

"You met someone?" Sammy tosses his empty bottle in the recycling bin and opens the fridge for another. The guy drinks like a fish. Or like a Squid.

"A woman came into the shop today. She was..." I trail off, not sure exactly how to describe Quinn.

At first, I thought she was shy, blinking up at me without words, clearly dragged into my shop by her sisters. But then sparks flared from her, and eventually, she roared to life with a glare and a tongue-lashing.

Fire. She was pure fire.

And I want to burn.

"That hot, huh?"

My cousin's comment brings me back to the present, and I shrug, trying not to give away how much the brief interaction rocked me.

"And you're worried she can't handle you in bed?" Damien smirks at me.

I scowl, mainly because he's right.

"The way I see it, you've got two choices. Get some practice under your belt until this isn't a problem anymore, or"—Sammy gives me an evil grin—"live a celibate life in tribute to the gods."

My eyes roll on their own, and I down another frosty swallow of beer while I finger the business card in my pocket.

Hours later, the paper still radiates warmth.

Chapter Five

QUINN

I am as cool as a winter breeze. As chilly as a mountain stream. As cold as the bottom of an iceberg.

Try as I might, the visualizing is hard to take seriously as I sit in my hot car under the intense midday sun. If only I could have grabbed the shady spot off in the far corner of the strip mall parking lot. But someone beat me to it, and the rest of the blacktop is a preheating oven.

Not that the heat is uncomfortable. Normally, I revel in it, letting the hundred-degree temperature feed the fire that is an innate part of my physical makeup.

But today is different. In a matter of minutes, when I work up the courage, I'm going to come face-to-face with the sexy ice cream god. This time, without my big sister backing me up to keep my fire at bay.

It's all up to me. Hence, the cold-focused meditation.

Maybe thinking of cold things isn't the right tactic.

He's nowhere near as attractive as you remember. Way too muscly. Probably spends all his free time at the gym, lifting and then taking pictures of himself in the mirror. And I bet he doesn't even like ice cream. He thinks the fat content is too high and would ruin his meticulously crafted washboard abs.

August is a self-obsessed meathead who hates dessert.

I silently repeat that last sentence like a mantra as I enter Land of Ice Cream and Snow.

Just before noon on a Wednesday, I'm surprised at how crowded the shop is. Every one of the heavy wooden booths is full, and the long table that looks straight out of a Viking's headquarters has a happy group of children squished onto the benches.

Despite the large amount of people, the place still holds on to a delicious chill. The fact that I can feel that cold is surprising enough to ease a bit of the tension from my shoulders.

My meditation seems to be working.

When August e-mailed about hiring me, we had a handful of completely professional back-and-forth correspondences. I felt sure he took my offer seriously when he asked for a list of my references. Proud of all the work I'd done in the past, I had no issue with handing over a list of names and numbers. Two days later, he responded with an enthusiastic request for my services.

Unfortunately, neither one of us clarified where I should meet him when I arrived, and he's nowhere in sight. Instead, a young girl is working behind the counter today. Playing it safe, I move to stand in line. After sampling the ice cream offered here, I wouldn't put it past someone to shank me if they thought I was cutting to the front.

"What can I get for you?" Her name tag reads *Marisol*, and her smile plumps up a cute set of cheeks.

"I have an appointment with August Nord. Do you know where I might find him?" I learned his last name during our e-mail exchange.

The girl's smile falters, and she drags her eyes over me.

I wonder what thoughts flit through her suddenly guarded brown eyes.

Today, I dressed for work, choosing my favorite red pantsuit and pairing it with a set of black suede heels. I opted for glasses over contacts, loving my *I'm a fucking professional, so deal with it* crimson frames.

Sometimes, women with red hair prefer to downplay the shade by wearing more muted colors. I, on the other hand, opt to embrace and amplify it.

Maybe this is why I still have trouble with starting random fires...

"Who are you?" the worker asks.

I can't tell if her tone is rude or not, but it's a valid question.

"I'm Quinn Byrne. The accountant he hired."

Some of the stoniness leaves her eyes, but her friendly smile doesn't make a reappearance.

"I'll let him know you're here." She whirls around and heads for a doorway that leads to the back of the shop.

A moment later, she returns on the heels of a man who is somehow *more* attractive than I remembered. Unfortunately, he's the perfect amount of muscle, and he has on an ice cream–stained apron.

Damn him.

Heat flutters under my skin, and I shove my hands in my pockets, praying to the goddess I don't melt every frozen treat in the shop.

"Quinn," he says my name with a smile that increases my heat, but surprisingly, the fire remains manageable.

Maybe I am getting better at this.

"Mr. Nord." I keep my expression cordial and my tone professional. Just because I'm not burning his shop to the ground doesn't mean I should tempt the fates.

We are business associates, and that's it.

August runs his eyes over my form, much like his employee did a minute ago. Only her gaze did not have the same hunger as his.

I shiver.

His mouth flattens as he clears his throat. "I have everything set up in my office, if you'll follow me."

I do as he directs, moving with him toward another doorway that opens to a short hallway.

"There's the restroom, if you need to use it today." He nods to a half-open door, and we pass by another with a sign reading *Supplies*. August turns the knob of the last door, opening it and standing back so that I can enter first.

The space is simple and cozy, much like the front of his shop. A computer monitor sits on a dark wooden desk, surrounded by neatly stacked papers and folders. Behind the desk is a large corkboard, notes pinned all over the thing. Taking a step closer, I realize the wall is covered in handwritten recipes.

I've entered August's creative space.

Mr. Nord, I silently correct myself. Need to stop thinking of him as anything other than a client.

"Will this work for you, Ms. Byrne?"

His switch to using my last name should set me at ease. Instead, annoyance sparks along my nerves.

I like the way he says my first name. I like it too much.

His imposing presence pushes on my senses, and I can't help turning to face him. The deliciously sexy ice cream shop owner hovers next to a table in the corner of the office. A cushy chair is pulled up to the workspace, and more stacks of papers sit in organized piles on the surface.

"Everything you said you would need."

Everything and more. In addition to the financial documents I instructed him to have ready, August—I mean, Mr. Nord—has arranged the perfect little area, with extra pencils, Post-it notes, a calculator, and even a laptop.

I have my own computer and supplies in my bag, but still, the gesture is sweet.

I mean, professional. A very professional gesture.

"This all looks good."

"Do you want me to stick around to answer any questions you have?"

I glance up, meeting his striking blue eyes. The icy color looks so refreshing, like an arctic ocean I want to dive into.

Dangerous heat pools under my skin.

"No." The word comes out harsher than I meant. I clear my throat, set down my bag, and glance back at him with what I hope is a pleasant but distant smile. "I'd rather focus on the numbers. Just the numbers. They often paint a clearer picture than people do."

Plus, numbers don't turn me on. Math has always come easy to me, and I enjoy it in the same way I enjoy brushing my teeth. No fire in my panties when I work through a particularly difficult equation. Just a sense of a job well done.

August—

Goddess-damn it!

Mr. Nord gives me a tight smile and a nod. Then he leaves me alone to work. And for a little while, I can breathe again.

I fall into a familiar rhythm, creating my own spreadsheets of his profits and spending, making sure all the values add up the same. The hours pass as I pore over receipts and invoices. My focus is only broken twice. Once when Aug—Mr. Nord quietly enters the room to set a cup of steaming coffee down next to me, leaving a bowl with creamer and sugar beside it before he exits without saying a word. The second time, he returns, holding a plastic bag.

"Ham, turkey, or veggie?" he murmurs, as if speaking too loudly will destroy all the work I've done.

I push my glasses back up my nose and glance at the clock on the wall. Six hours have passed without me realizing. As if my stomach arrives at the conclusion at the same moment, it lets out an unhappy growl.

"Turkey, please." For some reason, I speak just as quietly as he did and accept my dinner with a nod of thanks.

August retreats from the office, and I hate to admit how much I wish he'd stayed. But it's better he didn't. After pulling my hair up into a messy bun, I eat one-handed, eyes returning to my screen.

When I finally finish, my spine is launching a full-scale protest at its mistreatment. I stand and bend backward, reveling in the satisfying cracks that ring out from my vertebrae.

Despite the aches in my joints, I'm in a good mood. Land of Ice Cream and Snow is performing surprisingly well for a new business. Technically, Mr. Nord is still in the red, but that's to be expected with the store being less than a year old. The amazing part is that it appears he's approaching the much-preferred black quicker than most small shops would be. Not long until he's returning a true profit.

People in Phoenix love their ice cream.

From the meticulous way he's kept his finances, I doubt my conclusion will come as a big surprise. Still, I'm eager to share the good news. Or reinforce it.

I search for the clock again and stifle a gasp.

Ten p.m.?

I don't always keep normal business hours, with most of my work involving freelancing, but still. This is late, even for me.

I wander out of the office, up to the front of the store, only to find the shop closed.

Did he forget I was here?

But then I notice light shining from the back room. Following the glow, I discover where the delicious product is made.

The kitchen is pristine, big, shiny silver equipment filling the place. A mixture of decadent smells saturates the air, and my stomach alerts me that dinner was hours ago.

I find Aug—Mr. Nord at the very back, leaning over a tall worktable covered in ingredients, scribbling in a notebook. A black apron hugs his solid form, and I can't help focusing on the way his teeth bite into his full lower lip.

"I'm done." My voice rings out louder than I expected in the quiet kitchen, and I cringe when he jerks in surprise. "Sorry. I didn't realize it had gotten so late. You could've kicked me out a while back."

Mr. Nord turns to me with a grin so sweet, the sight makes my teeth ache. I'm not sure what I want to lick more—another cone of ice cream or the ice cream maker himself.

Bad Quinn! That is not *how professionals think.*

"I figured I'd give you till midnight before dragging you away. Didn't want to break your concentration." He leans back on his table, tapping a finger on a paper full of scribbles. "I know what it's like to get sucked into your work."

Moving closer, I try to read out what he's written.

"New flavor?"

He nods. "Want to be a test subject?"

"Hell yeah," I reply, reaching for the top button on my jacket.

Chapter Six

AUGUST

Quinn's manicured nails slip over her buttons, undoing them. She then clutches the lapels and slides the crimson jacket off her shoulders. The white collared shirt underneath is sleeveless, and I spy the outline of the top of her bra through the silky fabric.

A chill trickles from deep in my gut, spreading over my skin, threatening to spill into the air around me. Around her.

"Wha-what are you doing?" The question stutters out of me as I put the majority of my effort into suppressing my elemental reaction to her newly exposed freckled skin.

"As you've found out, I can't eat ice cream without getting messy. This is my favorite suit." She folds the jacket and glances around, searching for a spot to place it.

"Here." I hold out my hands, and she doesn't hesitate to pass off the garment.

When the material touches my skin, I almost drop it. Then I fight the urge to press the jacket against my cheek.

The fabric is warm.

Life as an Ice Elemental means days of perpetual cold. Some people might consider that a sort of torture, but I'm not uncomfortable in my frigid state. I like the cold.

However, once I was old enough to learn about the concept of warmth, the idea has always fascinated me. My mother, a baker, had attempted to explain the sensation to me, describing how the ovens she pulled her cookies and cakes from gave off an immense amount of heat. She regretted using that example the day she found me sticking my head into one of the appliances, the temperature set at the highest level I could manage.

I came out unscathed and still curious.

My father, the parent who'd provided me with my icy heritage, claimed he'd first experienced warmth when he met my mother. But he always said it with a teasing smile, so I never knew if he was serious, and I was always too nervous to ask.

What if he *was* just joking?

I shied away from the idea of going my entire life without getting the chance to know the sensation of heat. That would be like me approaching someone without taste buds and describing the delicious flavors of my ice cream. They'd always have the theory but never the experience.

But heat isn't a mystery to me anymore. The glorious discovery radiates off the woman in front of me.

I push aside my rush of excitement at Quinn's warmth, shoving it into a box in the back corner of the attic of my brain, along with my curiosity about kissing warm skin and sliding inside a hot-to-the-touch woman.

Back to the issue at hand. "Would an apron help?"

Quinn trails fingers down the front of her snowy-white blouse, and I try not to imagine mine taking the same path. "Do you have an extra?"

"You can use mine." I tug at the ties before slipping it off. Even though I want to place it over her head myself, I restrain the inappropriate urge and simply hand the garment off to her instead. The apron hits me mid-thigh, but it falls below her knees. Still, with her heels, Quinn easily meets my eyes, hers blinking wide behind a sultry set of glasses.

"What Frankenstein ice cream monster have you been creating tonight?" Her excited grin is almost too much. Every bit of her pulses with energy, like a steaming cup of coffee promising to taste delicious and bring on a new life to my tired brain.

I push the comparison aside and lead the accountant over to one of the waist high coolers, where I pull out a metal container full of a ruby-colored ice cream. My experiments start out in small batches, meant to be tested and approved before I commit to a larger production.

A cone in hand, I scoop out a generous amount of my new creation. As I pass the treat over, I hope it's not glaringly obvious what the inspiration was for the concoction.

"And this is..." Quinn doesn't wait for my answer as she sticks out her pink tongue to taste.

"Red Velvet Cake." Swirls of red mixed with pale white. The coloring is all her.

I'm just not committed to the taste. No doubt it's delicious. But does the dessert taste like *her*?

Having only ever interacted with Quinn in my shop, I'm not sure what she smells like. There are too many sweet scents in the air for me to distinguish hers. All I have to go off is her striking coloring and the hot feel of her.

New flavor combinations tumble through my mind. This time, with spice.

"Oh goddess, that is decadent," Quinn moans out the compliment, her entire focus on the cone in her hand. As she steadily devours it, the cool cream begins to melt.

With my focus fixated on the slide of her tongue and pursing of her mouth, my mind lags behind on her exclamation. *Did she say goddess?* No. I must have misheard. All my forceful wanting has me hearing her speak like an Elemental.

"What's the verdict on my finances?" I ask to distract myself from hopeful thoughts and the lustful sight.

In between hearty licks, Quinn gives me a rundown of her findings. She talks animatedly about the graphs she created of my revenue streams and payroll, which outline the ratios and how they'll change over time.

All her conclusions match with my financial plan.

Even though I wasn't concerned about my money, I don't regret hiring her. It never hurts to have a second set of eyes check everything out. Plus now I get to watch her eat more of my ice cream.

Stop drooling over a human, I scold myself.

One long trail of Red Velvet Cake has escaped her notice and traces the length of her forearm, steadily making a path to her elbow. Without thinking—because at some point my brain started to short-circuit at the sight—I reach out to swipe my finger across her skin, gathering the melted mixture.

Only when I've stuck my finger into my mouth do I realize exactly what I've done. Glancing up, I expect to catch her horrified stare.

Instead, Quinn's eyes flash hot, her attention adhered to my lips.

But then she blinks, shaking her head and stepping away from me. "So, Mr. Nord, your finances are fine. As long as you continue to keep your costs low, Land of Ice Cream and Snow will have no trouble returning a steady profit. I will e-mail the documents I created and send you a bill. Feel free to give me a call the beginning of next year if you'd like help preparing your tax documents."

As Quinn reaches for the apron ties, a protest shouts in my mind.

Next year? I can't wait that long to see you again!

"A date!" I blurt out, my tongue moving before I've thought the idea through.

Fucking hell, what is wrong with me?

Her hand pauses, and one perfect red brow curves up. "Excuse me?"

I clear my throat and stand straighter, committing to the impulsive offer.

Damien and Sammy have both been with plenty of humans. My dad married one.

Why should I let Quinn pass out of my life? All I need is a little self-control around her, and my powers shouldn't have any effect on our relationship.

"I want to take you out on a date."

Quinn simply stares at me. Her stillness is extra torturous because, while she contemplates what I said, more ice cream coats her hand.

Maybe, one day, she'll let *me* lick it off her.

"Okay," she murmurs and then holds my gaze as she takes a large bite out of her cone.

Chapter Seven

QUINN

August's text said to bring warm clothes, which is laughable. Like I'd ever need them. I could parade around Alaska in the middle of winter in a bikini and still be toasty as a loaf of bread fresh from the oven.

But he doesn't need to know that.

I pull into the parking lot of the address he sent me, and the reason for his instructions becomes clear. There's a warehouse-sized building looming before me, and the afternoon sun illuminates the business name.

Ice Zone.

An ice-skating rink.

Shit.

Ice cream and now ice skating? What is this guy, the abominable snowman?

I snort to myself. Yeah, right. That's as likely as unicorns or Ice Elementals.

As I park, I can't help the anxiety creeping through my veins. Maybe, if I were just meeting up with my sisters or some friends, ice skating wouldn't be a huge deal. But I'm supposed to walk into that place beside a drop-dead hunk of a man and not turn the entire rink into a puddle? My confidence in my self-control is spotty on the best of days.

You didn't melt his ice cream, I remind myself.

That's a halfway decent argument. When his finger trailed over my skin and then he licked the cream? I about perspired. In that moment, I was in need of a fainting couch, on the verge of a sexy-man-induced collapse.

But other than the heat pulsing quicker through my veins, there was no detrimental reaction. I kept everything contained.

So why can't I do that today?

This entire get together is basically one big experiment. Who's to say that even if I don't get too heated up that I won't find another way to screw up? My fire is worrisome, but at least it's a demon I know well. My ability to date a person is a whole other gauntlet I've never had to face before.

Maybe the stress of that will keep me from descending into a lust inferno.

The blacktop currently radiates more heat than I do, the air above the surface shimmering in miniature mirages. August lounges against the front of the building, an oasis in the middle of a desert. His arms sit crossed over his chest, biceps bulging against the blue fabric of his long-sleeved shirt.

How in all the heavens is he not sweating through that thing? If I were human, I'd be a sloppy mess in this heat.

But he stands, cool as a marble statue, and my doubts about my control return.

If the ice starts getting watery, I can pull out an excuse to leave early. Maybe pretend I twisted an ankle or that Harley called with an emergency.

No, I know! I'll tell him my period showed up, and I'm having massive cramps.

Guys never question menstrual issues. Not when the uterus is such a mysterious entity to them.

Tucking that perfect excuse in my back pocket, I skip up to him with more confidence. My giddiness fades slightly when I notice the corner of his beautiful, strong mouth dip down as his sapphire eyes track over my body.

"I told you to dress warm."

Is that what's got him concerned?

"I wore pants, and I brought a jacket." I hold out the windbreaker for his inspection.

"That's not going to be enough." August shakes his head, and then he has the audacity to bite his super fuckingly gorgeous, plump bottom lip.

That is all I need to get the furnace in my chest producing enough heat to last me for a decade.

Of course, I can't tell him that.

"I live in Phoenix. This is my winter gear. But don't worry." I reach out to pat his broad shoulder. "Like I told you, I run hot."

August still appears bothered, but he bends over to grab a duffel bag I just noticed. Unzipping it, he pulls out a felt scarf, a knit hat, a set of thick mittens, and one huge sweatshirt that reads *University of Alaska Anchorage*.

Maybe this guy *is* the abominable snowman.

Instead of handing the items to me, August takes the liberty of dressing me himself. His fingers, surprisingly cool, brush my chin as he wraps the scarf around my neck. I snort as he tugs the hat down far enough to cover my ears. Trying to be helpful, I drop my jacket on the ground and lift my arms in the air, so he can easily slip the hoodie on.

The minute the fabric passes over my head, my mind stutters in disbelief.

I breathe in deeper, not trusting my first instinct. But there it is again.

Once ensconced in the soft sweatshirt, I don't let him shove the mittens on my hands. I'm too busy grabbing the gray cotton and pressing it to my nose.

"What are you doing?" August's befuddled look has me considering the full implications of what I'm smelling.

I let go of the hoodie and step into his space so I can pinch the front of his shirt and hold it to my nose for inspection.

"Quinn—"

"Waffle cones." My voice comes out in a hodgepodge of wonder and agony. "You smell like waffle cones." I never thought the scent of sweet dough would make me horny, but I've never met a muscular ice cream god who smells like desserts. I'm tempted to glare around us, sure some other woman is going to shove me out of the way so that she can simultaneously climb and devour him.

"Sorry. It never completely washes out." Some golden hair flops over August's thick brows as he grimaces down at me.

I let go of his shirt to clutch his face in my hands. "Why would you try to wash it out? I'm one step away from consuming you right now."

His face flushes under my palms, and I suddenly realize how hot my skin has gotten. I stumble back, grabbing for the mittens, determined to cover my potentially incendiary skin.

Remember, he's a human. Fragile. Flammable.

If I want everyone to survive this date, I need to smother the inferno in my panties.

Just to be safe, I scope out the location of the fire extinguishers as August guides me into the building.

Chapter Eight

AUGUST

"You stay here. I want to see if I can make it around on my own." Quinn presses her hands against my chest until I glide back into the wall.

I chuckle at her demanding tone but switch to a contrite nod when she raises an eyebrow at me. "Show me what you can do."

She isn't graceful. Growing up around people who are used to ice, I've seen plenty of girls skate as smooth as dancers. On solid ground, Quinn can put their majestic movements to shame. But here? She's clumsy as a newborn deer.

Still, the sight of her choppy glide hits me with a strong wave of pride.

An hour ago, she was scared to put one blade on the glassy surface without clutching the wall in a death grip. When I offered her my hand, she let go, albeit reluctantly. It took a few turns for her to stop squeaking in surprise whenever someone passed us. Quinn started to relax into things when I asked her questions. Talking kept her mind off her feet.

Plus, I got to learn more about the copper-headed beauty. Like how she and her sisters grew up in Phoenix and now she rents a house with the younger one.

The idea of living with a sibling appeals to me. I've always wondered what it would be like to have that type of connection with someone.

Quinn clutched my arm and told me about some of their silly traditions. Apparently, the two of them have superhero movie nights every Tuesday. My date got animated when she related her family's history with comics.

"My dad went to a convention, and he saw this woman dressed up like his favorite villain. She had on a green spandex body suit covered in fake leaves, and some glorious red hair." Quinn tossed her own fiery mane over her shoulder while she told the story. "That was my mom. The two of them geeked out together, and they've been wildly in love ever since." She rolled her eyes as a smile creased her cheeks.

And something clicked in my brain.

"Quinn?" I asked.

There went that lovely eyebrow, swooping up in question.

"What are your sisters' names again?"

She groaned, covering her eyes with her hand, and then she immediately lost her balance and slipped down to one knee.

Without losing a beat, I bent over to wrap an arm around her waist, pulling her up and supporting her weight until she had her footing again. With her body pressed flush against mine, I could almost imagine a caress of warmth from her. But that had to be in my head.

And because she would need a certain level of expertise to navigate the ice while wrapped around me, I reluctantly let her go.

"Thanks." Quinn squeezed my hand before stretching her arm out for better balance. "I guess you picked up on our namesakes. Harley and Quinn. Then there's Cat, who luckily is the last of us or else our sibling would have been called *woman*. Or maybe penguin. My dad fell in love with a villain, so he decided to name his daughters after a few more."

From her light tone, I got the sense that Quinn enjoyed the story of their names.

"Do you have any weird family?"

I laughed then at her hopeful expression. If she was concerned I was too normal for her, she had a huge surprise coming. But even if things worked out between us, that reveal would come way down the line. Way, way, way down the line.

Instead, I answered as best I could, "I'm an only child, so no weird siblings. My cousin though, he's a character. Kind of a cocky bastard but in a way that you can't help but love him. I moved here to be closer to him and the group of friends he always talks about. Since I grew up with just my parents, the idea of a huge family has always fascinated me."

Over the hour, we continued trading stories back and forth—hers all about life with her sisters in Phoenix and mine poor attempts at describing life in Anchorage. All the while, I kept my ice stifled, even as the magic tried to spill out every time Quinn smiled up at me or squinted her eyes closed in laughter.

Now I see another of her joyous grins as she stumble-skates toward me, having successfully completed her first solo trip around the rink.

"I did it!" She pumps her arms in the air, barely ten feet away from me. And the universe decides to flip her the middle finger in the form of a kid in a hockey jersey zipping in front of her.

Quinn's face registers surprise before she twists in a clumsy attempt to keep upright. If I were closer, I could catch her. Instead, she lands with a hard thwack against the ice.

I wince in pity for her plump ass, specifically the right cheek, which takes the brunt of the impact.

"Shit. Quinn, are you okay?" I skate to her side, arms held out for her to use as support.

She grimaces. "I think I broke my butt."

Fuck. Tailbone injuries are hell to deal with. I bruised mine when I was thirteen, and it was one of the worst pains I'd experienced. If Quinn broke hers...let's just say, it's unlikely I'll get a second date.

And I *really* want a second date.

"How bad does it hurt? Do you need me to carry you off the ice?" Not a lot of guys would be able to make that offer, but there's not a single time I've felt unsteady on this slick surface. I was probably skating before I could walk.

"Help me up." Quinn grips my arms, and I gently pull her into a standing position, keeping an eye out for any indication that she'll go crashing back down. "Give it to me straight." Her tone catches my attention, and I search her serious face.

"What's that now?"

"You know what I'm asking." Her bottom lip quivers, and my heart just about shatters at the sight. Then she clarifies, "Did I flatten my ass?"

"Wh-what?"

"Stop putting off the inevitable and tell me!" Quinn grabs one of my hands, and with no qualms about being in public, she presses my palm onto her perfectly round butt cheek.

The only thing stopping me from squeezing is the knowledge that she's going to be bruised from her fall. Instead, I glance down and meet her mischievous eyes, which twinkle with hidden humor.

Somehow I keep an answering grin off my face. Playing along, I shake my head in mock worry as I rub the area. "I don't know. It's hard to tell. I think you need to remove these pants so I can perform a more thorough inspection."

A throat pointedly clears just behind my back, and I whip my head around to see a woman with a young girl clutching her hand. The mother glares at me before skating by us.

A solid weight presses into my chest. Quinn buries her head in my shirt as her entire body shakes with suppressed giggles. And just like that, my embarrassment fades. I wrap my arms around her and skate backward toward the exit, letting the redhead have her fun at my expense.

I'd do a hell of a lot more embarrassing things to hear Quinn's laughter.

My date only gives a slight wince when she settles on the wooden bench to remove her skates. I sit next to her, close enough that we brush arms but not so close that I'm crowding her.

"Thanks for bringing me here." Quinn tilts her head enough to give me a grin as she unties her laces.

All I can manage is a grunt because I'm waging a war in my mind.

This was a perfectly acceptable first date. I should tell her good-bye, promise to meet up with her soon, and then go back to my place to deal with all this pent-up lust. Dating a human is going to require some practice. I'm positive the main reason things went well today was because I bundled her up in an extra layer of clothes. Added protection against my unappealing icy habit.

On the other hand, every molecule in my body wants to pull her onto my lap, use my frosty hand to soothe the bruise forming on her ass and my mouth to devour her inviting lips. I risk another glance Quinn's way, only to catch her pressing the overly long sleeves of my sweatshirt to her nose again, eyes closed as she breathes in deep.

My mouth moves before my brain can launch another protest. "Do you like soup?"

Chapter Nine

QUINN

I have to dig through what seems like an entire produce section to locate the beer in August's fridge.

"Do you have a garden in your backyard or something? What's with all these veggies?" I stand up, glass bottle clutched in each hand, trying to envision what my refrigerator looks like. Last I remember, most of the space is full of take-out tacos and Chinese.

You'd think a Fire Elemental would be better at cooking things.

August chuckles and taps a drawer at his side. When I slide it open, the bottle opener is sitting right on top. We're not done with our first date, and already, I feel like we've started to develop a groove.

"In Alaska, fresh produce is expensive as hell. Plus, half the time you show up at the store and they've sold out of whatever you're looking for." He shrugs. "I have a hard time reining myself in here. It's like a gold mine of bell peppers. The first time I went shopping, everyone thought I was a country bumpkin because I kept exclaiming out loud over the prices. Walking out of the store, I felt like I had to make a quick getaway before someone tripled my grocery bill."

I giggle at the thought of August sprinting to his car, bags of kale and tomatoes swinging from his arms. He throws a quick grin over his shoulder while his large hands deftly dice an onion.

Growing up in Phoenix, I've never thought much about our unending supply of cheap produce. Water? Now that's something that's never far from my mind. Guess people tend to focus more on what they're lacking than on what they have.

"What else is different about Alaska? Other than the cold, obviously." I toss out the question as I wander into the living area of August's house. The place has an open floor plan, so we can still speak easily as I explore.

"Wildlife is bigger up north. Wasn't out of the ordinary to have a moose wander into our backyard. Sometimes a bear."

"Holy shit. Like a grizzly bear?" I plop down on his couch, enjoying how the overstuffed cushions attempt to swallow me in their comforting embrace.

"More often a black bear. But I did see grizzlies a couple of times. Kept my distance and lived to tell the tale."

"What else?" I keep my beer from spilling as I pull myself up from the couch.

"I'm sure you've heard about the darkness in the winter. Some people get used to it, but I've got to say, I'm loving this Phoenix sun."

I smirk across the room. "And I'm sure that has nothing to do with how our intense heat helps sell ice cream by the gallons."

August glances my way again, wearing a satisfied smile, and my heart beats quicker in response. Damn, the man should come with a safety warning. The way he makes my powers pulse feels like a five-alarm fire.

But I'm having too much fun learning about him to take the hint.

"I never considered opening my own shop up there."

"Alaskans don't like ice cream?" The idea of anyone not wanting the glorious frozen desserts August is able to craft baffles me.

I watch the back of his head shake as he focuses on the large pot he's been adding ingredients to the last half hour. A savory scent drifts from the stovetop. I'm not sure if it's the smell or the way his back muscles roll and shift whenever he reaches for the next item that has my mouth watering.

"Plenty do. My mom runs her own bakery up there, and when I started making ice cream, she sold it out of her shop." August washes his hands before wiping them on a towel and turning to face me. He leans back on the counter and sips his beer, those iceberg-blue eyes watching as I pull a cookbook off a shelf to flip through the well-worn pages.

"But you moved here." I'm not sure whether to form the statement as a question.

He told me why he moved here—his cousin. But who chooses cousins over parents? My mom and dad live a couple of hours away, over in Tucson, and I can't imagine settling anywhere farther from them.

August finger-combs his hair, and I trace the muscular curve of his arm out of the corner of my eye.

"Alaska never felt like my place. Something was pulling me south. I figured the best destination was to go where there was more family."

"Not a fan of the cold?" I ask, still trying to figure out how this gorgeous Viking of a man ended up in the middle of the desert.

He smirks, as if listening to an inside joke. "The cold is familiar. I'm looking for something different."

We hold gazes then, only the empty space of a room separating us. A stronger pulse of heat courses through my veins. Hoping some more alcohol will help my powers chill the fuck out, I take a swig of my beer. Unfortunately, the liquid has gone warm, unable to withstand the hot clutch of my hand.

I stifle a grimace and slide the book back into its spot.

"Come taste this," August says. "Need to know if it's any good."

I push away my worries and saunter over to the kitchen where August has resumed stirring the soup. I'm not particularly short, but his built figure still seems to loom over me. With one hand on the granite, I hoist myself up to sit on the counter.

August's mouth curves slightly, just a twitch at the corner.

He dips a spoon in the concoction and then cups his hand underneath, intending to catch any drips as he holds the silverware to my lips.

All my concentration goes to tasting the soup because I know, the minute I lock eyes with him again, I'll choke on the hot liquid.

If I was worried that ice cream was the only delicious food item August could create, all doubts drift away the moment his soup passes my lips. Spicy and sweet and creamy with bits of tender, shredded chicken incorporated into that savory mixture.

All my willpower is temporarily occupied by not moaning out loud. After I get myself under control, I attempt a quizzical expression. "Hmm. It's good. But I feel like it's missing something."

The concerned wrinkle in his brow is so adorable that I almost break.

"Is it the consistency? Too watery?" He pulls out a clean spoon and tastes the soup himself.

I shake my head, pinching my lips between my teeth to keep from smiling.

"Is it bland? Does it need more salt?" He sniffs at the brew, as if his nose will provide all the answers.

What's funny is, if August knew me a bit better, he would never bother asking my opinion on how to improve a recipe. My highest culinary achievement is fashioning a grilled cheese without burning the bread to shit.

"That's not it..." I trail off, as if considering the imaginary problem.

"How about the spice? Did it come on too strong? Or not enough? I have extra chipotles." August goes to reach for a shriveled red pepper on the cutting board.

I clap my hands, giving up on the game before he ruins perfection. "No! I've got it. To make this soup perfect, it just needs"—I grip the edge of the counter to keep my balance as I lean over and steal a quick kiss from his decadently soft lips—"a little sugar." I retreat from his stunned face with a wicked smile of my own.

As August remains still, no immediate reaction other than shock, a twinge of uncertainty pinches in my chest. *Did I read this entire situation wrong?* Most of the time, I avoid flirting and sexy glances in order to cut down on errant fires. Maybe what I thought was the sign of an interested man was really a guy thinking, *this is a cool chick that I want to be platonic friends with.*

Ready to laugh off my advance, using the excuse that I'm one of those lucky women who can get drunk on half a beer, I let out a surprised squeak instead when August steps in between my knees.

Both of his cool hands slide around to my butt and pull me forward until our chests are practically welded together, and his belt buckle presses delightfully against my center.

"I think it needs a hell of a lot more sugar than that." August's voice caresses my hot skin, smoother than ice.

All I can manage is a nod. He leans forward, his stare focused on my mouth, and I wonder if he fantasizes about my lips the same way I do about his. Then all ability to wonder floats away as he makes contact.

The taste and scent of him meld together, a heady mixture of warm vanilla and sweet molasses soaked in melted butter. I moan, needing to consume him.

My hands release the counter, allowing my arms to twine around his neck and pull him closer. My legs mimic the movement, hooking around his hips in a wanton demand. All the while, I feast on his delicious mouth.

August groans, deep in his chest, the sound quaking into my bones. His heavy hands push up under my shirt, spreading over my lower back. The rasp of his skin on mine is a strange combination of relief and torture. Every cell in my body grows overly sensitive as the fire at my core thrums through me, but his caress soothes the ache like aloe on a sunburn.

The twist and tangle of sensations muddles my mind, and for a moment, I forget to breathe. When my lungs burn with protest, I gasp, and August traces his tongue along the inside of my bottom lip. His taste refreshes me while also instilling a rabid craving that hooks my fingers into claws, clutching him tighter.

His hands match the motion, digging into the skin on my back, sending painful pleasure ricocheting down my spine. My hips rock into his, the press of his buckle finding just the right spot.

My sight blurs in and out of focus, all of my other senses overwhelming my ability to see. Stars burst in the corners of my eyes.

No, not stars.

Flames.

The kitchen is filling with fire.

Chapter Ten

AUGUST

A growl of protest rumbles out of my chest when Quinn shoves me away. Every inch of my skin joins in the denial of our parting.

That kiss...hell, tasting Quinn's mouth was better than any sex I've ever had.

Away from my shop, I've finally discovered her scent. Cinnamon. She practically burned my tongue with the taste. But there were hints of sweetness hovering on her lips. Honey. I want to create a batch of ice cream flavored like Quinn. And then melt it over her skin and lick it off her.

My dick, pushing against the zipper of my pants, seconds the idea.

The ice in my gut prickles through my body, sliding further over my skin and threatening to spill into the air. My powers seek out her heat, longing for connection the same way I do.

And like the chill, I reach for her. Only then do I realize there's a very pressing reason Quinn pushed me away. Instead of remaining on the counter, legs splayed for me to return to their inviting embrace, she's jumped down to stand in front of the sink.

And, from that sink, I watch a dark cloud of smoke twist with tendrils of steam and the occasional flicker of flame.

Shit.

Glancing over at the stove, I realize the towels I had hanging from the oven door are missing. That passionate kiss muddled my mind so much that I didn't realize the fabric must've come into contact with the hot stovetop.

Good thing one of us was able to keep our wits about us.

And I'm an asshole for the small twinge of disappointment that Quinn wasn't as affected as I was. Apparently, I'd be fine with my house burning down around us as long as she found my advances irresistible.

Properly chagrined, I move to take over the firefighter efforts, only to pause in horror.

As Quinn reaches for the faucet, her crop top rises up enough to reveal a decent stretch of her back. And there, on her already-pale skin, is a bright white handprint.

My handprint. I might have been able to convince myself she simply had sensitive skin, if it weren't for the bits of frost spiderwebbing out from each finger mark.

This has never happened before. In the past, women eventually pushed my hands away from them, claiming my touch was too cold. They would giggle and tell me to rub my hands together to warm them, thinking the chill was a temporary hangover from being outside in the Alaskan winter. None of them knew it was a constant state. In the end, I would simply grasp the bedsheets instead of clutching their soft bodies to me.

But Quinn didn't push me away. Not until something threatened our lives.

How was she able to put up with the discomfort? Frost directly on the skin for a human has to be painful.

Fire subdued, Quinn turns to face me, her expression surprisingly guilty as she traces her gaze over my body.

"Are you okay? Did you get burned anywhere?" Her voice has lost its confident, flirtatious nature.

I barely stifle the disbelieving laugh pushing at the back of my throat. She wants to know if *I'm* hurt?

Who is this woman, and why are the gods torturing me with her?

"No. I'm—" My voice leaves me as a shiver racks through her body.

Every beautiful curve of her shakes with the cold I left on her skin.

Her arms cross over her chest, as if trying to hold on to any little bit of warmth she might have left.

Did I steal all the heat from her? Would her lips have turned blue if I'd kept kissing them? Would the blood have slowed and frozen in her veins if she'd never escaped from my hold?

I want to fall on my knees before her, begging for forgiveness and promising never to lay another finger on her delicate human form.

But before I can, Quinn backs away from me, stumbling toward the door like a frightened deer.

"I just remembered. I promised Cat I'd eat dinner with her tonight. So sorry. Need to go." Her purse and jacket are hanging by the front door. She snatches them up and leaves at a speed that can only be considered fleeing.

And I'm left alone.

Curses tumble from my mouth, and I press my fist into the granite counter to keep from punching a wall.

I should've known better. But Quinn was too tempting, making me think of all the Elemental and human couples I'd heard of. For a moment, I thought that we could join their ranks.

But my powers cut off any chance of intimacy, and I find myself hating them.

Why can't I be like Damien or Sammy? Or descend from a less dangerous Elemental line, like Earth?

Doesn't matter. Wishing has never gotten me anywhere.

With frustrated, jerky movements, I pull a bowl and a spoon from my cabinets, resigned to eat without companionship.

Problem is, when I move to ladle out a serving, I find my dinner has frozen solid.

Fuck my life.

Chapter Eleven

QUINN

"I still don't understand why we're here." I climb out of the backseat of my older sister's Range Rover and glare at the beautiful house she brought me to.

"Because parties are fun. You remember what fun is, right?" Harley smirks at me, popping her bubble gum because she knows the sound drives me to murder.

"A *Squid* party. I've been proudly avoiding these since I was sixteen. Water Elementals are more likely to piss me off than cheer me up." I am definitely not whining.

She shrugs. "Anger is better than sulking. Cat says you've barely left your room in two weeks."

I gasp and then turn my fiery gaze to my younger sister, who suddenly seems to find her turquoise-painted toes extremely fascinating.

"I've been working. Remotely." That's only partly true. I've also been binge-watching superhero movies.

I was partway into my marathon when I realized a certain god of thunder strongly resembled August. At that moment, I paused the movie, left my room to grab a tub of mediocre ice cream from the freezer, and then resumed watching while drowning my self-pity in frozen dairy.

Dad would be ashamed. Pining after a Viking god? He'd much prefer I choose a billionaire with an obsession for bats or a journalist with a set of thick-rimmed glasses and a fear of green rocks.

But the heart wants what the heart wants.

Harley snorts, returning me to the present, and I'm betting, behind her sunglasses, she's rolling her eyes at me. We've reached the tall wooden gate leading to the backyard. She doesn't bother knocking, just pushes it open and saunters in. I don't think my older sister has ever entered a place without complete confidence that she owns every inch of ground in front of her. It's a level of confidence neither I nor Cat has ever achieved.

Past the barrier to the outside world is an oasis. Cat and I have a simple kidney bean–shaped pool at our rental, but the water wonderland in this backyard resembles a lagoon. The sides are fashioned out of smooth stones, and there are two waterfalls, one spilling out of a smaller, raised pool.

This setup, paired with the lush greenery, gives a sense of being transported to somewhere outside of our arid Arizona.

But I shouldn't be surprised when the house is owned by a Water Elementals. Damien has done well for himself. Last time I ran into the Squid, he was just a year out of college and more interested in the Phoenix nightlife than owning a home in a suburb.

"Now this is more like it. Let's find you a Squid dick to ride," Harley announces.

I throw up in my mouth. Just a little. "I'd rather live a life of celibacy, thank you very much."

"Celibacy? We don't use dirty words like that here." A deep voice, rife with humor, drifts over my shoulder.

I know that voice. I know a lot about the owner of that voice, too.

"Samuel." I turn to take in the shirtless Squid who did a subpar job of helping out with my little virginity problem.

"Quinn. Haven't heard from you in a while." He smirks before pressing a beer to his lips.

Objectively, Sammy is *get all the panties in the vicinity wet* hot. Dirty-blonde hair, dark eyes, sun-drenched skin, and a voice with a deep smoothness to it that gets you hoping he'll switch over to serenading you at any moment.

Problem is, Sammy is fully aware of how perfectly formed he is. What some people interpret as confidence, I know for certain is just cockiness. Which, ironically, doesn't help much in the bedroom.

"And you thought I'd call you, why?"

He stumbles back, dramatically clutching his chest, grinning all the while. "My poor heart. How could you be so cruel?"

A strong arm wraps around my shoulders, and I tense until I catch the scent of hibiscus and glance up to see a striking face framed in long ebony hair. Geneva.

"Sammy bothering you?" She glares at him.

I grin at one of my best friends, enjoying her coming to my defense whether I need it or not. "Nope. He's just lamenting the fact that he never got invited back into my bed."

Sammy scoffs. "Don't you know by now? I'm a one-and-done guy. But if I heard your sister right, you're on the prowl. Need some help picking out a bang buddy? My cousin is new to town—"

"Hell no. I'm not about to be passed around your family like some kind of party favor." I give Sammy's chest a gentle shove. "Go bother someone else."

"Fine then." He pretends to pout, but a mischievous light sparks in his eyes when he catches sight of my little sister. He saunters over to where she's leaning against the DJ booth, chatting with the Air Elemental spinning beats.

"Can't believe you slept with that guy." Geneva sounds so disappointed in me that I give in to the urge to pinch her side. She yelps, swatting at my hand as Harley chuckles.

"The girl was desperate." My big sister, such an ass. "Hence why we've come to the domain of Squids. She needs another water man to give her a good dicking without her risking pyrotechnics."

Goddess, I need to buy her a muzzle. "I am not here to get a 'good dicking,' as you so charmingly put it." I turn to my friend, who watches our family squabble with an amused smirk. "I had a bad date. Just here to let off some steam."

Geneva's sharp eyebrows dip, but she smiles and pokes me in the side. "Well no one better at letting off steam than a Pyro."

"Oh, we're playing that game, are we? Well, Miss Petal Pusher, you find a baby daddy yet?" I reach out to pat her flat stomach.

She shoves me away with a good-natured growl. "Fuck you."

Geneva isn't like most of her Earth Elemental relatives. In addition to their innate abilities to manipulate all growing things, they also tend to err on the maternal/fraternal side. She has so many nieces and nephews, I doubt she knows the exact number.

In her family, Geneva is the IUD-carrying black sheep.

Well, maybe there are two black sheep. Last I heard, her brother Aspen hasn't popped out any kids yet either. At one point, a long time ago, I thought something might happen between him and Cat. But that romance couldn't survive high school graduation.

"Now, children, don't fight." Harley slaps my butt in the affectionate way only she can master. "I'm off to locate the alcohol. If I don't see you chatting up a hunky guy within the hour, I'm going to feel obligated to intercede. Keep that in mind."

My big sister gives me a finger wave, and I return it, using just one of my own.

Geneva snickers into her red Solo cup. Coming from a large family, she knows the level of annoyance siblings can reach. When we're alone, my friend tugs me to a lounge chair, sitting us both down. "Tell me more about this disastrous date. My love life has been drier than this desert we live in. I want some juicy details."

I fiddle with the end of my long ponytail where it hangs over my shoulder. "He was a human."

"Interesting choice. For you, I mean."

I grimace and spill the rest of the sad story, ending with my chin resting on my fists, shoulders drooping in defeat.

"Wow. You've gotta stop taking *getting hot and heavy* so literally." Geneva elbows my side, trying to lighten my dark mood with her corny joke.

But I just sigh, stifling the guilt that still spikes through me at the memory.

I can't believe I was so irresponsible. *What if I hadn't noticed the fire?* I could've done even more damage. I could've hurt August. A shiver quakes over my body, a pale reflection of the fearful shudders I had to fight off after dousing his dish towels. In the moment, the stress had me shaking, my mind reeling as I berated myself for being so careless.

Lesson learned. Humans are not for me. Not unless I want to send them to an early, fiery grave.

"So, you're on the prowl for a Squid? Looking for a man who can put out any fires you start?" Geneva scans the crowd of partiers.

"I'm not feeling a hook-up." That's only partly true. I'm not feeling hooking up with a random guy. The only person making my lady parts tingle is a particular ice cream shop owner.

"Okay. Maybe don't sleep with anyone. But it never hurts to chat with some cute guys. Maybe that'll help with your control. We just need..." Geneva trails off, and I glance up to find her mouth hanging open. Quickly, she swallows and clears her throat. "Sorry. But I just spotted a gorgeous hunk of man meat. And he looks new."

I follow her line of sight, only to have my mouth pop open in shock for an entirely different reason. Across the way, holding a beer and chatting with a vaguely familiar Squid, is the cause of my current depression.

August Nord.

"By all the gods and goddesses." I mutter the oath as I shove up from my seat and stalk around the pool.

I knew Squids were arrogant douche bags who often struggled with responsibility, but I never expected them to throw an Elementals party and then invite a human to it!

If my eyes weren't so fixated on the Viking of a man on the opposite side of the pool from me, I'd scan the guests to see if I could pick out any other human attendees.

But August has all my attention.

Taking this pool party seriously, the guy only has on a set of swim trunks. The black fabric rests low on his hips, displaying a beautiful set of chest muscles, plus that glorious V that points to all the good bits.

As I approach the two men, a familiar-looking girl skips up to them in a blue-polka-dot bikini. She smiles up at August as if he were a marble statue of manliness in need of worshiping, and I wonder if that's how I stare at him, too. Then I remember her face.

She's the girl who works at Land of Ice Cream and Snow.

So not only a human, but also an underage one? These Squids need to pull their collective head out of their collective ass.

The teenager rolls her eyes at something the dark-haired Squid says just before I reach the group.

"Stop being such a dork, Damien," she commands with a confidence I did not possess at her age.

And Damien! I didn't recognize him with his face clean shaven and hair carefully styled. The guy looks like an adult instead of the college kid who'd buy Sammy and his friends beer when their fake IDs didn't work. Damien used to have major *I'll help you mess up your life* vibes.

Looks like he's moved on to more destructive behavior if he's exposing our kind to humans.

"August!" I try to mask my panic with a friendly, casual smile. At least, I hope that's how I've arranged my face.

The ice cream Viking of my dreams whips his head around to stare at me with wide eyes.

"Quinn." He steps toward me, reaching out a hand, only to drop it a moment before our skin touches. "What are you doing here?"

After asking the question, a surprisingly intimidating glare creases his eyebrows. My heart hurts at the angry expression, even when he directs it away from me and toward Damien.

I know I practically set his house on fire...but *he* doesn't know that. And though I never texted him after our date, he never texted me either. So this reaction brings an unexpected amount of sting with it.

"Funny. I was about to ask you the same thing." My statement is more directed at Damien than August.

A moment ago, I was simply furious with the Squids for inviting a human to an Elemental party. But now, the hurt from August's unjustified reaction only amplifies my anger.

All I wanted was to get drunk midday on a Sunday. Now I've got this shit to deal with.

Damien doesn't seem to mind the pair of glares he's being hit with. Instead, he glances between the two of us with a curious smile on his face. Obviously he's not going to be any help with escorting the staff of Land of Ice Cream and Snow out of his backyard before they witness something they shouldn't.

"You two know each other," the Squid murmurs to himself with a satisfied smirk.

"She's his accountant." This from August's employee, who I'm surprised to find scowling at me, her beautifully tanned arms crossed and feet spread wide as if preparing for a fight.

"Ah. Yes." Damien nods and continues with his annoying little smile that makes me want to wring his neck.

"Damien," August growls out the Squid's name. "You told me this was an"—he flicks his eyes to me and then back to the dark-haired man—"*exclusive* party."

I don't have time to get offended over August's insinuation because a familiar screech cuts through all the party noises.

In unison, everyone turns to watch Cat fly into the air, recently tossed by a grinning Sammy. My little sister lands, fully clothed, in the middle of the beautiful pool. She emerges a moment later, sputtering and cursing.

No one can piss off my normally sweet, friendly baby sister better than a Squid.

"You goddess-damn son of a bitch!" Cat's short hair glows red, sparking and smoldering, until full flames sprout from her skull in a fiery crown.

The entire pool begins to let off steam. Sammy, grinning like my sister just gave him the highest compliment, sets his beer down and whips off his baseball cap.

"Hot tub!" he shouts before cannonballing into the water a foot from the furious Pyro, dousing her flames with his splash.

A few others laugh and dive in after him.

The series of events all happened so fast. It takes me a moment to register the disaster of my sister's public display. My brain kicks into desperate survival mode, and I turn back to August, who has his eyes locked on Cat's still-literally-fuming head where it bobs just above the water's surface.

Without thought, I launch myself at him, twining my legs around his trim waist, wrapping one arm around his neck, and clapping my free hand over his wide eyes.

"You're hallucinating!" I shout, sure if I say it with enough conviction that he'll believe me.

"Quinn—" August begins, but I talk over him.

"Someone roofied you! Slipped you some shrooms! Probably Damien."

"Hey!" The Squid might sound more offended if he wasn't snorting out chuckles.

I glare over my shoulder at the host of this disastrous party. "What the hell is wrong with you? Get the girl out of here!" As I hiss furiously at the amused Elemental, the young human continues to glare daggers at me.

Damien shakes his head, his aqua eyes crinkled in hilarity. "You mean, Marisol? My sister?"

The word acts like a hint to a puzzle. Suddenly, connections tumble into place. Glancing between the annoyed girl and the chuckling man, all of their similarities become clear. Copper skin, round cheeks, thick black hair, eyes fashioned from a color pulled straight from the waters of a Caribbean beach.

"She's a Squid?" I whisper as my brain works through the last few bits of the equation.

"Yep," Damien answers with a cheeky grin and no additional information. The bastard.

August's employee is a Water Elemental. He's at an Elemental party. *Does that mean...*

I peel my hand away from August's eyes to find him staring up at me with awe. "Are *you* a Squid?"

"No, he's not! And I think August would appreciate it if you stopped climbing all over him!" Marisol snaps out the chastisement, and I spare a glance her way.

Clearly, the little Squid's powers are not jealousy or anger-induced because her scowl tells me I'd be fighting off a tsunami if that were the case. Still, she's got a point. I move to loosen my legs from August's waist, only to have a cool arm, solid as iron, clutch me tighter to his chest.

When I meet his searching gaze, my heart pumps harder, and heat pulses with the beats, pooling heavily under my skin.

"Ice."

I tilt my head, confused by his one word.

He clears his throat and starts again, "I'm not a Water Elemental. I control ice."

Ice. August controls ice.

Every cell in my body clenches in excited joy when the full meaning of his confession registers.

Ice Elemental.

"Oh my goddess." My hands cup his cheeks, the cold brush of his skin making sudden sense. "You're a fucking unicorn!"

Chapter Twelve

AUGUST

I must have misheard Quinn. Not a huge surprise, what with her long, hot legs wrapped around my waist. Skin against skin, she's lucky I've maintained any brain function at all.

Still, I correct her, "Um, no. Unicorns aren't real."

"I didn't think Ice Elementals were real, but here you are." She gazes down at me like I'm the Holy Grail.

Her admiration is addictive. I want to sprawl out in a lounge chair with Quinn spread over me like a warm blanket, her eyes on me with this same expression for hours.

Instead, I remember that we're at a party full of people, including my impressionable, young employee. And while Quinn knows my secret, I've yet to fully identify hers.

My arm practically groans in protest when I loosen the instinctual clutch I wrapped around her waist when she first tried to retreat. But while I want her pressed against me, spicy, sweet scent filling my nose, if I keep her in my arms much longer, a particular part of my body is going to make itself known.

Hiding a boner in a swimsuit is a near-impossible task.

The moment I release my hold, Quinn blinks rapidly, glances down at her vine-like grip on my body, and relaxes her legs. Still, she doesn't jump away from me or stutter out apologies. Quinn keeps her hands on my shoulders until her toes touch the ground, slowly sliding down my chest.

It's all I can do not to grunt like an animal.

"What an interesting business relationship you have. Is this how you treat all your clients, Quinn? Because, if so, I think I need someone to check over my books." Damien's eyes flash with barely suppressed laughter.

I'm tempted to shove him into the pool turned hot tub.

Speaking of hot, that display Cat just put on gives me a good idea as to why Quinn is at this party.

When I heard my name and turned to find her staring up at me, I was ready to pummel Damien for not only inviting a human to this gathering, but *this* human. The one who's been tormenting my dreams and fantasies for the past two weeks.

But if my suspicions are correct, Quinn isn't a human at all.

"Sorry, Damien. My schedule is full. You'll just have to *handle* your own books. I'm sure you've had plenty of practice with that."

Quinn smirks over her shoulder, Marisol gags, and I cover a laugh with a cough.

Then she turns her attention back to me. "You're an ice god named August? You sure you're from Alaska and not Australia?"

I can't keep from staring at Quinn as I register her odd question. She looks adorably sexy today with her ruby tresses pulled into a high ponytail and another pair of cutoff jean shorts hugging her round ass. A white tank top hints at a bathing suit underneath, and from what I can tell, it's black and stringy.

Shaking my head, I try to coherently answer her, "First off, my great-great-a few more greats-grandfather is the ice god, not me. Secondly, Australia?"

She tilts her head to the side. "Their winters are during our summers. Here, August equals hot. And while you are extremely steam-worthy in the looks department, you'd think your mom would've given you a chillier name. Like February."

"People aren't named February." I fight a smile.

"Why not? We've got Aprils and Junes. I'm sure there's a May wandering around somewhere. And then there's August. Why not a February?"

"August is a nickname. My actual name is Augustus. Does that set your mind at ease?" My hand still sits on her waist, my thumb tracing the edge of her shirt, wanting to explore underneath the fabric.

"Augustus Nord, the Ice Elemental. Nice to meet the real you." Quinn grins up at me, the freckles coating her cheeks condensing all the more. One of her hands moves to shade her eyes against the bright midday sun as she continues to stare into my face, eagerly studying me as if I am a grand prize she's won.

The idea that this sexy, warm woman could be so fascinated with me has me stumbling over my next words. "So. You. Fire, huh?"

Shit. I sound like a caveman.

Quinn only smiles wider. "Yes. Me fire."

"And me water. What's the big deal?" Marisol snaps.

I glance over to see her glaring at the back of Quinn's head.

Maybe the guys weren't too far off about the whole crush thing.

"Come on, Merry Berry. Let's chat with some other guests. Be good hosts, you know?" Damien slings an arm around his sister's neck and turns her away.

"But August—"

My friend cuts Marisol off as he drags her along beside him, "Now, you know how much I hate cursing in front of you, but today, I think I need to expand your vocabulary. Ever heard of the term cockblock?"

Thankfully, the siblings move far enough away that I don't catch any more of his educational talk. I'm not sure how things will go during Marisol's next shift at the shop, but I hope Damien can convince the high schooler that crushing on a man close to fifteen years older than her will not end well.

"Who's running the shop right now?" Quinn's question pulls all my attention back to her stunning face.

The sunbeams absorb into her skin, which then gives off its own heated radiance. Standing so close to her, I can finally experience the warmth of the sun. Or more accurately, the warmth of her.

"One of my other employees, Denise. She usually handles most of Sunday on her own. I figured I need at least one day off a week." The fact that I can form a coherent answer is impressive with Quinn's hot hand resting on my forearm and the fingers of her other twiddling with the end of her ponytail.

"Mmhmm. That's nice. Means you can attend the occasional party. Meet some more people like you."

She hasn't stopped grinning, and I'm finding the expression catching.

"Are Fire Elementals like me? Have to admit, never really spent time with one before." But, hell, do I want to.

She's like me. She knows my secret and is perfectly fine with it.

"Well, some people say we have quicker tempers." Quinn flicks her eyes over to her younger sister, who's heaving herself out of the pool in a soggy sundress. From the way steam rises off of the fabric, I'm betting Cat will be dry soon.

"I think I can deal with that." The jean material of Quinn's shorts is rough against the pad of my finger. I want something smoother, like the pliable flesh of her lower back. To reach, I just need to slide my hand up ever so slightly.

Giving in to temptation, I sneak my hand further under her shirt, finding the scorching satin of her skin.

The moment my thumb makes contact, a visible shiver traverses Quinn's entire body.

The sight shocks me out of my lust-induced disregard of her safety. I drop my hand and step away, silently berating myself for being so careless.

"August?" Quinn's joyous expression flickers into a frown.

She reaches for me again, but I evade her touch, for both our preservation.

"I'm sorry. This can't happen."

"Can't happen?" Quinn's shocked words come out as a whisper that I easily hear despite the party noises. Around us, people drink, laugh, and converse with the steady beat of music in the background.

"For me, relationships, they don't work." I'm fucking this explanation up.

Quinn wrinkles her nose, gaze confused. "What do you mean?"

"My powers. If we...when I ..." The idea of telling Quinn my ice is all tied up in my arousal freezes the words on my tongue.

How do I say this? Quinn, I'll lose my mind with pleasure when I'm inside you, but you'll feel like you're being fucked by an iceberg.

Shame forces me to move farther from her. "I'm going to hurt you."

"We're both Elementals." Her scowl has turned fierce now as she crosses her arms over her chest. Even pissed off at me, she's glorious.

But that's because she's all heat and passion. Quinn is fire, and the frost inside me will just snuff her out.

"We're fire and ice. We don't go together." The words hurt, saying them out loud. But I suffer through.

When she opens her mouth, readying another argument, I move past her, making sure not to let even an inch of me touch any part of her glowing, freckled skin. She needs to see the danger I am to her, the risk she'd be taking, getting close to me.

"August—"

"No, Quinn. Just watch." I crouch down by the edge of the pool and plunge my hand into the water.

Since one of the guys started serving burgers from the grill a minute ago, most everyone has gotten out to grab food. Sammy is the only one left, climbing a ladder out of the deep end.

The second Quinn wrapped herself around me, my powers took notice, building in my gut and pricking at my skin. Now I fix my stare on Quinn's beautiful, annoyed form, imagining peeling each piece of clothing off her until I get her down to that black bikini and then removing that, too. With my teeth.

The ice spiderwebs from the palm of my hand, freezing the entire pool solid in a frosty wave. My cousin yelps and jumps out at the last second, narrowly avoiding having his leg encased in ice.

"Quit being an asshole, Auggie!" Sammy flips me the bird from across the pool. "This'd better be back to normal by the time I'm done eating!"

I ignore his glare to return my attention to Quinn. Her shocked eyes trace over a surface as solid and smooth as the one we skated on for our first—and only—date.

With an intense amount of effort and only after ducking my head to cut off my view of her, I'm able to pull most of the chill back into my skin. I blink and peer over the water. A few basketball-sized icebergs still float in the pool, but with the hot day, I doubt they'll last long.

Standing up, I meet Quinn's eyes for the last time. "You're fire. I'm ice. We don't mix."

Chapter Thirteen

AUGUST

"I've got to say, you've done a hell of a job with this place. I'm impressed, Auggie." Sammy leans on one of the heavy wooden tables as he digs a spoon into a scoop of the daily special.

Since the guy rarely offers a compliment without a joke attached, his genuine sentiment hits me right in the chest. Kind of like he ran up and hugged me.

"Thank you." I grin at him across the counter before moving to the cash register. I debate if I should remove the drawer of money yet. There are still a few minutes left before we close, and I'm in no hurry to get out of here, so I leave it in.

Never know who might straggle in at the last second.

"I'm proud of you, too, August." Marisol blinks up at me with a wide smile.

That is until Sammy snorts, and she shifts rapid-fire into a glare directed at him. He pretends not to notice, eyes only for his dessert.

I shake my head and try not to roll my eyes. Ever since the pool party last week, Marisol has either stepped up her crush-induced commentary, or I've just been noticing it more. Either way, I'm going to have to figure out a way to let her down easy.

"You two can head out whenever. I've got this." I use a cloth to wipe the last traces of fingerprints off the glass protecting the ice cream.

"I don't mind sticking around to help." Marisol sidles up to me.

"You might want to check with your chauffeur before you start making plans to stay late, Merry Berry," Sammy scolds as he tosses his trash in the can.

The little Squid whirls on him. "Don't call me that!"

"Why not, Merry Berry? I thought you *loved* your nickname."

The two of them continue to bicker as I wipe down the tables. Most people would find their snipping annoying, but I enjoy the feeling that comes with witnessing their inconsequential arguments. A sense of belonging. Like I'm part of this family, so they don't mind having it out in front of me. They're still going at each other when I make it back to the counter.

Then the bell above the door jingles, cutting off their squabble. All three of us turn to eye the last-minute customer.

Marisol mutters a curse, Sammy lets out a chuckle, and I clutch the granite counter, the surface growing cold under my palms.

A certain Fire Elemental, who has permanently lodged herself in my brain, saunters across the hardwood floor in a set of lethal red heels. A dress, the same flaming bright color, hugs every single curve she has.

The devil herself, temptation personified, fills my shop with her presence.

"Quinn Byrne. Funny seeing you here." Sammy steps in front of the Pyro, cutting off my view. It's all I can do not to growl at the loss, paired with his familiar tone.

"Samuel. Look at you. Someone might mistake you for a professional." Quinn sidesteps the Squid and flicks a finger at the shoulder of his perfectly tailored suit.

My cousin turns, keeping his eyes on her and a cocky grin on his face.

I hate to admit it, but they look good next to each other. Like a high-powered couple ready to dominate the corporate world. I, meanwhile, have on jeans, a T-shirt, and an ice cream–stained apron.

"I can be a gentleman when I want." Sammy straightens his cuffs.

Quinn and Marisol scoff at the same time, but when the redhead smiles at my employee, she gets a glare in response.

"So, is this a major Elemental hangout or something? All the Squids looking for their ice cream fix?" Though Quinn's question is aimed at Sammy, she takes another step toward me, her heels clicking on the hardwood.

I'm torn between retreating into my back office and locking the door, or circling around the counter to toss the little fire starter over my shoulder and carrying her back there with me.

"You do know how much I like sweet things in my mouth"—Sammy's confident grin brings a sick feeling to my stomach—"but I'm just here to pick up this prickly pear." He wraps his arm around Marisol's neck and ruffles her hair while she hisses at him, reminding me of an angry cat. "And to support my cousin, of course."

Quinn's confident step stutters, and I finally meet her eyes. There's heat in them but not as much as what's infusing her cheeks.

She flicks her gaze between Sammy and me as the pale skin behind her many freckles flushes. "You're August's cousin?"

Her reaction sets off warning bells in my brain. Still, I keep my mouth shut and silently pray to the gods that she'll turn around, leave my shop, and stop tormenting me with her irresistible appeal.

"On a first-name basis, huh? And how is it that you know my cousin?" Sammy shoots a smirk at me.

I'm tempted to flip him off but worry about letting my icy shield crack even that much.

"I'm here to seduce him."

Silence settles over the shop.

Ice, slick and heavy, condenses in my gut and threatens to spill out of my skin.

Despite her blush, Quinn holds my gaze with her own determined one. Out of the corner of my eye, I catch Marisol's hands curling into fists.

Sammy's mouth bobs a couple of times before he lets out a grumble that finally breaks some of the tension, "You never bothered seducing me."

"Sorry, Squid. One and done, remember? Besides, you're not the one I want."

The inside of my chest shudders with the frost trying to force its way free, all brought to the surface by her words and the alluring sway of her hips.

The growing chill reinforces the danger Quinn is in.

"Well, I can tell when I'm not welcome. Let's go, Marisol." Sammy's pout from a second ago has disappeared as quickly as it rose to the surface. Meeting my eyes, he offers a wink.

"I'd rather stay." My employee crosses her arms over her chest and glares.

"Not up to you, Merry Berry."

And before Marisol can protest further, my cousin scoops her up in a fireman's carry. The sixteen-year-old shrieks a protest, pounding on his suited back while Sammy turns to face Quinn.

"Don't let Auggie's stoicism scare you off." He smirks my way, and I glare in response. "He's dying to get laid."

Marisol gasps, Quinn grins, and I grind my jaw so hard that my teeth protest.

My cousin and his struggling Squid cargo are almost out the door when he offers up one last comment. "I think he'd appreciate a little ass play once you dislodge the icicle that's shoved up there!"

Then my outrageous buffer is gone, and my once-spacious shop suddenly feels as small as an ice-fishing shack.

With precise steps that remind me of a tiger stalking prey, Quinn approaches the counter. She spreads her palms flat on the surface and leans forward just enough that I catch a hint of cleavage down the neck of her dress.

"What does a woman have to do to get serviced around here?"

Chapter Fourteen

QUINN

"We're closed." August's response is frigid.

So that's how he's going to be?

"That's not what the sign outside says. According to it, I still have five more minutes to indulge in some ice cream."

He grunts, which I choose to interpret as agreement.

The second I walked into the Land of Ice Cream and Snow, I knew that cracking this Ice Elemental was going to require some effort.

Good thing I'm planning on enjoying every minute of it.

I've always wanted to seduce a man.

"Hmm. Now, what do I want?" I tap my fingers on the counter that separates us. The chalkboard catches my eye, and I can't help the triumphant grin that spreads over my face. "How about a big old scoop of today's special? Looks like that's the *Fiery Queen.*"

If it's possible, his attempt to act like an ice sculpture takes on a new level of rigidity. "We're out."

"Oh, really?" I saunter over to the glass display where customers can peer down on the variety of flavors, each one designated by a handwritten label. Up front and center, I spot a half-full container with a little tag that reads *Fiery Queen* in block script. "Because, as far as I can tell, you've still got a bit left." I press my hands to the glass, enjoying how the heat from my skin fogs the surface.

August doesn't admit to lying. He just stomps over to the ice cream and snatches a cup from the neat stack behind the counter.

"No, wait." My protest stops him before he can scoop out my treat. "I want a cone."

The man growls, but I'm having too much fun with playing the temptress to worry about whether the sound is sultry or menacing.

August replaces the cup and grabs a waffle cone. I can't wait to have the crispy dough in my mouth, knowing the flavor will taste exactly how the delicious man in front of me smells. If my plan works, ice cream is not all I'll be using to satisfy my craving.

Even as stress radiates off of him, August forms my dessert with smooth skill.

"Here." He's gruff as he extends the offering to me. I make sure our fingers brush as I accept the cone. He snatches his hand back as if burned.

Not yet, but maybe soon.

Keeping my gaze on him the entire time, I drag my tongue across the creamy, frozen treat in a slow lick. August's eyes don't leave my mouth.

The intensely delicious flavors distract me from my mission as they bombard my tongue. For a moment, I drop the seductress role as I fight to keep my eyes from rolling back into my head.

"Bless the goddess, this is fucking amazing. What's all in this?" I savor another slow lick.

August's clenched jaw relaxes a hint, and he grumbles out an answer with sheepish pride, "Honey, cinnamon, whiskey."

"And this is what I taste like to you?"

That gets him to shut back down, shutters dropping over his eyes. He steps back and crosses his arms over his chest, as if that'll somehow block my advances. Like he thinks I'm going to climb over the counter to get at him.

Silly ice cream god. That's not my plan at all.

I'm going to get the Viking to come to *me*.

I take my own backward step, moving just far enough away that I'm sure August has a full view of my outfit. No point in denying that I know

I look like sex on a Popsicle stick. This dress has hung alone and forlorn in the back of my closet for close to a year. When I tried it on in the store, the crimson fabric felt like a second skin, so I immediately bought it. But since that moment, I've never found the right occasion to slip it on.

Until today.

Eyes on August, I enjoy another lick of my cone, briefly reconsidering my plan as I experience the glorious taste of Fiery Queen.

The payoff will be worth it, I remind myself.

I hold the cone away from my face. Not too far though. Close enough that I might bring it back for another lick at any moment, but far enough that I clearly want to talk. "You left Damien's party pretty fast."

He grunts.

"Pity. Wouldn't have minded spending some time in the water with you."

August scowls. "If you like water, you're better off with my cousin."

I see he picked up on the past between me and his relative. Have to admit, I didn't expect to keep my affections within the family.

But just because the two men are cousins doesn't mean I find August any less enticing.

"I had a cherry that was in bad need of popping. Sammy helped me out. It's probably worth noting that I never requested a second round." I affect a stage whisper. "This might be news to you, but your cousin is slightly full of himself. Not the best quality in a bed mate."

The Ice Elemental snorts and then glares as if he's mad at me for making him laugh. "You need to finish up and head out. I'm closing."

"Of course. I'll get right on that." Even as I agree with him, I don't make a move to eat any more. Instead, I encourage the rising heat in my body to decimate the perfectly sculpted scoop.

Standing in the middle of August's shop, I let the sweet treat melt in my hand. Rivulets of ice cream trickle over my fingers, like sugary veins forming on the surface of my skin.

"Quinn," August growls. "Eat your gods-damn ice cream."

I bite my lip and blink the widest eyes I can manage at him. "What if I want *you* to eat it?"

August shoves a hand into his messy golden hair, muttering curses and looking anywhere but at me. A chill rises in the air, pushing back against my heat. I watch in fascination as frost scatters over the taut skin on his exposed forearms.

What would it feel like to touch that? To lick it?

"I think you should leave." He won't look at me. Won't even truly tell me to go.

Because August wants this, too.

The only reason he's holding back is because he thinks his powers will hurt me. But this Ice Elemental has no idea how hot my fire roars, especially around him. August might as well be a blacksmith pumping the bellows in his forge, feeding the flames under my skin with pure oxygen.

He's going to have to do a lot more than gently suggest I leave to get me to walk out of this shop.

"Hey, August?" I affect an innocently curious tone.

Something in my voice has him glancing up. But his crystal gaze doesn't reach mine. Instead, his deeply blue irises focus on my arm. The one that clutches my ice cream cone.

Streams of Fiery Queen have trailed the entire length of my forearm, collecting at my bent elbow and dripping onto the dark hardwood floor beneath my knockoff Louboutin heels. I mourn the waste but remind myself that it'll be worth it if my plan works out.

While he's distracted, I push on with my question, suppressing an evil grin as I go. "When you're fully aroused—you know, hard, ready for action, on the verge of begging to get inside a woman"—August's throat bobs as he swallows, and his glare flicks up to my face—"does that frost cover your entire body?"

He glances down at his arms, scowling, annoyed that his powers are giving away so much of his inner turmoil. His thick fingers rub the frozen surface as if they can erase the evidence. "This is a bad idea."

Ignoring him, I trace a finger through the soft ice cream in my cone. With it thoroughly coated, I slowly suck the whole finger into my mouth, enjoying the taste and the way August's eyes track the movement.

Once I've lapped up all the delicious cream, I shoot him a grin. "Then let's be bad."

I don't know what part of my performance was the last straw, but August's stoic resistance cracks. Before I can blink, he's around the counter, gripping my shoulders in a tight grasp.

A soothing coolness seeps from his palms as they press into my overly warm skin. I want to lean further into him, but the frustrating man keeps me at an arm's distance.

"You don't know what you're asking."

Staring up at August is like standing at the foot of a jagged, snow-capped mountain. The sight is glorious...daunting...terrifying in a way that makes one question if the magnificent image was meant for any eyes other than the gods.

He steals the breath from my lungs, but the light-headedness reminds me of what it's like to summit such great heights. I want to climb him.

"Quinn?" Apparently, my silence was enough to cause worry. His eyebrows dip, and his fingers press deeper into my shoulders. The Ice Elemental's ruggedly sculpted face loses its frosty shield, and his inner turmoil lies bare.

The heat pulses, a living thing under my skin, and I don't bother fighting the power begging to be released.

As I keep my gaze on August's face, a reddish light flickers, casting interesting shadows over his scruff-covered chin and his high, round cheekbones. His eyes widen, tracing over my body, where I know small flames have started to form.

Silently, I say a thankful good-bye to my outfit. Not even a jaw-dropping crimson dress can survive my powers. I've never mastered that level of control.

But I know, deep in my bones, the flames will never injure August. The same way his ice won't hurt me.

Time for him to learn that, too.

Chapter Fifteen

AUGUST

Fire rises from Quinn's skin as if she were a piece of kindling. Only *she's* the source of the flames. They trickle over her, dancing and moving with a silent rhythm. The edges of her tantalizing red dress blacken and smolder to ash.

Too shocked by the sudden appearance, I forget to remove my hands from her shoulders. Then, when the sparks meet my flesh, I'm too mesmerized by the sensation to retreat.

By all rights, I should be shouting in pain, my hands on fire. Instead, the living heat makes contact with my natural frost, and a hiss echoes through the shop. Steam rises from where we're in contact, and a decadent warmth races down my arms to fill every hidden corner of my body.

My eyes threaten to roll back in my head, and Quinn lets out a satisfied hum.

"You can't hurt me, August. You can only make me feel good."

The finger she was sucking on a moment ago trails down the front of my apron, leaving scorched fabric in its wake. Her own dress is half gone at this point, the fire eating it as eagerly as I want to consume her.

Letting her go is more painful than holding on, but I do it. Some of the confident swagger leaves Quinn's posture. I'm sorry to see it disappear, but I'm on a mission.

My steps hit the ground heavy and leave icy prints behind.

"Stop, August. I'm sorry. You don't have to leave. I will."

When I reach the front door, I glance over my shoulder to see the Fire Elemental clutching the singed edges of fabric together to keep the material from crumbling off her body.

"Too late," I inform her, flipping the lock and switching off the Open sign. "If you wanted out, you shouldn't have shown up wearing that dress."

This time, I'm the one stalking her, prowling through my shop to approach my now-grinning quarry.

"So you're going to stop being noble?" Quinn's hair crackles with live flames.

I fist the strands, smothering the heat with my frigid palms, and tug her head back until she has no choice but to stare into my eyes.

"The things I'm going to do to you will have me burning in hell. But as long as the fire is your doing, I have no complaints."

Then I brave the inferno of her gaze and press my lips against hers. Heat spills through my body, burning my throat in painful pleasure that has me dragging in a deeper breath. Quinn is a hot spring I want to soak in for the rest of my life.

She gasps and groans as I pull us closer together. When I press my hand into her lower back, I realize the dress is completely gone. I don't have time to mourn its loss when there's a naked Quinn in my arms.

Cupping her bare ass, I lift her until she can wrap her legs around my waist. With just a few steps, I have Quinn perched on the surface of one of the heavy wooden tables. Plenty of my ice cream creations have graced this surface, but I doubt any of them have tasted as delicious as this woman.

The thought has me breaking our kiss and drawing back enough to glance at her hand. What was once a perfectly formed cone is now a crumble of fractured waffle pieces, stuck to her palm with traces of melted Fiery Queen.

"I have a strong grip." Quinn grins up at me, and I smirk in return.

"I'll be wanting to test that out at some point."

She gasps out a delighted chuckle that melts into a moan when I grab her arm and drag my tongue over her ice cream–coated skin.

Perfection. I thought the specialty flavor was decadent on its own, but paired with Quinn, the concoction morphs into ambrosia.

Maybe it's animalistic, but I don't let her go until I've consumed every drop of Fiery Queen she let spill over her. By the time I'm done, she's writhing and panting, leaving scorch marks on the heavy wooden tabletop.

Still hungry, I release Quinn's arm to place my hand on her chest, resting my palm between her heaving breasts and pressing until she lies back, completely on display before me.

Then I pause, worry flickering through my mind, dimming my arousal as I realize Quinn is shivering. I go to remove my hand, spotting frosty marks on her freckled skin.

"I'm sorry—" I move to step back.

"No!" My retreat fails when she wraps her scalding palms around my wrist, pulling my frigid hand to its previous position. "More. I love the chill."

"You don't..." I trail off as Quinn lifts her head to glare into my eyes in aroused defiance.

She drags my hand over her own naked body. Crystals scatter along her bare skin as I watch, fascinated. When the side of my finger brushes her puckered nipple, a groan spills from her throat as her head drops back and her spine bows off the table.

"Fuck, Quinn," I all but growl, now fully convinced her shivering arose from pleasure.

"Yes. That. Do that." She gasps out the command.

I'm tempted, but my hunger still demands a taste of her essence.

Tugging my hand from her clutches, I grip her thighs, pushing them wide as I kneel down to glimpse the glistening core of her, surrounded by beautiful, fiery curls.

My tongue sweeps across her folds, just as I would lick a scoop of ice cream. I vow to use her as my cone one day. But for now, I savor and tease pure Quinn.

The original Fiery Queen.

Soon I find myself gripping her hips with a steel hold, so I can continue my ministrations as she twists and writhes. I press her to the table with one forearm while I suck on her little nub of pleasure and push a finger past her entrance.

Nails dig into my scalp, and my name spills out of her lips on a shout. The smooth, slick walls of her pulsate around my finger.

As she gasps out pants, lying loose-limbed on the table, I stand and strip off the apron and shirt Quinn burned holes in during her seduction. My pants, still intact, get shoved down only as far as my thighs, and I fist my throbbing cock.

Despite the pleasure and need muddling my brain, one rational thought intrudes, and I let out a curse.

Quinn rises up on her elbows, a single eyebrow curving in question.

"I don't have any condoms," I explain. Not a product I thought I'd need to supply at my ice cream shop.

The naughty Fire Elemental smirks at me as she bends one of her knees to prop a foot on the table, putting her pussy on full display. The red heels are gone, either burned up or discarded.

"This is about to get to volcanic levels of hot, and I doubt Trojan makes Elemental condoms." Quinn licks her bottom lip. "I'm on the pill and have a clean bill of health."

I grin. "Thank the gods. Me too." Realizing how those words might fit together, I scramble to clarify. "I mean the health. Not the pill. When they make one of those for men, I'll pop them every day for you."

Her laugh rings out, as mesmerizing as staring into a campfire. The sound dances around the empty shop, and my chest tightens at the idea of hearing the joyous declaration every day.

Placing the head of my cock at her entrance, I hold Quinn's smoky gaze with my unforgiving one. "To be clear, this is in no way a one-and-done situation."

It's not a question, but I still wait for her response. She sits up straighter, bringing her sweet cinnamon scent with her. Hot hands cup my shoulders, fingers pressing into my muscles, nails digging into my skin. Marking me. Claiming me.

"I'm not letting you go." Her whisper is fierce, and I respond by sliding into her warm embrace.

We move together, slow at first, steam rising from all the places we touch. As I pump inside my Pyro, I grip her neck, pulling her in for more burning kisses. She rakes trails of fire down my back with her nails, spurring me on faster.

Sparks fly from the ends of her ruby hair, and the frost that gathers in my gut continues to melt and spill into her.

I reach between us, pinching her nipples to elicit more beautiful noises from her. She groans into me, our mouths melded together. My hips rock, my fingers knead, and my balls tighten.

I'm torn between reaching my climax and spending hours buried in her.

Should have known the demanding witch would steal the decision from me.

Quinn breaks our kiss to lean down and drag her teeth along the pulsing vein in my neck. Meanwhile, her scorching hand reaches between my legs to gently cup my balls. In her warm palm, she strokes them before giving just a light tug.

My last bit of control shatters. With a shuddering groan, I push as deep into her glorious heat as I can go and ride out my climax with my nose buried in her silky, sweet-smelling hair.

I come back to myself with the caress of her fingers tracing random designs over my back. Her cushion-soft lips press into the hollow of my throat.

"August?" My name in her husky, scorched voice has me wondering how long before I can get my dick hard again.

"Mmhmm?" Apparently, my voice hasn't fully returned. I cup the back of Quinn's head and tilt mine to meet her eyes.

She stares up at me, mischievous smile playing over her kiss-swollen lips. "You wouldn't happen to have some spare clothes lying around? I seem to have misplaced my dress."

Chapter Sixteen

QUINN

As August goes into his back office to search for something to cover me, I visit the small bathroom to clean up. In the mirror my skin is flushed, my hair is a mess, and there are little spiders of frost on the places where he held me.

I've never felt more beautiful.

When I walk back out, August still hasn't returned. I slip behind the front counter, just in case some curious kid walks by the front door and decides to press his face against the window. I'd rather not have the police called on me for indecency. The lights in the shop are off, thank the goddess, but there's still enough of a glow from the kitchen that I can see.

Staring out at the space with its rustic decoration, it's almost as if August has carved out a small piece of Alaska and brought it here for us all to experience. I have very little claim on the man, but I can't help feeling proud of him.

It's also sexy as hell that he's a successful business owner who made his dream come true. Maybe as time goes on, he'll let me lay claim, and then I can be as proud as I want. Also have access to unlimited ice cream.

Thinking of ice cream, my stomach clenches, reminding me that instead of eating my glorious treat, I let the whole thing melt onto the floor. And after a rousing bout of sexcapades with August, I'm ravenous.

One of the perks to getting ravished in an ice cream shop should be a post-coital icy treat.

I reach for a scooper before approaching the glass case that holds all of August's delicious creations. A scoop of Fiery Queen will hit every possible spot that his tongue didn't.

The container's door slides open with a soft swish, and I lean closer to discern which metal pan holds the flavor I'm looking for.

It takes me less than a second to discover a catastrophic problem.

There's no ice cream. Not anymore.

All that exists in this display case is flavored milk.

Every bit of the ice cream is melted.

Desperate to prove that my eyes are lying to me, I reach out with my bare hand. I plunge a finger into room temperature liquid.

"I don't have any pants, but this extra-large T-shirt should keep you decent enough until you get home." August walks out of the back hallway, holding a huge navy blue shirt that proclaims *Land of Ice Cream and Snow* across the front.

The guilt must be clear on my face because his grin falters and his step quickens.

"What's wrong, Quinn?"

"I'm so sorry. I-I thought I had it under control. That being with you fixed everything." The words hurt to say as I force them from my shame-tightened throat.

August's steps echo through the shop as he approaches me. While he stares down at the destruction, I snatch the shirt from his hand and tug it over my head. My naked body embarrasses me because I can't help thinking about the ruin my sexual urges bring with them.

"There wasn't much left. It's not a big deal," he offers.

"But this isn't all the ice cream you have, is it?"

August scratches the back of his neck, then tilts his head toward the kitchen. I follow him, even though I want to go hide under one of the tables. Better yet, I want to rewind ten minutes. Back to when everything was glorious.

Inside the brightly lit room is a cooler large enough to fit a human body. August pops open the top.

I moan in self-disgust.

Soup. It's all fucking melted as soup.

He doesn't bother to shut the lid, instead turning to cross the kitchen to where a heavy metal door takes up a portion of the wall. When he unlatches it, I realize there's a massive walk-in freezer.

I don't dare follow, worried that the heat might still be leaking out of my pores without me realizing.

"Everything in here is still frozen," August assures me, stepping back into view and offering a conciliatory smile.

The guilt isn't done with me though. Not when I'm standing next to what must be gallons of melted mess.

"What about this?" I point to the cooler. "Can you refreeze it?"

August grimaces, then quickly smooths the expression off his mouth, clearly worried about me seeing it.

"You can't, can you?" Mortification burns through me, though the heat is nothing compared to what I must have been putting out just minutes ago.

"No." My fantasy man's shoulders shrug as he returns to my side. "I mean, technically I can. But it's a health hazard. It's okay, though. I can always make more." August's large hand reaches for me, but I step away, my heels clicking from my retreat. I cross my arms over my chest, probably looking like I'm trying to defend myself. But I'm not the one who needs protection.

"How long will it take to replace all of this? How much will it cost?" I whisper the questions, scared of the answers.

"Don't worry—"

"August! I melted half your stock! How are you not furious with me right now?"

"You didn't mean to. It was an accident."

I try not to flinch, but I can't help it.

An accident. How many accidents do I have to have with my powers before I admit that I'm a menace? Even though I don't mean to cause trouble, I can't pretend I don't know that it follows me around like a destructive shadow.

"I should go." Without waiting for a response from him, I hurry toward the front door. My fingers are fumbling with the lock when he catches up.

"Quinn, wait."

I don't look at him. I can't. "Let me know how much stock I ruined. I'll pay you back."

The metal latch slides free, but the door doesn't budge. That's when I realize a huge Viking hand hovers above my head, holding the door closed.

"I'm not worried about the money."

A huff of disbelief escapes me.

"You're a new business. Of course you should be worried about the money! This isn't a free cone you hand out on a whim, August. I melted at least a day's worth of product. Probably more." I whirl around to glare at him. It's that or I burst into tears. "You should be interrogating me right now. Trying to find out if I work for the competition."

A smile twitches at the corner of his mouth, and it makes me want to pull my hair out by the roots. "If you are a saboteur, I doubt you'd tell me."

"Unless I'm trying to lull you into a false sense of security!" My emotions are on a rampage, spilling out of my mouth in nonsense. At least nothing of what I'm feeling is lust.

The neediness for August and his body doesn't even hint at resurfacing when I see that he's starting to full on grin. That he's not mad.

Just like that, he's already forgiven me.

Making the same mistake my sisters do.

I don't need coddling or jokes or work arounds.

I need a fix.

Because I'm a problem.

I'm a walking, talking equation with no solution in sight. I thought August was the missing component. Turns out he's only a means to a mildly less destructive result.

This isn't good enough.

I'm not good enough.

Don't any of them see that?

"I need to go home." I turn back toward the door, not wanting him to witness the extent of the self-loathing I'm descending into.

"I..." August starts, then lets out a laugh on a sigh. "I want to go with you, but I do need to figure out what needs to be replaced."

"You should. Take stock of the damage."

"Quinn," he whispers my name, his breath brushing against my neck as he leans down. "Kiss me?"

If it had been a demand I might have been able to pull on my bitch cape and fly off into the night with a sassy *Hell no!*

But the question is clear in his voice. The doubt. And it makes me feel like a whole different kind of destructive.

I'll probably get whiplash from the back and forth of facing away, then facing him again. This time, when I turn, I do it fast enough that his eyes can't catch mine. My arms fling around his neck, wrapping python tight. I plaster my body to his and offer the kiss he asked for. I make it deep but quick, scared of my own lust. Just as I feel the shift in his shoulders that proceeds his hands dropping to my waist, I let go.

With him too distracted to keep the door shut, I make my escape.

Only my hurried walk across the parking lot in red heels and an XXL T-Shirt doesn't feel anything like freedom.

That will forever exist in the space under August's hands.

A place I'm not sure I'll ever get to visit again.

Chapter Seventeen

AUGUST

"She's avoiding me." My thumb picks at the label on my beer as I sit at the kitchen island in Damien's house.

"I could give you her address. You could show up at her house." Sammy makes the offer with his head buried in the fridge.

The three of us have made a habit of getting together for a drink a couple of times a week. For some reason, I thought they might be able to help me with my relationship problems.

I stare at my cousin with disbelief and disgust. "You mean like a stalker? You want me to stalk Quinn because she won't return my calls?"

"Is it stalking if she likes you?" He punctuates his point by popping off the lid of his bottle.

Damien and I meet eyes across the room, then answer in unison. "Yes."

Sammy throws his hands up, spilling half his beer with the gesture. "Well then all those romance movies are full of stalkers!"

"What are you talking about?" Damien waves his hand, and the puddle on the tiles forms into a golden bubble that floats its way to the sink while Sammy keeps on with his dramatic flailing.

"I'm talking about, *Sleepless in Seattle, There's Something About Mary, This Means War, Love Actually*, I could go on."

"Could you? I didn't realize you were such a rom-com expert." Damien smirks.

"Anyone who doesn't like happy endings is a heartless bastard," Sammy announces.

"That's fiction, though. I don't think real-life stalking ends the same way." And I find it concerning I have to explain this to my cousin.

"Yeah. You're not going to be crying tears of joy. You'll be crying tears of 'Oh shit! She just pepper sprayed me in the face!'" Damien gives Sammy an evil grin as the other man rolls his eyes.

"Who's pepper spraying Sammy? And can I help?" Marisol strolls into the room, glaring at the blonde Squid. I guess she still hasn't forgiven him for hauling her out of the shop like a bag of potatoes last week.

Still, I can't pretend like I'm not grateful for him helping me out then. I doubt I would have gotten to debauch my shop with Quinn if the two of them had hung around.

Also, Marisol came to work the next day all business. She hasn't spoken to me in anything other than a professional manner. No subtle flirting. No giving me moon eyes.

At least, not where I can see.

Something seems to have gotten through to her that crushing on her older boss is a dead-end street.

Everything should be falling into place in my life.

If only Quinn weren't avoiding me.

"No one is pepper spraying me, you little demon. We're only debating the proper way to pursue a woman."

"Well, I'll give you a free piece of advice. Don't pepper spray her."

Damien snorts just as he tips his beer for a drink, resulting in coughing and swearing and all of us laughing.

Once the room calms down, Marisol pipes up again. "So whose love life did I just save with my words of wisdom? You finally find a lady that'll give you more than ten minutes of her time, Sammy?"

My cousin affects a cocky grin. "Why would I need more than ten minutes?"

A smile tugs at my mouth. "I can't imagine why Quinn never wanted a repeat with you."

My cousin glares at me, and I realize there's not an ounce of jealousy in my chest. Worry, sure. Discomfort, yeah. But not because I think Quinn wants to leave me for him. I'm just worried she wants to leave.

"Seems like that trait runs in the family," he mutters.

I forgot how much of a dick Sammy can be sometimes.

Feeling petty, I freeze his beer. In retaliation, he pulls a palmful of water from the sink and directs it at the crotch of my pants.

"Children! Behave!" Damien tries to keep his face stern, but I can tell he's fighting off laughter.

"You're not dating Quinn?" The question brings the focus of the room back to Marisol, and I don't like the hopeful glimmer in her eyes.

Even though Sammy and Damien will aim jokes at me and give me a hard time, I know two things.

One, they do actually want me to be happy.

Two, they do not want sixteen-year-old Marisol chasing after me. If only to keep me from freezing their entire alcohol supply.

"She's just gone a bit radio silent on him," Sammy says.

"Rough patch, nothing more," Damien adds.

Marisol's head bobs around the room, her gaze finally coming to rest on me. "If she's blowing you off, then she doesn't deserve you."

A grimace tries to claim my face, but I keep it contained. "I don't think she's avoiding me for no reason."

"What's the problem? She seemed pretty eager to see you when we were there." Sammy waggles his eyebrows, and Marisol scowls at him.

"I think it's because she..." I trail off, trying to figure out how to phrase this without letting my young employee know I fucked a woman on one of the tables at Land of Ice Cream and Snow. "She has a similar problem with her powers that I do. And she let them get out of hand. At my shop."

All three Squids look confused, then understanding dawns on two faces, along with shit-eating grins.

"There were some problems with things getting...too hot?" Sammy's eyebrows do a suggestive waggle.

"Are you saying that Pyro set a fire at the shop?" Marisol's horrified question has me shaking my head adamantly.

"No. No fire. Just heat. We realized she melted some of the stock, and she felt bad about it. Still, I thought we left things off on a good note." Well, maybe not the best note. But at least with the understanding that things between us weren't over.

My cousin holds out his beer to me in silent request, his eyes flicking to my pants with an unspoken offer.

I tug at the ice, and simultaneously feel the dampness of my jeans retreat.

We're quick to forgive.

"You're not going to get any answers if you don't talk to her," Damien points out.

"And you're not going to talk to her unless you show up at her house," Sammy adds.

"Show up at her house? First pepper spray, now stalking? How do you even get women to talk to you?" Marisol gives Sammy a look of disgust, but he only throws her a wink.

"All charm."

I block out their back and forth and my mind grapples with the problem.

If I'm not willing to show up unannounced in Quinn's life—and I'm not—how can I fix things?

Unless Quinn got what she wanted from me already.

Maybe she and my cousin have a few things in common when it comes to their sexual conquests.

Maybe she doesn't want anything fixed at all.

Chapter Eighteen

QUINN

Most people avoid driving out into the desert, period. Much less when their activities might turn their car into a roiling fireball of unusable destruction.

I make sure only to travel as far as I know I can walk back to civilization if the worst should happen. If I do demolish my transportation and my means of communication during this practice session, then at least I know I won't die. A normal, non-Elemental human might because of sun exposure and heat exhaustion.

Me? I'll just have a cranky, hungry hike to the nearest gas station.

Hopefully, not in the nude.

I haven't seen another car in an hour, and the last building I passed was a good ten miles back. Which means I'm—cross my fingers—safe to go about my fiery business.

Dust rises in a burnt orange cloud as I pull off to the shoulder, driving a short way into the desert. Not far, but enough that I'm hoping no one spots my Jeep and tries to tow it.

Then I hike.

Again, not far. I'm not worried about the skin-blistering temperature or anything. But I do have a habit of getting lost. I'm good wandering around the sandy landscape as long as the only danger is the heat.

Despite my goddess ancestry, I can still easily die from lack of food and water if I'm stuck out here for multiple days.

I might not be human, but I am mortal.

Dodging the occasional cactus, I try not to consider how painful the walk back will be if my boots get scorched to pieces.

"I can control it. I know I can." I mutter the words to myself and the small lizards that scurry away at the crunch of my boots.

When I've almost lost sight of my car, I come upon what I've been searching for. The rock is big enough and flat enough for me to sit on if I cross my legs. The pose is preferable anyway, seeing as how I'm trying to get into a sort of meditative state.

I know one of the things that helped Cat gain control of her rage-induced powers was immersing herself in the world of yoga. She tried to teach me the structured breathing and meditation practices, but I found the sitting and doing nothing to be a major snooze fest.

Numbers have always been the calming aspect of my life. When sexy thoughts creep into my mind I drown them out with calculus. But I can't focus on equations when August is kissing me.

So here I am, in the middle of nowhere, nothing to distract me, an entire day to practice.

I make sure no bugs or other creepy crawlies are in my general vicinity before settling myself, eyes closed.

First things first, setting a base of calm. I count to eight as I breathe in, and eight as I breathe out. Over and over again. Just like Cat taught me.

Boring. But I do it.

I try to clear my mind of the emotional turmoil of these last few weeks. With my mental hands, I push aside the devastation at discovering I had ruined a decent portion of August's ice cream supply. I tamp down on the insecurity of his original rejection at the pool party. I avoid the doubt that I'll ever have full control of my powers, therefore leaving me to live a lonely, romance-free life.

Instead, I force my brain to do nothing more than follow the count of my breathing.

The practice seems to be working, and when I'm sure my mind has been relaxed for a few minutes, I let in a few specific thoughts.

Thoughts about August. The way his hands felt trailing over my body. The way his mouth fit perfectly against mine. The taste of him mixed with the cinnamon of the ice cream. The refreshing coolness of his bare skin rubbing against mine.

How it felt to have him inside me.

Heat unfurls in my chest, the fire hungrily eating up the fuel of my lust-soaked memories.

And as the fire rises, I envision wrapping my arms around it, pulling the flames in close to my chest so they only exist within my body. Denying them the freedom to spill out into the world.

At first, I experience a spike of triumph that my hold on the power is working.

But I quickly realize I don't need to use my arms to contain the force. I need nothing more than a slightly cupped hand around a candle flame. The heat of my desire is entirely manageable rather than an uncontrollable onslaught.

And that's a problem.

I need the full inferno to rise up in me. Because it will if I ever allow myself to be intimate with August again. If I can't bring forth that mass of heat, then I don't have the chance to learn how to fight it.

When I finally open my eyes, the sun has shifted positions. A glance at my watch shows I've been practicing for two hours.

Two hours of getting nowhere.

"Goddess damn it." The sweltering air evaporates my words.

At least Cat will be happy to hear I've figured out how to meditate.

Across the way, on a rock, sits a tiny lizard.

"Stop staring at me," I grumble, shooting the reptile a scathing glare.

The thing's tongue sneaks out and licks its own eye.

"Ugh! Gross. Get out of here!" I wave my arms in what I hope is an intimidating display. The creature scuttles away. "Weird ass lizard," I mutter at its retreating form.

This isn't going to work.

I gaze around at the barren landscape. The terrain holds a certain kind of beauty, with its rusty colors and forbidding plant life. Unfortunately, this desert is not sexy in the slightest.

Thoughts of August will only get me so far.

It's him, the actual man standing in front of me, that revs my engine until it combusts.

I wonder how weird it would be for me to ask Sammy to try and get me a shirtless photo of August. One I could bring out here and stare at and maybe use to call up the fire storm.

That wouldn't be odd. Right?

Maybe if I stuck my hands down my pants and started to get things going...

The lizard is back.

"Fine!" I stand up and kick a small rock toward the peeping tom. "I'm going, you creep!"

Today was a giant bundle of complete uselessness.

Chapter Nineteen

AUGUST

My first thought is that the flash of red is a reflection off a car windshield. My next guess is that I'm hallucinating because it's been over a week since Quinn sauntered into my shop and eviscerated all other sexual encounters for me.

The thought has my eyes trailing over to the table where she'd been sprawled out naked. A group of teenagers lounges there now, none the wiser.

I don't feel bad, especially because I made sure to scrub the area down. I'm not a monster.

Still, despite every trace of our encounter being washed away, there's no soap in the world strong enough to bleach out the memories of Quinn. Quinn raking her nails along my chest. Quinn crying out my name, begging for more of my icy touch. Quinn with little flames dancing over her bare skin, each one flaring to life because of the lust I inspired in her.

Barely stifling a groan, I glance back out the front window.

And I lose my breath.

She's here.

Out in the middle of the parking lot, Quinn stands still, facing my shop. At this distance, I can't make out her facial features, but it doesn't matter. I will her to start moving again. All I want is to hear the chime of the bell at the front door, telling me she's stepped inside. That she's not avoiding me anymore.

Instead, the Pyro turns her back and walks in the other direction.

"Hell no," I mutter. Then louder, I tell Marisol, "Watch the register."

I still have on my apron as I shove open the glass door, charging out into the noonday sun.

As if sensing my approach, Quinn glances over her shoulder. With her sunglasses on, I can't see the expression in her eyes, but her pillowy lips part.

Will she wait for me to catch up?

No.

Quinn doubles her speed, which admittedly is not very fast. The gait she uses is some strange shuffle step. It's like she wants to be caught. I'm more than happy to oblige.

"Quinn Byrne!" My voice comes out low and growly, and her shoulders go up to her ears. "You better pause that cute ass right where it is!"

That earns me a gasp and a glare, of which I get the full effect because she decides to swipe off her sunglasses in the process of shooting it at me.

All I care about is that she's stopped.

I meant what I said to Sammy. I would never show up at Quinn's house uninvited.

But she's in my territory now. Came here of her own free will. And I'm not about to let her scurry away without saying my piece.

"This cute ass is *my* ass, and I'll do whatever the hell I want with it! And maybe I don't appreciate you shouting about it in a strip mall parking lot!"

Quinn stomps her foot to emphasize her point, and the movement draws my eyes downward.

"What are you wearing on your feet?" I can't help asking. Even though I need to have a serious conversation with her, I still want to know every little odd thing about the Pyro.

"I...what?" Clearly my question threw her off balance. Good. I think I need to keep her at least a little unsteady if I want to get any answers.

"You can't tell me those are real shoes." All that's between her and the scorching hot blacktop is a thin strip of foam on each sole. I'd be worried about the material disintegrating and her feet catching fire if that weren't a normal thing for her.

"They're disposable flip flops," Quinn uses a tone that automatically adds the word *Duh* on the end of her statement.

"You wear disposable shoes?" *Is this some weird Arizona thing I don't know about?*

"Not usually. They're for pedicures. Why are we talking about this? I'm leaving." She scowls at me, daring me to stop her.

She's here for a pedicure? My determination wavers. But then logic steps in, acting the savior in a way it usually doesn't.

"How many nail places are there in Phoenix?"

Quinn only blinks at me, her russet lashes sweeping against soft cheeks I want to cup my hands around. From her blush, I can guess her skin would be warmer than usual.

"It... It doesn't matter! I like that one." She shuffles a step closer to her Jeep. My movements only mirror hers, but with my longer legs, I get a good deal closer.

"Really? You like the one right next to my shop. That's the *only* reason you're here?"

"Obviously. See?" She waves a hand at her feet. "Painted toes."

Quinn isn't lying. There does seem to be a new color on her nails. It's a light, almost crystal blue, and the sun reflects in a delicate coat of sparkles. The combination reminds me of ice, while the pinpoints of shine bring to mind the hundreds of freckles scattered over Quinn's face.

"I want to suck on your toes," I mutter without thinking.

I've never had a foot fetish, but every inch of Quinn tempts me.

All of a sudden, she's lunging forward.

Eager for her, I spread my arms wide.

But Quinn doesn't climb me like at the pool party or wrap her arms around my neck to pull me in for a scorching kiss. Instead, she makes a desperate grab for the bottom of my apron, crushing the material between her fists.

"You can't say things like that!" Her voice comes out breathless but also angry.

I realize why when she loosens her grip. The edge of my apron is charred, as if the cloth caught fire.

Hope and ice spread through my chest.

My words turned her on so much she set my clothes on fire?

She's not over me. I'm not a one and done. Whatever is wrong between us, it's not a lack of attraction.

"You still want me."

Quinn's head jerks upward, shock slackening her face before she smooths it away.

"What I want and what I can have are two different things." She reaches for the car door handle, and I don't stop her. I never want Quinn to think I'd use my size to manhandle her.

But I don't back down. As she settles in the driver's seat, I continue to push my point.

"Not when it comes to me. You want me? I'm yours."

I'm hit with another glare, and we face off for a minute. Then all of a sudden her face crumbles and her forehead hits the steering wheel. Taking this as a crack in her armor, I push more. "I don't usually do this."

"What? Chase women around parking lots?" she mumbles.

The snort that escapes is involuntary, and I keep talking to gloss over it. "No. I don't do that. Not very often anyway."

Fiery eyes meet mine, and I lean on the window sill, trying to soak in every stinging caress.

"What I meant was, I haven't ever tried a relationship. But I want to. With you."

"I. Melted. Everything." The words grind past her teeth, sounding angry, even as hopelessness glimmers in her gaze.

"And until you convince me you did it on purpose, I'm not holding it against you." My hand reaches into the cab of the Jeep, and my skin tightens from her heat.

That can't be good for the upholstery.

I catch a lock of her crimson hair between my thumb and forefinger, fascinated by the silky texture. Then I let the strand fall away and retract my arm.

"I'm a mess," she whispers with a harsh tone that morphs the words into a plea.

"You're passionate." With a sigh, I find myself lowering my chin to my crossed arms, wanting to use every bit of my energy to memorize the shape of Quinn's face, the fall of her hair, the spicy scent of her soap. Just in case I can't convince her to give me a chance. "Put our powers to the side. If we were humans, would you want to date me?"

A scoff bursts from her chest. "Don't be obtuse, August." Before I can take her response the wrong way, Quinn keeps going. "I lost the ability to form coherent words the first time we met. And do I have to remind you our first date we both thought the other was a human? So yes, obviously, I want to date you."

"Then date me."

"Stop making it sound so easy!"

"It is, and it isn't."

Her fingers curve into claws, and she reaches over, miming strangling me. "I don't care if you're a sexy Viking man with a heart of gold. I will murder you if you don't start making sense."

I lean closer, letting Quinn's hands have full access to my neck if she wants it.

"The choice is easy. The relationship will take some work."

Her scowl softens, so I keep up my argument.

"All of this is new. We're both volatile. But that doesn't mean we give up without trying."

The annoyance seems to relax out of her muscles, and instead of choking me, she lets her hands fall to my collar bones.

The touch is everything I've been craving this past week. Warm. Intimate. Her.

"I want to get better. I hate how I can't control my powers," she admits.

"Let me help you."

"What if it takes a long time? Years?"

The thought of Quinn and I together for a long stretch of time doesn't bring on any worry or fear of commitment. And the idea of waiting doesn't have me fighting impatience. I want her to be happy, and if her haywire powers means I become a permanent fixture in her life, I'll take it.

At least, I'll take the excuse until I can convince her to fall in love with me for me. I'm determined to do that, I decide in the moment. Because I can feel myself careening down that path, and I don't want to go alone.

"Then the sooner we get started the better."

She watches her fingers as they fiddle with my collar, and I enjoy the intimacy of the casual act.

"We can't have sex in your shop again."

"If we went too fast and you want to wait, I'll respect your decision." I won't say I'm overjoyed about not getting to explore her naked body any time soon, but I want whatever makes her comfortable.

"Not having sex in your shop doesn't mean not having sex." The tips of her fingers continue to tease my skin. "But we need to be smart about it until I've gained some control."

"And what does smart sex look like?" My voice has gone surprisingly raspy. Probably because my body has so many emotions fighting inside it. Excitement, lust, need, annoyance that I have to go back to work, and an ever-growing wave of contentment.

"Well, the more water there is around me, the better. So I guess smart sex looks like shower sex."

Shower sex. Quinn wet. Her back pressed against tiles. Her legs wrapped around my waist. Taking her as I hold her in my arms.

The fantasy almost has my knees buckling.

"Yes."

My immediate affirmative response earns me a naughty smile. She leans in quickly to give my bottom lip a small bite but pulls back before I can capture her mouth.

"Okay. If you can promise to be patient with me and only have smart sex, then…"

She trails off, the tail end of her words leading me forward.

"Then…?" I prompt.

Quinn cups my jaw, her nose wrinkling adorably as she scratches her nails in my beard.

"August Nord, you just negotiated yourself a girlfriend."

Pure joy spears through my chest, and I know I've got on the biggest, goofiest grin. "Then kiss me."

Quinn leans forward, but stops just before her mouth touches mine, and her grip on my face keeps me from crossing the final inch.

"Only smart kisses."

"I'll keep you cool," I promise.

She relents, and finally I have her back. Her kiss is chaste, nothing I'd expect from the woman who walked into my shop and burned away her dress to tempt me. I still revel in the innocent touch, feeling my ice prickle over my skin in response. As I press kisses along her sealed lips, I encourage the chill to pass to her.

The action goes against my every instinct. All my life I've been trying to keep the frost from affecting anyone around me.

But this is what Quinn needs. Me.

Then her hands firmly press me back as her eyes blink away a fog of passion.

"You should get back to work," Quinn tells me, and I watch in fascination as her breath puffs out in a small vapor cloud, as if we're standing outside on a cold winter day.

"I don't want to," I mutter but step away from her Jeep nonetheless.

That earns me a saucy smile. She slips her sunglasses back on, and I mourn the loss of her gaze.

"One of us has to be responsible. Today, I guess it's me." There's the sound of her slipping her keys into the ignition and the engine starting. Her hair floats around her, tangling in the breeze from her air vents. Quinn fiddles with a dial and the swoosh of AC disappears.

"You busy tonight?" All I want is to shut my shop down and climb in the passenger seat. But Quinn is not the only one giving in to responsibility. Still, I need firm plans, a clear time for when I'll see her next. I can't handle any more of this avoiding shit.

"What did you have in mind?" Her shaded eyes turn toward me.

"Looking to take my girlfriend out on a date."

Quinn bites her lip, but that doesn't stop the curve of her mouth. "I guess it sounds like I have some amazing plans. I'll text you my address." Then she extends her arm out to me, fingers splayed. "Want to give me another icy shot for the road?"

Hell, I've never had someone ask me to use my powers unless it was to chill a six pack. But Quinn wants my frost against her skin.

Sandwiching her palm between both of mine, I let my stare drop to her cleavage. With that glorious sight in front of me, the cold spills out easily. I watch in fascination as goosebumps crest over her exposed skin in a wave.

She asked for this. She wants it, I have to remind myself.

"Thanks, boyfriend." Quinn retracts her hand.

Then the Pyro shifts her Jeep into drive and pulls away.

And I'm certain she took a piece of me with her.

Chapter Twenty

QUINN

"I'm too hot," I mutter to myself, staring into my mirror. The black dress I have on is doing all types of glorious things for my boobs and my waist and my hips.

Damn. I look good.

Which is kind of the problem.

For this date with August, I need an outfit that says... *Don't bother looking anywhere else because I'm the sexiest thing in this room, but don't try to have sex with me because I might set the building on fire.*

It's a hard line to balance on.

"Oh, I love that dress." Cat drops her bag outside my door and comes to stand beside me in the mirror. The sack full of her tutoring materials sags in defeat, and I feel a kinship with the thing.

"Yeah. It's a great dress. Too great. Forget August, *I* want to take me to bed." My hands trail over the perfectly tailored pencil skirt. Despite the material reaching my knees, the way this garment outlines every curve I have is indecent.

"Got it. You're looking for subtle sexy. I think I can help." Cat jogs from the room, and I pin my hopes on her. While I wait, I slip my feet into the peep-toe pumps.

"Goddess, I'm not even trying. I'm a masochist. Or an arsonist." Because I seem hell bent on starting a fire tonight.

When my sister returns a minute later, I'm still checking myself out in the mirror, as if I'll find the exact right angle to make this dress work. Or not work.

Maybe if I walk hunched over like a gremlin...

"Found it! You need my sexiest cardigan," Cat announces.

She said the words as if they make sense. But they don't.

"I'm sorry, what?"

"This is one of my sexiest cardigans." My sister pulls on the garment and starts striking some poses, as if I just needed to see it in action to understand.

If anything, I'm more confused.

The thing is chunky, and maroon, and has done nothing in its short clothing life to deserve the moniker *sexy*.

At a loss, I find myself asking, "Could you explain your reasoning?"

Cat rolls her eyes at me like the answer should be obvious.

"For starters, it's red. One of the sexiest colors." She runs her fingers over the sleeve.

It's maroon. Still, I nod for her to continue.

"And then look at this knit. Look how loose the pattern is!" My baby sister holds a corner of the cardigan up in front of her face, where she can easily peer at me through the weave.

She's not wrong...exactly.

But I wouldn't call her right either.

"And a loosely knitted cardigan is sexy because...?"

"Are you kidding me?" Cat throws her arms in the air as if she's being asked to explain a simple addition equation to me. "Just imagine if I was naked under this thing. You would see my *nipples*."

I would also see her nipples if she were wearing nothing but a clear plastic tarp, but that doesn't make plastic tarps sexy.

"So," I speak slowly, honestly trying to follow her thought process, "you're suggesting I wear the cardigan, and *only* the cardigan?"

My sister scoffs. "Of course not. I'm saying that August's imagination will go wild when he sees this over the dress."

I have to sit on the bed, feeling a little dizzy on the twisted road that is Cat's logic. "Okay, let me see if I understand what you're saying. You think if I wear this dress," I gesture at my body, "with that maroon—"

"*Red.*"

"Fine. That *red* cardigan over the top, it'll inspire August to imagine what I would look like if my dress disappeared, but the cardigan remained. Do I have that right?"

Cat grins. "Exactly. It's hot, but not *too* hot."

"It's definitely not too hot," I mutter to myself.

"What was that?"

"Nothing," I'm quick to respond. "Why don't you leave that on my bed. I'm going to check in with Harley."

Cat shrugs and does as she's told while I head out to the backyard.

A familiar sight greets me. My older sister being a pool mooch once again.

"Don't you make a decent amount of money?" I ask, standing next to the lounge chair where she suns herself. My hands rest on my hips as I glare down at her. "Enough to get a place with your *own* pool?"

"My my, Quinn. I never knew you to be so crass. We are well-bred young ladies. We do not discuss such vulgar things as *money.*"

My eyes roll on their own. "If I couldn't discuss money then I couldn't do my job. And stop pretending like you're some innocent Southern bell. I'm surprised you've yet to tan topless."

A wicked smile curls her lips. "What a delightful idea." She moves a hand to reach behind her, and I lunge forward, grabbing her wrists.

"No way in hell. Take your tits out at your own place."

Harley smirks. "You're right. I wouldn't want to show you these beautiful globes of perfectness right before your date. Might give you a complex."

"Someone thinks highly of themselves." I retreat a step. "You know, I came out here for your help. But you're making asking for advice super unappealing."

My big sister waves a dismissive hand. "Ask away. Tell me your woes."

"This dress." I move back further so she can judge the whole look. "What do you think?"

Her chin dips and raises as she scans the outfit. "I don't expect you'll be wearing it for long. August will want to rip that number off you. With his teeth."

"Damn." I plop down on the lounge chair across from hers. "That's what I'm afraid of."

"Not seeing the problem. I thought you liked the guy."

"I do. A lot. But I want to get better control of my powers before we fool around again. And if he's giving me *fuck me* eyes all night, combustion is guaranteed."

"Then why'd you think that dress was an option?"

I can't help my petulant shrug. "Because this is a date, and I still want him to think I'm attractive."

"Ah. Balancing act. I see how it is." Harley snaps the bubble gum she's been chewing as she ponders my predicament. "Why don't you borrow one of Cat's *sex doesn't interest me* cardigans?"

Our little sister storms out from the house at that moment. "I'm totally interested in sex! And look at this one." She twirls in front of us, triumph on her flushed face. "It's *black*. And formfitting. There are thousands of people who would fuck me in this. Hundreds of thousands!"

Harley lowers her sunglasses to the tip of her nose, gaze running over Cat. Then she snorts and goes back to reclining. "They'd fuck you because you're hot. They'd fuck you in spite of the cardigan."

Steam starts to rise from my little sister's head. But then she sucks in a deep breath, lets it out slowly, and all indication that her power was taking over disappears.

I envy her control.

"Whatever the reasoning," Cat speaks, her voice steady, if slightly strained, "it sounds like both Harley and I say that a cardigan is the answer."

"Fine," I mumble. "I guess that maroon one'll work."

"It's *red*."

Doesn't matter if it's technicolor, as long as it keeps me from setting the restaurant on fire, then the dick deflater is doing its job.

Chapter Twenty-One

AUGUST

I don't have a lot of dating experience. Truth be told, I've never had a girlfriend.

There's been a handful of women I took out a few times, things got intimate, I got cold—literally—and one of us would break it off.

Now I'm parked outside of Quinn's house and the night seems full of potential. So much so that if I could sweat, my shirt would be damp right now. At least in this instance I'm happy about my ability to keep my body cool.

And that becomes a hell of a lot easier when I knock on the front door and the woman who opens it takes my breath away.

Quinn grins up at me, all her freckles creasing with the expression. A tight black dress hugs her close as a red sweater covers her shoulders. I wonder if she wears the outer layer because she's worried I'll give her a chill.

Self-consciously, I make sure none of the ice gathering in my chest spills out.

"Goddess bless, August. You look so good in dressy clothes." My date steps forward, running her hands over my button-up shirt. The heat of her touch seeps through the fabric, and it's all I can do to fight off a moan of pleasure.

As I struggle with my response, Quinn presses her front to mine, then crosses the last few inches to brush her lips against my mouth. "Give me some ice. I need it with you looking like this."

She's asking for my chill?

Just like in the parking lot, I'm eager to comply, and this time I'm not able to stifle a groan as the power slides from my skin to hers.

Quinn shivers, but from her expression, she likes it.

"Ready to go?" We have to go now before I carry her into the house, locate the nearest surface to bend her over, and hike up the skirt of this sinful dress.

"Definitely." She grabs a purse, then we're down her front walk and in my car.

On the drive, the air between us is charged. There's tension, uncertainty, lust, and probably a handful of other emotions I can't identify. Just when I think I might go wild from the buildup, Quinn reaches over to lace her fingers through mine, claiming my free hand.

But she doesn't just passively hold it. No, Quinn is too curious for that. Instead, she raises my hand up, running her free fingers over the back, tracing the veins and bones under my skin. Examining me.

What is she looking for?

"When your power comes, what does it feel like?"

I clear my throat a couple of times. "You mean what does it feel like... when I'm turned on?"

Quinn chuckles. "No, I think I can guess at that. I mean after you feel lust, your power rises, and then it makes itself known. How is that for you? For me it's like a second pulse under my skin, pressing to get out."

"Really?" I'd never imagined that Elementals felt magic in distinctive ways. But why wouldn't they? The powers themselves are different.

"Yep. Then that second pulse gets so hot everything boils over. Like a pot of water left on the stovetop for too long."

Fascinating. "It's in my gut." I clear my throat and try to think of a better way to describe it. "The ice is deep in my belly, then it seems to scatter over the top of my skin."

"Hmm," Quinn makes the happy noise in the back of her throat. "That's why you get a nice frosty coating."

I don't know that I'll ever get used to the way she likes my cold. Still, the satisfied tone she uses has my power responding, and I let it go enough to form a web of frost across the back of my forearm.

And the woman in my passenger seat practically purrs.

My dick gets half hard, and I carefully retract my arm from her hold. "Gonna need you to stop making those noises if you want me to make it through this date."

A rosy blush spreads underneath Quinn's freckles, but the grin she gives me is wicked.

A few minutes later, we walk into the restaurant Damien recommended. The place does Mexican food with a fine dining flare. Apparently, the head chef was on one of those reality cooking shows, making the place popular. Still, my friend was able to pull a few strings and get me a reservation.

After the mess made of our first date, I want to show Quinn I'll pull out all the stops for her.

The woman at the front podium finds our name on the list and directs us to follow her. The place boasts low mood lighting with most of the tables set up for two diners. We're not the only ones having a date night.

The thought makes me smile, makes me hopeful that I'm doing this right. That I'm not going to screw up this chance I have with the woman of my dreams. My eyes drop to the strong, shapely curve of Quinn's calves as she navigates through the restaurant.

More like the woman of my fantasies.

When the hostess leaves us to our table, I'm about to help Quinn to her seat.

That is until my date speaks.

"Oh hell no."

At Quinn's mutter, I glance around to see what's wrong. *Does she not like the restaurant?* Damien said the food was delicious, but I'll leave in a second if she wants to go somewhere else.

Before I can ask, the Pyro steps up to the table and leans over it. Reaching out, she uses her bare fingers to snuff out a little tea candle that rested between the two plates.

She smirks at me over her shoulder. "No need to add any more fuel to this fire."

Ah. I grin in return, then pull out her chair. A charming stain of red brushes across her cheeks as she takes a seat. The waiter comes by to take our drink orders, then leaves us on our own.

"I have a confession." Quinn leans forward, voice lowered in a conspiratorial whisper.

"What's that?" I keep my response just as quiet.

She bites her lip and my eyes fixate on how her perfect white teeth pucker that delicate skin. "This is the first time I've been out with a guy at a restaurant."

For a moment, I can't comprehend her words. When I try to run them through my brain, they just don't make sense.

"You mean *this* restaurant?"

The ruddiness returns to her cheeks, but she shakes her head.

"Nope. I mean any restaurant. Period."

"How?" is all I can think to say.

Quinn sips from her glass of water and shrugs. "I mean, I've been asked out. So I guess I had plenty of opportunities. But I turned them all down."

I wonder how many *plenty* is. But then I realize the number doesn't matter because I'm the one she said yes to. Laying my hand on the table, palm up, I make a silent request.

Quinn smiles wide and slips her hold into mine.

Heat seeps from her skin, pulsing up my arm, through my chest, filling my body. My eyes threaten to roll back in my head, and I barely stifle a moan.

Curse all the gods. Or maybe bless them. I don't know. All I can think about is the pleasurable agony of limiting myself to the smallest of touches with this woman.

"What I'm saying is," she murmurs, "that I'm a restaurant date virgin, and I'm glad you're my first."

No need for dinner because I just swallowed my tongue.

"That was a weird way to put it, huh?" Quinn squeezes my hand before letting go. "I spend too much time with Harley. She speaks in a constant flow of sexual innuendo, and that's rubbing off."

When I struggle to get words past the blockage in my throat, I go to take a sip of my water, only to get bashed in the nose with a block of ice. "Damn it," I mutter, setting the glass down and pulling the power back under my skin.

"What is it?" Quinn stares across the table at me with concern.

"Nothing." My eyes track over the freckles on her face, loving how they darken in this low lighting. "Only, you look amazing. Of course, you always look beautiful, so I shouldn't be surprised."

"Even with this thing?" Quinn plucks at the knitted cardigan she has on over her heart-stopping black dress. One side has slipped off her shoulder, as if the garment is teasing me.

"You look especially good in red."

My date smirks at me, and slowly the expression morphs into an almost vulnerable smile. "I like you. A lot."

Her statement doesn't have me fighting off frost because I don't get hit with an onslaught of lust. Instead, her sincerity fills me with hope. And anticipation.

Could I convince this amazing woman that I'm worth more of her time? Can I get her to keep coming back to me?

"I like you more than ice cream," is what my mouth decides to declare.

Quinn's eyes go wide. Then she grins so big and gorgeous, I notice our waiter stumble a step as he returns to our table. Luckily, the guy had enough balance to keep our drinks from spilling.

When the waiter asks for our orders, Quinn and I both take a hurried glance at the menu. I pick the first item I spot with the word steak included.

Alone again, Quinn sips her wine, watching me over the rim. I consider how best to apologize for my juvenile compliment. Seriously, I sounded like a preschooler.

"More than ice cream, huh?" Her tongue sneaks out to catch a stray drop of wine at the corner of her mouth.

I have to reach under the table to adjust myself. "Yeah...I mean—"

"What's your favorite flavor?"

"Huh?" I respond, too off balance to be articulate.

"What's your favorite flavor of ice cream that you've ever had?"

Quinn leans forward to trace a finger down the back of my forearm where it rests on the table. "I need to know exactly what I'm beating out."

My brain goes blank. *Name my favorite flavor?* Try naming any flavor when I have her fingers on me. Remembering my own name is a struggle.

Still, with a herculean effort, I'm able to jumpstart my memory, cycling through all of the scoops I've ever sampled.

Capturing Quinn's hand, I keep her from drawing more mind-numbing patterns so I can focus.

"Did I ever tell you I studied ice cream making in college?"

"Really? That's a major?" The sultry notes have left her voice, replaced with interest.

"Technically the major was Food Science. But I had a focus in ice cream. My one professor was originally from Canada, and she would craft this maple nut ice cream that had everyone drooling. Me included."

"Oh goddess, that sounds decadent. Do you ever make it?"

I shake my head. "Tried once, but it was a sad comparison. Can't copy perfection."

Quinn is quiet, seeming to focus on the task of unfolding her napkin to lay on her lap. Then she meets my eyes.

"And you like me better than that maple nut?" Her question is both curious and hesitant.

A grin stretches my cheeks as I hold her gaze. "I'd rather eat you any day of the week."

Chapter Twenty-Two

QUINN

I wish I had a relationship road map. All this jumping around we're doing is making it hard to figure out exactly where I am. Or where I should be. We've mixed up all the steps and added in a few extra.

- Business associates.
- Dating.
- Not speaking.
- Sharing our most intimate, supernatural secret.
- Avoidance.
- Seduction.
- Sex in his ice cream shop.
- More avoidance.
- Making out in a parking lot.
- Flirty date that cannot lead to more.

At least, not yet.

I thought I had a handle on the situation, but then we sit down at this restaurant, and I can't help wanting to fast forward. Or maybe rewind. Whatever gets me back to August's hands all over me like we're alone in Land of Ice Cream and Snow again.

So you can melt everything? Or maybe you'll just fully commit and set this building on fire.

These diners did not pay for those kinds of pyrotechnics.

Luckily, shortly after our food arrived, August asked me about my work. I love my career, but math doesn't make me horny in the slightest. Plus, my date doesn't seem to mind as I wax on about spreadsheets.

There are some exciting aspects to my job though.

"I ran the numbers five times and they didn't change. The owner hired me because he was worried one of his employees was skimming off the top. The guy set up hidden cameras. Turns out, all his employees were on the up and up."

"So, who was it?" August leans forward in his chair.

"His wife! Since she knew his schedule and had keys to everything, she snuck in when he was gone and took cash from the safe and altered the receipts."

"Wow. That's some sneaky shit."

"I know! There's an Airhead in town who works as a PI. I gave the owner her card. Apparently, the wife had a boyfriend on the side with gambling debts." I fork up a bite of my spicy corn dish, enjoying August's baffled look. After a swallow of wine, I smirk at him. "Bet you thought the job of an accountant was boring."

The Ice Elemental grins at me across the table. "Nothing about you is boring."

And there he goes again, heating me up. His words are like a hand reaching inside me, throwing another log onto my internal fire. I down half my glass of water, hoping it'll help.

Since him complimenting me is having such a dangerous effect, I decide to shift the conversation his way.

"Enough about the exciting world of accounting. Let's get back to what's important." I point my utensil at him. "Ice cream."

August chuckles. "What do you want to know?"

We're getting to the end of the meal, which means I'm craving dessert. If I am being honest, I don't want to bother with whatever this place has on its menu. If I could choose, we'd pay our bill and head to the Land of Ice Cream and Snow.

But I can't go there anymore. Not until I get control of my powers.

Hopefully that happens in my lifetime.

"Flavors. How do you think of them? Any major fails? What are you working on now?"

My date's smile widens, and in between bites of his tacos he waxes poetic about his culinary craft.

And I'm simultaneously fascinated and pissed at myself.

Why did I think this direction of conversation would help put a restraint on my attraction?

Would it be weird if I dumped the rest of my water on my lap to cool down my lady parts?

Probably. This joint is too classy for that.

The waiter must somehow telepathically pick up on my neediness because he chooses the moment August is going into detail about the strawberry rhubarb sherbet he's crafting to deliver us the dessert menu.

Since I know a visit to his shop is out of the question—as well as licking every inch of the man—I search for the most decadent item available.

Chocolate lava cake.

Fitting, seeing as how if anyone were to puncture me with a spoon, they'd discover my middle is a melted mess, too.

August opts for the tiramisu.

The man lets out a happy hum when he spoons up the first bite.

I, meanwhile, squirm in my seat and shuck off Cat's cardigan in an attempt to cool my skin.

"This is on my list of flavors to try creating. Just want to choose my favorite local coffee shop first and buy a few bags of their beans." August explains all this as he studies his treat, picking apart the layers with a keen eye.

"Sounds delicious," I murmur, my gaze tracing around the room until I spot a guy chewing with his mouth open.

Gross.

Perfect.

The sight of a stranger's saliva mixing with soggy food bits quickly stifles my arousal, and the magical pulse slows from a rush to a trickle.

But what really helps is the blast of chilly air I'm hit with.

Glancing across the table in search of the source, I realize August has lost interest in his dessert.

The Ice Elemental is staring at me, and despite the huge meal we just ate, he looks hungry.

"You took your cover-up off," he rasps.

Damn the gods.

My *sex doesn't interest me* shield is down, and now August has an unobstructed view of my perfect cleavage.

My internal heat picks back up again, which causes the skin of my chest to flush red.

August's swallow is visible and has me longing to lick his Adam's apple.

"I need to pee!" The proclamation comes out in a panic, and I almost knock over my chair as I stand up and stride toward the bathroom. Multiple people give me strange looks as I dodge around tables in a desperate bid for the restroom.

Alone in the tiled space, I turn the cold tap on the sink, thrusting my hands and then my forearms under the stream. I wish I could douse my entire body, but trying to climb into a sink is a good way to get booted from this fancy restaurant. Instead, I splash my neck, the cool droplets sizzling immediately like grease on a hot grill.

"Damn the gods," I mutter out loud this time, glaring at my reflection. "Don't fuck this up. You're a badass, and badasses don't burn down buildings." Shutting off the water, I pace and fan myself while sucking deep, hopefully calming, breaths. "He's attractive, but you can handle it. Just focus on his flaws. Like how he..."

...

...

I got nothing.

"Come on. No one is perfect. Flaw...flaw...think of a flaw ..."

He's related to Sammy.

But that's not really August's fault.

He was just staring at my chest for a good minute.

But who can blame him? My boobs are awesome.

I'm scraping the bottom of the barrel of what can be considered a failing when my memory snags on something.

"Socks!"

The woman who opens the bathroom door the same time I shout the word gives me a startled look and hesitates to move forward. Like she's scared to use the facilities if there's an odd woman yelling out clothing items in the same room.

Whatever. If she doesn't need to pee bad enough to ignore me then she can hold it.

I return to the sink to dunk my hands under cold water again as I focus on August's flaw.

The guy dressed up for this date, wearing nice slacks and a button-up shirt that stretched over his chest in a beautiful way. He even had on a shiny pair of black dress shoes.

That he paired with *white* socks.

The faux pas!

When August sat down and his pants leg inched up, I saw the color clash and dismissed it. Now I focus all my attention on the one thing August tripped up on.

White socks with black dress shoes? So not sexy.

The woman eventually decides to join me in the bathroom, so I can't give myself any more pep talks. After drying my hands off, I head back out to the dining room. When I reach the table, my date gives me a concerned look.

"Everything good?"

Forcing my eyes away from his caring expression, I drop my gaze to below the table, getting a clear view of his ankles.

Look at those white socks. They're so bright. I bet he'd wear them during sex.

Stop thinking about sex!

"All good!" I decide the best course of action is to simply not look at him, focusing on my dessert instead. The problem is combining the taste of chocolate in my mouth with being near August is a new equation that equals inferno disaster.

"They came by with the check while you were in the bathroom. I hope you don't mind that I paid."

This catches my attention, and I pop my eyes back up to scowl at him. "I do mind. Tell me how much I owe you."

"Would you believe your meal was free?" His attempt to appear innocent fails.

"No."

"Even if it's Redhead Day?"

That has me fighting a smile, twisting my lips to the side as I try to maintain my indignation. Before I tamp it down enough to respond, August holds up a staying hand.

"How about, since I chose this date, I cover it. You choose the next date, and you cover that one. Does that work?"

Scooping up the last of my dessert, I ponder the offer, then nod. "Acceptable."

His wide grin is a warm glow in this dim lighting.

"What's got you so cheerful?"

August reaches a hand across the table to snag mine. "To me, it sounds like you just agreed to go out with me again."

"Well, duh." Even white socks couldn't keep me away.

But the way my internal flames respond to the teasing of his hand tell me this date should probably wrap up soon. We've risked enough tonight, and I need to recuperate.

Seeming to think along the same lines, August rises from his chair and scoops up my cardigan, holding it for me to step into. When we're back in his car, he doesn't start it right away, turning toward me like he plans to say something.

In a panic, I speak first. "I have an early meeting tomorrow." Not a lie, as long as you consider nine a.m. early.

"No worries." August gives me a small smile then buckles his seat belt and starts the engine. "I'll take you home."

Damn. I sounded way too eager to be done with this date. When really, what I'm anxious for is figuring out some method to control my powers when I'm in his presence so I can rip his clothes off whenever the urge takes me.

"Are you free Thursday night?" I ask. "For our next date?"

August pauses with his hand on the gear shift, tilting his head to look at me.

"Let me check with my staff. Just need to make sure someone is at the shop."

Okay. That's kind of a yes. A responsible *I have other responsibilities* yes.

But gods, I'm so in my head about stepping the right way, saying the right thing, not thinking too many dirty thoughts. Our communication suddenly seems stilted, and I worry we're moving in the wrong direction on the relationship map that I don't have access to.

The drive back to my house is quiet. I keep opening my mouth to start a conversation, but I'm concerned that the more I learn about him, the sexier he'll become, and then I'll accidentally melt his tires in the middle of the highway.

I know from personal experience that is no fun, and not something AAA is used to dealing with.

When we reach the street in front of my house, I breathe out a sigh that is half relief, half disappointment. Then I want to stab myself in the leg when I glance over to see August's tight mouth.

What is he thinking?

Probably all the wrong things.

When his car rolls to a stop, August lets out his own sigh. One of defeat.

Oh no. No no no.

"Listen, Quinn—"

"No," I say, the second before I lean over to his side, clasping his sturdy jaw in both my hands.

Tires be damned.

When I press my mouth to his, August doesn't respond at first. That is until I lick his lower lip. Then he's all in. Suddenly, I'm sucking on the most delicious popsicle stick, the chill seeping through the whole of my body, taking the strain off all the internal muscles I was using to stifle my heat for the last few hours.

As we make out, and August gets turned on, everything becomes easier.

It would be great if I could count this as a solution.

But it's not.

I need control all the time, not just when I'm pressed up against a lusty Ice Elemental.

Still, I allow myself this treat, shivering as he groans. The sound reverberates down my throat, and I want to consume more of him.

That's not smart though, so I pull back. Retreating is difficult to do. Partly because I only want to get closer, but also because there's a strong arm wrapped around my waist.

"Gods, Quinn," August moans, dropping his forehead to mine. The longing in his voice matches the twisting in my chest, but I also find myself smiling with hope.

"You're bordering on blasphemy," I murmur.

"You're a goddess," he responds.

That has me chuckling, the sound deep and husky. "Okay. Now I definitely need to get out of this car before they smite you with a bolt of lightning." The Goddess of Fire can be a jealous bitch, or so the legends say.

With reluctance, August lets his arm fall away, and I reach for the door handle.

"Did you have fun?" The question comes as I'm about to step out, and I can't help thinking his voice was tinged with a note of doubt.

Another reason I despise the wall my power erects between us. I never want August to question how much I want him. Glancing over my shoulder, I let my desire show. The eager force curves my lips in a wistful smile.

"More than you know. And more than is safe."

Then I leave, exhaling in relief when I spot a set of four fully inflated tires.

Chapter Twenty-Three

QUINN

Date number two, post ice cream melting fiasco.

Maybe not the best way to keep track of our interactions, but those who forget the past are doomed to repeat it and all that.

I arranged everything this time, and I'm hoping my choice of seeing a movie will prevent this encounter from going up in literal flames. All explosions are to strictly remain on screen. And there will be plenty of props going boom, along with manly shouting and knife fights. I opted for the most action-packed film playing, reasoning I'll be distracted enough to not focus on the amazing man beside me. I can use this time to simply get used to being around him.

At least, that's what I told myself when I ordered the tickets.

I'll be able to ignore him. I'll be able to ignore him. I'll be able to ignore him.

I chant this mantra to myself as August holds open the door to the theater.

"Want to get some snacks?" he asks, tilting his head toward the concession counter.

You mean, do I want something to keep my hands and mouth busy so I don't try sexually mauling you for the next two hours? "Yes. Definitely."

And that's how August and I end up debating the merits of different movie-theater-themed flavors of ice cream.

"Gross. Buttered popcorn ice cream? You can't be serious." The giant handful of the real stuff I shove into my mouth after the statement is delicious, but I can't fathom it in ice cream form.

"I am." He eats a more socially acceptable amount of kernels. "The main flavors I'd be trying for are butter and salt. People love butter and salt."

"People also love ketchup. That doesn't mean they want it frozen in a cone." The thought makes me want to gag. "And I should tell you now, if you make a ketchup ice cream, I will boycott your shop." Not that I've been going there lately anyway.

Memories of the destruction I caused keep me away.

August grins. "I promise not to make ketchup ice cream, but I think this buttered popcorn idea could work. I'll have to experiment."

"Oh no. Dr. Frankenstein is going to create himself a frozen dairy monster." I smirk at my date as he chuckles.

Unfortunately, the sound of his laughter is more delicious than any of the many snacks we bought. My tastebuds tingle, like my ears are connected to my tongue and they demand said tongue lick the lips of the man at my side.

Shoving another massive handful of popcorn in my mouth is like trying to extinguish a bonfire with a Dixie cup of water.

The lights dim, and I breathe a sigh of relief.

But the reprieve doesn't last long.

Despite us sitting in a dark room not facing each other, I am completely aware of the guy next to me. There's no denying it. August has a presence. And it's not just his coolness, which drifts over to me in a teasing caress. The Ice Elemental has mass. He takes up space and that aura pushes outside of his skin.

Not like he's man-spreading, though. He's not trying to take my space away from me. It's more that I cannot ignore that I'm near him. In *his* space.

The previews aren't even through, and I want to plaster myself to him. My bones heat to the point of melting until I could easily slip out of my cushy seat to a puddle on the ground.

Now that I think about it, my time on the floor could be very productive. For example, I could get to my knees, move in between his legs, unzip his pants—

Too hot! Warning! Too hot!

I suck down on my straw rather than his dick, hoping the icy soda will help neutralize my heated insides.

Unfortunately, the ice cubes seem to have already melted from their proximity to me, and now I'm grimacing at the taste of watery soda. Not helpful in the slightest.

Then the movie starts and I discover the inconsiderate director decided to make one of the first scenes that of the muscly, attractive lead actor stepping out of the shower.

Damn the gods. I'm getting bombarded with sexiness from all directions!

A second fiery pulse beats heavy under my skin, and I duck my chin, closing my eyes in hopes I can stifle the powerful force.

But I'm distracted by a deep voice whispering close to my ear. "Quinn? You okay?" Turns out August's low murmur is even sexier than his chuckle. Especially when the puff of his breath stirs the hair at the nape of my neck, bringing with it the scent of Junior Mints, which he's been consuming since we sat down.

"I'm fine," I mutter back, not liking the bitter taste of the lie on my tongue, but not sure what else to do. It's not like I can demand that August be less attractive. Even if he could manage that, the request wouldn't be fair.

This is my problem to deal with. My dangerously wayward libido to suppress.

The movie rolls on, and a sudden car chase catches my attention. The fast turns and near misses set off little sparks of my adrenaline, but in a completely acceptable way. Then one of the pursuers makes a wrong turn, goes off a cliff, and their car crashes, exploding into a giant fireball.

Reminds me of my orgasm. The thought pops up without prompting.

Then the image sticks, and I'm taken back to the last moment I felt like combusting into a firestorm of lust.

Sprawled out on a table, August thrusting between my legs as he pinched my nipples and groaned my name.

Little pinging noises from my lap draw me out of the erotic memories.

Oh no.

What I thought was an empty bag of popcorn now has a new handful for me to shove into my mouth. Apparently, my heat decided to pop the last few kernels rolling around at the bottom of the bag.

This is not good.

Safe bet I'm one step away from melting the film strip. Maybe setting the entire screen on fire.

"We need to go." Damn the gods and the quiver in my voice. I'm not usually the hesitant, nervous girl. Maybe I'm not as outrageously unfiltered as my older sister, but I know how to command a room. Confidence is a cape I normally don easily.

But around August, I turn into a mess.

I want to be normal for him. We should be two people who can have a relationship like everyone else in the world. Not that I know exactly what a *normal* relationship looks like, but I doubt regular couples contain a person who constantly fears their lustful urges.

"Okay." August doesn't pester me with questions about why, or sigh in disappointment that he's missing out on the ending of the movie. Instead, he gathers up our drinks and snacks in his big hands and gestures for me to lead the way out of the theater.

This response only makes him more attractive, which in turn makes things worse.

Why do I have to deal with a heat surge just because a guy is acting decent? Is my bar set that low?

From the way my second pulse kicks up, I guess it is.

Luckily, the sun has already set by the time we get outside. Not that a summer night in Phoenix does much to cool me off, but it helps more than the blazing heat of midday would.

"What's going on?" August asks, his voice gentle as he guides me toward a bench down the street, where we sit side by side.

Do I have to admit this? Didn't he feel the intense heat radiating off me and know how heavy the danger was looming?

My internal furnace had to have been hard to ignore, especially for a man who runs so cold.

I sit on the bench for less than a second before I'm up, pacing in front of him.

"Quinn?"

"I felt myself getting too hot." My sandals slap against the blacktop as I work out my irritation with tense steps.

Silence falls between us, and when the lack of noise becomes stifling, I glance at August from the corner of my eye. The guy appears thoughtful, his brow crinkled, digging deep wrinkles into his forehead.

"You wanted to deal with it on your own." The groves in his skin disappear as he speaks, like he finally understands something.

Somehow, I stop the agitated movement of my feet, shifting to face him. "Well, yeah. Why wouldn't I want that?"

August shrugs. "I figured if you were worried, you would ask me for help."

That has my mouth bobbing. Words fail me as I realize I didn't consider that option. It was hard enough to admit the problem, much less ask him to be my solution to it.

"I..." The sentence hangs unfinished. I shouldn't have started speaking until my brain came up with a response.

The Viking ice cream god stretches out his hand, an offering that hangs in the air between us. Inviting me to accept a little bit of something from him now, even if it's just a molecule of comfort.

After hesitating, I lift my own hand, twining my fingers with his. August tugs enough to let me know what he wants, and I give in, settling in the man's lap.

"You don't ask for help much, do you?"

I never really thought about it, but as I consider the idea now, I realize he's right. "No. I don't. Not with this." A sigh gusts out of me, and I let my head fall to his broad shoulder.

He strokes my thigh, leaving a soothing cool trail along the path that he touches.

"Can I ask why not?"

My thumb traces over the lines on his palm as I consider how best to describe my hesitance. "Probably because admitting my powers are getting out of control is the same as admitting I'm super turned on. And that's never been a topic I've wanted to discuss with people around me. Like my dad, or my sisters."

A firm kiss presses against my hair.

"Do you mind if I know?"

Though confessing my lack of control chafes, I don't care if August knows how attracted I am to him. "No."

"So maybe you could tell me. In the future. And I could help."

I play around with this idea in my head.

Could I imbue some more confidence into my sexuality, along with some vulnerability?

Wasn't that the whole point of me going to August's shop and declaring my intentions? Burning off my dress was a pretty clear statement.

But the whole melting incident tore away at that confidence, leaving me doubting myself all over again.

Still, one stumble doesn't mean I can't try to get back on the right path. That I can't work hard at controlling this on my own, then ask for some help if I realize I'm struggling. When I asked August to cool me down in the past, the request was playful. A way of flirting with him and showing that I *liked* his powers. But could he be my training partner?

Maybe this doesn't have to be disappointment after disappointment.

Maybe this could be how I approach learning.

And if August is up for being teacher's aide, maybe we could start exploring the topic deeper.

Chapter Twenty-Four

AUGUST

I'm being too pushy. Quinn is allowed to approach dealing with her power however she needs.

All I want to do is let her know that I'm here to help, but this is probably coming off more as me demanding to take part in her process.

The decent move would be to loosen my arms and let her climb from my lap.

So why can't I do that? When did my hands decide to make their own decisions?

One of them rubs circles on her back, still picking up a steady heat through her T-Shirt. The other basks in the small caresses of her fingers. She idly traces the bones in my hand while keeping quiet, her brow furrowed with her deep thoughts.

I fight the urge to lean forward and kiss that little dip. The move would only lead to me trailing my mouth over the other interesting curves of her face. I might be tempted to use her riot of freckles as a guide, each one a pinpoint on a map I would make sure to visit.

Ice gathers in my gut, and I realize I've started to grow hard under her taut ass. Luckily, before that becomes too obvious, my Pyro suddenly stands.

"Okay. I think I can do that," she declares.

"Hmm?"

Quinn grabs my hands and pulls me off the bench.

"I think I can tell you when I need help. Let's practice!"

"Yeah, sure." Her eagerness has me smiling. "How you want to do this?"

"Let's go to your place and have sex."

By the time my slow mind makes sense of Quinn's words, she's already towed me halfway across the parking lot. That frost in my stomach? It spreads, threatening to coat my skin.

"Hold up." My feet plant in the asphalt, immobilizing us, and she frowns back at me. "Are you serious?" Not that I don't want her to be. Far from it. I'm just having trouble keeping up with the swerves in her thought process.

"Yes." Quinn moves in close to me, wrapping her arms around my neck until our bodies press flush together. "I haven't been able to stop fantasizing about you, and I want to practice asking for help. What better way than to do the deed? That's when I'm at my hottest."

"Yeah you are," I mutter, the memory of her naked body sprawled out on the table in my shop as I thrust into her splashes across my mind, and my dick continues to rise along with my ice.

Quinn's smile is wicked. "Meet you at your place." She presses a quick kiss to my lips, stepping away before I can deepen it, then jogs to her car. "Race you!" she calls before diving into the driver's seat.

And I thought a fancy dinner was a good date.

Moving quick, I'm in my car, revving the engine to life. I don't care if Quinn beats me to my place as long as I don't leave her waiting. Keeping that fire burning in her eyes is my main goal. I want her hot to the touch, and I want her to beg for my soothing caress.

When I pull into the driveway of my small house, Quinn is leaning against the front door, fiddling with a strand of her red hair. My keys are barely out of the ignition before I'm jogging across the expanse of tiny rocks that cover the front yard.

As I go to unlock the deadbolt, a set of scorching hands lands on my waist. The heat is so intense, I wonder if she's burning through my shirt.

If so, this would officially become my favorite piece of clothing.

Once we're inside and alone, I reach for her again, but Quinn skips back.

"Shower?" she asks, one eyebrow raised.

"Hell yes." I don't care how high my water bill gets.

Taking the lead, I navigate to the bedroom, through which is a full bath with glass doors boxing in the shower.

"Turn the water on cold," she demands. From the heat waves rolling off her, I understand why.

I'm just about to let my chill surround her when I stop myself. Quinn hasn't asked for help yet. She wants to do this on her own for the time being. And when I glance over my shoulder I discover my Pyro has her eyes shut as if concentrating hard.

As she takes a moment for herself, I slide open the shower and turn the faucet as cold as it will go.

I'm going to see Quinn soaking wet.

Just the thought has my cock standing at attention, making my pants uncomfortably tight. I want them gone, but this encounter is under my woman's control.

"Should I take my clothes off?" I ask.

Quinn's eyes fly open. "Yes." Her one word sizzles in the air.

Thank the gods.

I whip my shirt over my head, then unbutton my pants and tug down the zipper. While the denim had done something to control the tent in my pants, the stretchy fabric of my boxer briefs does nothing to camouflage how hard I am.

Quinn makes a noise deep in her throat that has my balls tightening.

Then she repeats the moves I just made, pulling off her blouse and sliding her shorts down her toned legs. For the first time, I notice that her freckles continue their scattered path over her stomach. The small flames that coated her skin when we hooked up in my shop blocked that view before.

But now I can admire the sexy little dots. And imagine licking each one.

"If you're going to look at me like that, I need to be under the water." Desperation and command weave themselves together in Quinn's voice, and when I feel her hungry gaze on me, I wonder how long I'll be able to make this last. Committing fully, I tug off my underwear then step into the frigid spray.

Well, frigid for someone with a normal body temperature. This feels just fine to me.

But I don't want *just fine*. I want Quinn's body reminding me what heat feels like. I want fire against my bare skin.

I want to burn.

Through the glass, I watch as my date reaches behind her to unhook the lacy black bra that cups her breasts the way my hands long to. I bite my knuckle to stifle a groan at the sight of her tight red nipples.

Is their color always so dark, or is there a flush over the tight tips? Are they begging for my attention?

When her thumbs hook in the waistband of her matching panties, I swallow. Once, twice, a third time, and I still feel like I'm going to choke on my tongue.

"Take them off." The pleading seeps out of me, even though I thought the words would stay in my brain. There's a strange noise that briefly distracts me. A high-pitched, repetitive pinging. A quick glance down shows that my arms are now coated in frost, and the noise is from the shower spray colliding with the icy surface.

Quinn smiles wide, then does as she's told. The beautiful red curls at the apex of her thighs call to me as insistently as her nipples. So many places I want to touch, to caress, to kiss.

But she's still on the other side of the room.

"What are you waiting for?" I growl.

Quinn's chest expands on a deep breath, and I watch her arm herself with confidence.

That's it. Come to me as the badass you are.

She steps under the water.

Chapter Twenty-Five

QUINN

The spray from the shower head might as well be room temperature for all the effect it has on my core heat. But the point of the water is not really to balance me out. The point of doing the deed here is to douse any stray flames that pop up from my skin.

No, what really helps stabilize me is the cool slide of August's hand around my waist as he pulls me deeper into the shower.

Goddess, he's glorious.

His body is so big and solid, I want to plaster myself to him. Rub every inch of me over his unyielding surfaces. One of those sturdy pieces I want to slide inside of me.

And a wave of giddy joy flows through me when I realize I don't have to hold back. Every option is open to me right now as my Viking ice cream god stands at attention before me.

This must be what a goddess experiences when she receives the perfect offering.

Time to inspect my prize.

"Quinn—" Whatever August's sentence was, it gets cut off on a choke as I lean in and lick my way along his collar bone. His hips jut forward as if his dick is desperate for attention.

Instead of reaching down to stroke him, I step up against August, pressing our fronts together, trapping his member between our hips and using my wet body to slide over him.

"Gods," he mutters, his hands reaching to palm my ass and pull me closer.

I've already got him praying. I must be doing good work.

Not that a moment of paying homage to August takes any effort. Stroking my fingers across his tight back muscles is the most fun I've had in a while.

I never thought I would get to do this. Before August, I'd started to lose hope. But here I am, and here he is, and for a moment my gratefulness overwhelms my horniness. My hot caresses pause as I give in to the urge to hug him.

"Thank you," I murmur against his pec, watching my breath fog over his frosty skin.

This sweet, sexy man could have his pick of partners. Sure, he has worries about his ice, but clearly the guy has better control than I do. I'm betting he could've made a relationship work with most anyone. He's not as defective as me.

But still, I'm the one he wants. The one he's patiently working with.

"Quinn?" This time his voice holds a question as his hands rub circles on my back. The touch is cool, making me shiver in anticipation.

My mind does a rapid play-through of what's coming up. Hot eager kisses, hands stroking and clutching, August spreading my legs and sinking into me.

"You're going to be inside me," I moan.

August jerks, as if I hit him, then a deep sound rumbles from his chest. Two wet hands cup my face, tilting my chin so he can fuse our mouths together.

He doesn't taste like ice cream. He tastes better.

As our tongues tangle and our breathing meshes, I sample the flavor denied me my whole life. Lust.

A solid pressure pushes against my back, and I realize August has maneuvered me against the tiled wall. Just like that day at Damien's pool, I hitch my legs around August's waist. Only this time, there's not a single bathing suit between us.

"Can I?" The query is spoken against my lips in the same moment the head of his cock strokes through the wetness of my folds.

"Yes. Now!" *Am I whimpering?*

Since that day in Land of Ice Cream and Snow, when this man made me come harder than I ever managed on my own, all I've wanted was another chance to revel in the fullness of him hard and wanting inside me again.

There's an inferno under my skin, swirling, pulsing, demanding to get free.

Breaking off from August's kiss, I lean my head back against the wall and shut my eyes, battling between the amazing pleasure between my legs, and the terrifying power wanting out.

My man presses his open mouth against the pulse in my neck as his cock eases inside me.

"Oh!" That's the only coherent word that escapes my throat, the rest a jumble of choked gasps. Steam rises from my skin, filling the shower stall.

August continues to caress my neck with his mouth and tongue, using his grip on my ass to hold me steady during the leisurely thrust of his hips. Every time he retreats and returns, all the muscles in my lower abdomen flutter and tense, building toward an explosion.

A seemingly unstoppable heat force follows the build of my orgasm, like lava creating a destructive river down a mountainside.

When my hard fought control threatens to slip from my hands, I finally relent.

"August! Cool me down. I need it."

From the erotic groan he lets out, the Ice Elemental is only more turned on by my request. A refreshing chill brushes my nipples first, eliciting a gasp from me. Then the wintery touch trickles over my skin, delicate yet persistent.

Glancing down, I'm mesmerized as I watch the ice crystals on August's skin transfer to mine. The flowery patterns last for only a moment before melting, but then, a second later, they reform. I realize the snowy designs appear along with his thrusts, as if every time August slides inside me, he's gifted with a new burst of power.

How did this man get more sexy?

For fucks sake, he's liable to make my brain combust. Except, my brain is not what he ends up setting off.

"Close." His voice is gravely against my ear, his breath more refreshing than mint gum.

"My clit," is all I can manage back.

Expecting August to follow my command, I grasp his shoulders tighter, preparing for the moment one of his hands moves away from supporting my weight.

But his grip doesn't shift.

The cold does.

Suddenly, there's a focus to the chill. Frost coats my thighs then the tips of the curls his dick disappears into. Then the sensation dips lower, between my folds, his power so strong he's basically manifested himself a third icy hand. When the pressure circles my clit, my mind goes blank.

When consciousness returns, every muscle in my body is clenching and tensing in time with heated waves of pleasure. August's chest pins me to the shower wall as his cock stays buried deep in me. From the now uneven jerking of his hips and panting groans, I can guess he found his release soon after I claimed mine.

Suddenly, the pair of us are sliding to the floor. Not entirely graceful, but August clutches me to him as he settles in the bottom of the tub. He ends up with his back on the porcelain and me as his heated blanket. Water sprays against my back, the constant pressure acting as a massage to ease my still twitchy muscles.

The rapid rise and fall of his chest eventually evens out to his normal steady breathing.

"That's the smartest sex I've ever had," August announces, his fingers digging into my hair and kneading my scalp.

A sound like a purr comes from my throat. "Oh yeah. Very educational."

And I'm wondering when the next lesson can take place.

Chapter Twenty-Six

AUGUST

The scene is so similar to the one from a couple of weeks ago that a surge of panic goes through me.

Once again, I'm looking out my window and seeing Quinn in the parking lot, staring longingly at my shop before she turns to walk away.

What the hell?

Is she avoiding me again?

Since chasing after her worked last time, I decide that's the best route I can take.

"You good on the register?" I ask Marisol.

"Yep. I got it," she says while fashioning the perfect scoop of Fiery Queen in a sugar cone. My customers love the flavor. I think it might become a staple for the shop.

Just like the woman who inspired it.

Not bothering to take my apron off, I dodge around the counter and power walk across the floor and out the front door.

"Quinn!" My call has her stopping and turning. This time at least she doesn't try that silly shuffle run to escape from me. When I get closer, I glance at her feet and see she has on those temporary sandals again. This time her toenails are painted a petal pink color. Gods, they look like candy.

"Hey." The Fire Elemental wears a tight smile on her face and has her hands shoved deep in her pockets. The posture makes me uneasy, but I try not to read into it without all the facts.

"Hey. Why didn't you swing by the shop? I think I can get the owner to give you a cone on the house."

That has her brows dipping in a scowl. "Stop giving your ice cream away for free."

Her expression clears when a chuckle sneaks out of my throat. "Sorry. If you come in, I'll promise to charge you full price." Another thought occurs to me. "Or you don't have to get anything at all. I know not everyone is as dessert obsessed as I am. If you're tired of ice cream, I won't guilt trip you about it."

"Tired of your ice cream? Are you serious?" Quinn stares at me like I just spoke in a foreign language and expected her to understand me.

"Yeah. I get that it's a once in a while thing for people. Not a daily treat."

"Oh my gods. You *are* serious. How could you think I'm tired of your ice cream? If your ice cream suddenly took on human form I would cheat on you in a second. And I wouldn't even feel bad about it. I would suck that ice cream dick on the daily."

"I..." Words are slow in coming with that imagery in my head. "I'm not sure how to feel about that."

Quinn glares at me as her arms cross defensively over her chest. "Feel damn lucky your ice cream is not on the verge of being personified."

"So..." I have to shake my head to get rid of the fantasy of Quinn dripping ice cream onto my dick and then sucking it off. That's too sexy for a Tuesday lunch hour. "If you *do* like my ice cream—and want it on the daily—why didn't you come by the shop when your pedicure was done?"

Quinn's mouth snaps shut with a click of teeth, and her eyes look anywhere but into mine. "Come on, August. You know why." Her voice is low. Dejected.

"No. I don't." Frustration has me finger-combing my hair. I fight off nausea as I voice the dark thought that I don't want to be true. "Is it because you don't want to try dating anymore? You're done with me?"

The Pyro jerks as if I hit her. "What? No!" Quinn shuffles forward and fists my apron. "We are not done. I just can't go in your shop right now."

Relief has my heart rate slowing, but then I focus on her last words. "Do you have somewhere to be?"

The muscle in her jaw tightens before she pushes out a gust of a sigh. "No, I'm working from home today."

"So why can't you come in the shop?"

"Gods, August. Because I'll just ruin more of your livelihood!"

Ah. Back to this.

"We talked about this. I'll keep you level. Especially because I'm not asking you to come in for a hook-up. I just want to catch up with you. See how your day is going."

She moans, her forehead dropping to my chest. "That only makes you *hotter*. And now that we've slept together, I know exactly what you're packing under this." She gives my apron a half-hearted tug.

My instinct is to say something flirty back because when Quinn tells me her mind is on my naked body I don't want to direct it anywhere else. But turning up her heat is the opposite of my goal. She needs to feel centered and in control so she can come into my shop.

"What can I do to help?"

My Pyro shrugs, head still resting on my peck. "Put a bag over your head? Or maybe one over your whole body?"

The half-hearted suggestion has me fighting against laughter. Trying to soothe her, I stroke my hands up and down Quinn's arms.

"Don't have a body bag on hand. Sorry. Anything else?"

She sighs out her frustration before tilting her chin back. "I'm not going into your shop today. I need time."

I try not to show how disappointed I am. I don't want her thinking I blame her. My annoyance is with this whole situation.

"Okay. I won't force you."

Quinn nods then drops her eyes to watch as her fingers trace up the straps of my apron until her arms drape around my neck.

"Kiss me," she murmurs. "So I can practice some more."

As consolation prizes go, this one I can handle.

Pinching her chin between my thumb and forefinger, I maneuver her mouth into the best angle for my lips to caress hers. After the first touch,

I almost stop because a buzzing starts up in my back pocket. But whoever is calling my cell can wait. If Quinn isn't coming inside to visit me at work then this is all I get of her until our next date.

She smells like nail polish but tastes like spice, her lips parting to allow my tongue inside. Everything around me is hot, and I'm not sure how much can be attributed to the summer day in Phoenix versus the woman in my arms. Either way, my body soaks in the sensation, reveling in what is still new.

Quinn's hold on me tightens, her grip in my hair an erotic sting. I find myself pushing her back as I kiss her until her body is wedged between mine and the scorching metal of her car. She doesn't seem to mind.

My back pocket buzzes again just as my hips jerk forward, seeking. The irritating sensation is bothersome as a fly in my ear. I want to swat it away, ignore it. But the distraction reminds me that we're in a public parking lot in front of my business. Not the best place for an overheated make-out session that might leave me covered in a coating of frost.

Breaking away, I pant in hard bursts while staring down at Quinn's freckled nose. She blinks up at me, licking her lips. The sight has me groaning.

My phone pauses its vibration, then starts right back up again.

"Fucking persistent," I mutter as I reach for my cell, all the while wishing I'd left it inside. I'm not sure who I expected to see calling me, but the sight of my dad's number shocks most of the lust out of my brain.

He never calls.

Not that I don't talk to him. Only it's always my mom who dials me up then puts the phone on speaker so the three of us can chat.

The fact that he's tried to get ahold of me repeatedly in the past few minutes has my muscles tensing as I step away from Quinn and press to accept the call. A sense of foreboding sits heavy on my shoulders.

He doesn't waste time.

"August. Thank the gods. Your mother is in the hospital."

Chapter Twenty-Seven

QUINN

August looks ill as he talks to the caller. The sight has me itching to snatch the phone away and chuck it across the parking lot. Or maybe scorch it to a useless pile of ashes. Then I'd have him to myself again with no disconcerting conversations to take away the fragile times of happiness we find in our new relationship.

However, I doubt the best move as a girlfriend is to destroy his property. I've already done enough of that.

"What happened?" His voice, which only a minute ago was full of growly pleasure, now sounds winded, as if the phone call is physically demanding.

The speaker on the other end doesn't talk loud enough for me to hear, despite the fact that August still stands relatively close. If he decides to walk away from me for more privacy, I won't fault him for the move. Just because we agreed to try the relationship thing doesn't mean he's going to be ready to dive into the harder, more intimate topics a few weeks after we went official.

For a moment, I imagine that our relationship isn't a handful of days old.

What if it was months, or years?

The idea of stepping up to August, wrapping my arms around his waist, and holding him steady through this torment of a phone call makes my bones ache.

Goddess, I want that.

To be someone's steady force rather than their fire hazard responsibility.

But the control to get myself where I need to be, so I can be here for someone else, takes time.

So instead of engulfing him with my body in a strange display of solidarity, I put my best effort into waiting patiently. Into being here for him if he needs me when this call is over.

It's the least I can do when I just asked him for the same exact thing. Patience.

This is what relationships are really about. It's not all hot sex.

Hopefully it's a little bit of hot sex.

Guilt spikes through me as I realize the direction my thoughts have trailed down. August is getting some kind of bad news, and I'm sitting here thinking about the next time I can get him out of his clothes.

I chastise myself and refocus on him. He's still listening to whatever is being said on the other end of the line, so I do my best to read the situation through his body.

Every one of his ample muscles is tense. I bet his jaw would feel like granite if I poked it, from the way he's clenched it shut. The blue of his eyes has seeped into a stormy dark color, reminding me of thunder clouds over an ocean.

Damn, this must be bad.

The urge to jump him fades away, again replaced by the need to push off of my Jeep and wrap my arms around him. Solely for the purpose of comforting.

August almost looks scared.

What could frighten a six-foot-something supernatural being?

"What do you need me to do?" His question startles me, and I realize that he had gone so rigid, I began to imagine him as an immobile statue carved from ice.

The thought of his frostiness, and the fact that he said my warmth was such a welcome sensation to him, gives me an idea.

I can embrace him without invading his space. Support him while keeping distance. He wants me as his girlfriend? Well here's my best effort.

When the world gets cold, I'll keep him warm.

Normally, lust super charges my powers, forcing the fire past whatever feeble barriers I've constructed. But when I'm not turned on, I still have access to my magic. I can tug at the fire, ignite the spark of it in my veins.

I do that now, directing the warmth outward, mentally forming it into a pliable material that I can wrap around something. Or someone.

My invisible blanket of heat settles over August's shoulders. Just as I envision it touching his skin, the thunderstorm gaze flicks to meet mine, holding me still. Not that I had any plans to move.

August's eyes widen as the phone remains pressed to his ear. I can see the moment he realizes what I've done because the tension in him eases. Not completely. Not even fifty percent. But there's the barest centimeter his shoulders drop, and I'm proud of myself for succeeding that much in an attempt to master this good girlfriend responsibility.

August steps forward, laying his hand on my bare arm in silent thank you.

"I'm coming."

For a second, I think he's talking to me, and I'm on the verge of telling him there's no hurry. That he can talk to whoever is on the phone as long as he needs to.

Then I realize he *is* talking to the person on the phone.

"I'll call you when I have my flight booked. Okay. I love you. Bye, Dad."

Flight?

My brain works through the few facts I have as August disconnects the call.

His parents live in Alaska. August is leaving.

Don't panic. There's nothing to panic about.

Even as I try to reassure myself, I can feel my blood pressure creeping upward.

We just agreed to try things, and now he's leaving.

August slides the phone into his back pocket, and he simply stares at the ground, his hand still resting on my arm.

I should be patient. I could let him tell me what is going on in his own time. But I can't seem to breathe without also asking my question.

"Is something wrong?"

August's head jerks up, and in his eyes I see a lost look. "My mom is hurt."

"Hurt? How? What happened?"

He heaves a heavy sigh, his eyes closing as his forehead drops to rest on the edge of the car behind me. "Apparently she was climbing a ladder to hang a bird feeder and she fell off. She's in the hospital."

"Oh goddess. I'm so sorry. How bad is it?"

"She has a few broken bones. And she hit her head. She's awake but disoriented. So I don't know."

I push more of my heat toward him, not sure if it's helping, but I need something to do. Some way to comfort him.

"You're flying up to be with her?"

"That, and if she's in the hospital, there's no way my father is going to leave her side. Which means there's no one to look after the bakery. Even if this all ends up being short-term, I don't want them to go into debt because they lost their means of income."

The plan is completely selfless. And maybe that's why I feel the need to be selfish for him.

"What about *your* shop?" His new business. Leaving now could set him back in the same way he's worried for his parents.

"I'll...figure something out." Almost absentmindedly, he leans down to press his lips to my forehead.

Then he turns to walk away. Leaving.

Shit. It's way too conceited to stop him and ask where this leaves us. He's as rattled as a man plowed into by a bus. I'd be surprised if he could pair two coherent thoughts next to each other.

His mother is in the hospital with a head injury. He doesn't need me harping on him about labels and parameters. I can do one of two things for him right now.

I can back off, keep my mouth shut, and push the drama of us away from him so he has room to breathe and think.

Or I can squash the drama completely by doing what we agreed; I can be his girlfriend.

Only, what exactly would a girlfriend do?

I've never been one before, so my frame of reference is limited. This relationship is so new, I have no firm ground to stand on.

A girlfriend would probably tell him she hopes his mom is okay and offer to give him a ride to the airport, right?

The idea sounds reasonable. But also, surprisingly cold. And not in the good way, like August's version of cold. Maybe it's the Fire Elemental in me, but I want to burn that version of a girlfriend to the ground.

How can I send him off on his own when he looks like an abandoned Saint Bernard alone at the dog shelter?

No. No way. I cannot be that kind of girlfriend.

Which means I have to be another version. A girlfriend persona that fits me.

A plan forms in my mind, and I love it because for once, I finally don't feel the need to worry about myself. I can worry about someone else for a change.

I shove away from my Jeep and forget about my pristine, painted toenails as I jog across the parking lot after August. He's so lost in his thoughts, I have to grab the back of his shirt to get him to stop.

"Quinn?"

"I'll come with you."

Chapter Twenty-Eight

AUGUST

I didn't hear her right. I couldn't have.

But here she is in front of me, a firm tilt to her mouth and determination in her eyes.

"What?"

"I'll come with you," she repeats.

I did hear her right. But she can't know what she's saying.

"My parents live in Alaska." She must've forgotten.

"I know."

"So that's where I'm going. Alaska." My words come out slower, as if that'll help her grasp their meaning.

"Got it. August and Quinn are going to Alaska." She points between the two of us.

Though she's forming words that appear to make sense, my brain still can't fully comprehend them. Or maybe it's because I don't want to hope only to be disappointed.

"You...why?" The second I ask, I'm worried my question might sound harsh. That I might have offended her.

But Quinn only holds out her hands, palms up, as if offering herself to me.

"Isn't that what girlfriends do? Be supportive? Be there when their man is in a crisis?"

Automatically, I'm driven to point out that she could be supportive over the phone or with video calls. Quinn doesn't need to fly across the country with me.

But I stop myself.

Because I want her to come.

"Yes." I nod, slow at first, then with more vigor. "Definitely. That is what they do."

I expect a quip back, some short joking response. Instead, Quinn steps in close, wrapping her arms around my waist.

"When are we leaving? I just need to rearrange some client meetings, pack a bag, and I'll be good to go."

There's a sudden blockage in my throat, and I can't answer her right away. We stand in the parking lot, holding each other as the afternoon sun cooks the pavement around us. Not that either of us mind the heat. In fact, I find warmth in Quinn's embrace and the sensation comforts me. Pair that with the fact that she initiated this affectionate gesture on her own, and I'm in ecstasy.

People aren't often eager to hug cold objects. I've gone a lot of my life with little physical contact. Mainly trying to keep the people around me comfortable.

Having Quinn actively entwine her body with mine eases the mental turmoil I'm dealing with about my mom.

At least, a little.

"Tomorrow. I want to fly out tomorrow."

"Of course. I can book—"

"I'll get the tickets." No way is she paying for her flight. "You just go pack. Make arrangements. I'll make mine."

"Okay. August?" Quinn tilts her head up, meeting my eyes.

"Yeah?" My fingers flex, wanting to hold her closer, needing the connection and support she offers.

"I'm going to be a kickass girlfriend for you."

Fear for my mother has smothered most of my other emotions, but that surprises a chuckle out of me. But not a disbelieving one.

"I never doubted that." I lean down to steal a kiss, feeling slightly guilty that even while I worry about my mother, I can still long for Quinn.

There's no way to articulate how much it means to me that she's willing to travel with me. A short while ago, she was sprinting across a parking lot to get away from me, and now she's putting her life on hold to support me.

With an extra bit of effort, I break off from the taste of her, worried I might forget the world around me if I don't return to it immediately. My hands cup her cheeks, and I can't help brushing my thumbs over her wildly freckled skin.

I don't have to say goodbye. She's not making me choose between a family emergency and giving this new relationship my full attention.

"Thank you," I murmur.

"We'll figure everything out. Go get Lois in order."

"Lois?"

She smirks. "Land of Ice Cream and Snow. Lois. Just trying to cut down on the mouthful."

"Do you think it's a bad name?" This is not the time for this discussion, but my emotions have all risen to the surface, including my insecurity.

Quinn covers my hands where they cradle her face. "I love the name. You are a clever dork, and I only date clever dorks. If you ever even consider changing it, I'm leaving you." The threat loses all edge as she grins while delivering it.

Unable to hold back, I dip down for another kiss, wishing this day could just consist of us bantering and kissing and eating ice cream.

But the world likes to threaten my happiness. I release Quinn, all my regret billowing out on a sigh. The tempting Pyro steps away, but I grab her wrist, reaching into my back pocket. Metal clinks together as I pull out my key ring, detaching one from the set. The metal warms quickly once I slide it into her palm.

"When you're packed and ready, come to my house."

"You want me to stay with you tonight?" There's a note of doubt in her voice. Like worry.

"We'll be smart. I'll just hold you." It's not like I'll be able to sleep anyway. And I want her near me.

After a brief hesitation, Quinn nods and pats my chest. "I'll grab us food. See you soon."

This time when she turns to go, I let her walk away, content with the fact that we'll only be apart for a few hours.

The strange mixture of hope and worry puts me in a daze as I walk back into the shop. Even though Marisol gives me an expectant look, I walk past her to my back office, needing a moment to get my thoughts in order before I talk to anyone.

Sitting behind my desk, I allow myself one minute, a full sixty seconds, to wallow in fear for my mother.

Then I shake myself and open my laptop.

After our tickets are bought, I go to the kitchen and review our stores. Luckily, my excitement about Quinn these past few days resulted in major inspiration that I poured into my craft. I've been spending more time than usual concocting additional batches, feeding off of the joy that my life was suddenly filled with. But I'll still need to stay late tonight to mix up as much as I can.

When I have a full tally of the product and a rough estimate of how much more I can make, I return to my desk and draft an email to my weekend manager. Denise is great at keeping things in order on my rare days off, but she really only knows the basics. I hadn't planned on handing over the reins of my shop for any length of time, and I know for a fact that this is one of at least two jobs she works.

The shop will need more than her part-time attention to keep on track.

A vague idea forms, and I wonder if I'm reckless for the amount of trust it would require.

Desperate people can't be choosey.

I return to the front of the shop, finally approaching the counter.

"And what has you running around like a headless chicken? Is that Pyro on her way over? Looking to melt everything again?" Marisol asks, judgment coloring her every word.

I knew it was a mistake to tell her the cause of our loss of stock.

"Marisol—"

"No, no." She holds her hands up in mock surrender. "What does it matter what I think? I'm only trying to help you have a successful business."

"Marisol," I growl now, second-guessing my decision, "I need your help."

That shuts the teenage Squid up.

Luckily, there are no customers waiting to be served. I'm able to lay out the situation, and all the snark falls away from my employee's face.

"I'm sorry. That's awful. Your mom... I hope she's okay."

"That's what I plan on finding out. We're going to have to be open limited hours while I'm gone. I'll make more ice cream tonight, but I'm not sure when I'll be back by. When you run out, the shop will have to close until I'm back."

Her face falls at this, but then her spine goes straight, and she gives me a nod I'd have to describe as mature. "Of course. Let me know what you need. School doesn't start for another few weeks, so I can take on extra shifts."

"That's what I was hoping. And if you're open to it, on the days that Denise can't be here, I'd like you to be acting manager."

The young Squid's eyes go wide, and she leans forward, her expression almost worshipful. "Acting manager? Really?"

"It's a big responsibility. You would be in charge of counting the till at the end of the day. Making sure all the money is where it is supposed to be. Opening and locking up the store. Keeping things running as smoothly as you can until I get back. Are you ready for that?"

The enchanted quality of her gaze flees, and I find myself staring into the eyes of a determined young woman.

"I understand, and I am ready. You can trust me, August. I swear I won't let you down."

My hand reaches out to squeeze her shoulder before I turn back toward the office, intent on typing up detailed instructions on how to keep Land of Ice Cream and Snow running while I'm gone. How to keep Lois alive.

The nickname Quinn came up with gives me a small bit of happiness in the middle of the turmoil.

It's nice to have people around me, so I don't have to shoulder this all alone. I wonder if the immediate support Marisol offered is what it feels like to have a sibling. If so, it seems my trek south may have resulted in exactly what I was looking for.

Hopefully I didn't make this move only to have to leave permanently.

Chapter Twenty-Nine

QUINN

"You can't be serious."

"I have never been more serious in my life," I declare.

August stares at the shirt I just handed him, then back up at me. "You want me to wear this? Why?"

Luckily, I was able to swing by one of those novelty gift stores on my way to his place last night. I had time to browse, seeing as how August stayed late to beef up his ice cream stock before leaving town. Among the raunchy party games, neon beer signs, and rudely shaped mugs, I found a horrible piece of clothing that was perfect for my purposes.

"Because," I gesture emphatically at his beautiful muscular body, "of that."

"You don't like my shirt?" August's mouth twists as if he's fighting a frown, eyes dropping away from my face. He fingers the edge of his shirt, a navy blue piece of cotton that hugs him like a second skin and has the logo of Land of Ice Cream and Snow printed on the front.

Bless the goddess, August looks so sad, I feel like I've kicked a puppy. A sexy, handsome puppy.

"Not like it?" I scoff. "I'm *obsessed* with it. I want to rip it off you, then wrap myself in it. I would mummify myself in that shirt and happily be entombed in a sarcophagus for all eternity."

My gushing chases away the mopey look in August's eyes, but he's still obviously not grasping the importance of this wardrobe change. It's like he has selective memory when it comes to how his looks affect me.

Even now, when he's worried about his mom and I should be offering concern and words of support, I can't help remembering the cool deliciousness of his mouth against mine.

Then, as if the universe knows how weak I am, a subtle scent teases my nose, so tantalizing I can't help a gasp.

"Wha—" August's question cuts off when I crowd his personal space, pressing my face to his chest and breathing in deep. My suspicion is proven right.

"I knew it!" I can't keep the accusation out of my voice. "Waffle cones. For goddess sake, August. I need you to *try* to be unsexy. At least for the flight."

"But I'm not trying to be sexy." He almost looks chagrined, as if apologizing. It's infuriating.

"That's even worse! Do you know how sexy not knowing you're sexy is? *Do you?*"

"I know you're sexy," August offers with a placating smile, and I don't know whether to kiss him or shove him.

"Of course I am! I have a rocking body and a head of hair a succubus would be envious of. But do you see what I'm wearing? I have Crocs on." I wave toward my feet. "*Crocs.*" There shouldn't be a need to point out the loose, shapeless T-shirt and holey sweatpants I've also pulled on.

"I like you in Crocs."

"You. Are. Impossible." I pinch the bridge of my nose before growling at him. "Go get in the shower."

"But I—"

"Get in the shower, now. *Please.*" I try not to imagine him getting all wet and sudsy. "I need you to scrub your skin until you smell like something other than dessert. Then, hopefully, we will get through this plane ride without me setting the engines on fire."

A wave of cold brushes over me, and when I glance up, I can see the Ice Elemental's pupils have dilated.

"That's what this is about?"

"Of course it is. I'm not trying to be some creep by telling you that you're asking for it because of how you're dressed. But you've got to know how much you turn me on simply by existing. Can you *please* just work with me to tone this all down?" My hands outline his Viking body of deliciousness again.

Biting his lower lip, August holds the T-shirt I bought him up to his chest. I searched the racks for the most annoyingly offensive shirt that I thought wouldn't get him into an argument with a random person on the street. And then I grabbed the largest size the store carried.

This is how we end up with August contemplating an XXXL black number that proclaims him to be a member of the FBI.

AKA, Female Body Inspector.

It is horrendous and does a lot to douse the literal and figurative fire in my panties he normally inspires. That is, as long as I focus on the shirt, rather than the handsome head above it.

"Okay. We'll do it your way. But I promise nothing will happen. I'm going to keep an eye on you, okay? I'll keep you cool. Make sure our powers are balanced. You won't hurt anyone." August sets the shirt aside and pulls me into a comforting hug.

"You didn't at the shop," I mutter against his chest. I try not to sound accusatory, but it's an important point that needs to be made. Now that we're so close to leaving, I can't help wondering if my gesture of support is turning into another burden for him to carry. *Am I a bad girlfriend?*

"I was distracted then. This time I won't be. I won't make a move. We'll just be a normal couple, flying to visit my parents. We can pretend we're years down the road, and all the passion between us has cooled."

I snort. "Sure. Like I'll ever stop drooling over you."

August pulls back slightly to grin down at me. "I'll spend the whole flight telling you embarrassing stories from my childhood. Those should take the edge off."

With his sugary scent twining around me and his hard body pressed up against mine, I doubt how successful his plan will be.

"Doesn't hurt to try."

Chapter Thirty

AUGUST

"Everyone thinks I'm a douchebag." At least ten different women scowled at me while we walked to our departure gate.

Quinn finishes buckling her seatbelt before glancing up with an apologetic smile.

"Well, I know that you're sweet and amazing and totally not a douche."

"I guess that counts for something."

She gives my shoulder a playful swat, but I notice when she sets her arm down on the armrest, there's a quiver in her hand. Quinn is on a knife's edge of panic, and the plane engines haven't even rumbled to life yet.

I honestly don't think she has a reason to worry. With minimal concentration, I continue to let the chill seep from my skin and settle over hers.

Leaning in close, I lower my voice to a whisper as other passengers shuffle by us. "The ice cream melted because I was distracted. I'm not distracted today. I swear, I won't even let the temperature rise a couple of degrees."

The Pyro's only response is a tight-lipped smile and a nod.

"Is there anything I can do to help you calm down?"

She sighs, but the exasperation seems to be directed at herself. "You're not supposed to be comforting me. I'm supposed to be comforting you."

Focusing on keeping Quinn's powers neutralized is doing a good job at taking my mind off my mom. Maybe focusing on my state of mind would be just as helpful to her.

"Okay, then comfort me. Talk to me."

"About what?"

"Anything. How do you know Sammy. Thoughts of him aren't going to... raise your heat levels. Are they?"

Before I have a moment to discern if I'm jealous, Quinn snorts. "Not likely."

"Then he's the perfect subject. Tell me how you know him, but you didn't know Marisol."

"I do know Marisol, actually. Or I did. It was years ago though, so I completely forgot. I met her when she was younger. Just a little tyke tottering around after her brother."

I can envision that. A miniature Marisol demanding the attention of a surly, teenaged Damien.

"Perfect. This is the story I want to hear." Settling back into my seat, I'm thankful that despite my last-minute booking, I was able to snag two spots in the emergency exit aisle. Sitting anywhere else is always hell on my long legs.

Quinn takes a deep breath, and from the corner of my eye I notice her fingers loosen, just slightly, from their white-knuckled death grip.

"We grew up next to a Squid family. The Aguados. Do you know them?"

My knee-jerk reaction is to glance around warily, trying to see if anyone is listening in on our conversation. When I was young, my parents drilled into me that I couldn't talk about my powers in public. They were worried, and rightly so, that if people found out, I'd become some freak of nature the government would insist on studying. Probably the worst fear of any Elemental parent, especially now, in the age of smartphones and security cameras.

But Quinn, despite her agitation, doesn't even lower her voice.

Trying my best to cover my initial discomfort, I simply shake my head.

"Yeah, I don't think they're related to Sammy or Marisol. Just another family like us that moved to town and was able to get in touch with some of their own." She's talking about our fellow Elementals on a plane full of humans, and Quinn doesn't show an ounce of hesitation. She's completely mastered the art of speaking about the dual worlds without giving any indication what she's saying might be odd.

Her confidence soothes my nerves, and I realize just how tightly wound constantly hiding this important piece of my life has made me.

Since moving to Phoenix, I've never been so open.

Unaware of the revelations in my head, Quinn keeps on with her story.

"So the Aguados, which was really just Ms. Aguado and her son Rafael, were one of those neighborhood families you get super close with. Rafael was my age, but he and Cat always got along better. Our moms were best friends. Marisol and Damien visited the Aguados a couple of times, but Damien was like four years older, and Marisol was still in diapers, so it wasn't a primo my-kids-play-with-your-kids situation. I guess that's why I barely saw them when I was growing up. Then high school comes around, and that's when Rafael met Sammy and they started hanging out. There were a couple of others in their group, too. You know, Squids stick with Squids or whatever. They had some wild parties, and I'm pretty sure Damien was their beer supplier."

"Did you ever go?" The idea of having a large enough group of friends to throw a party in high school has me envious. In my teenage years, I tended to be a loner. Back then I had less control over the chill. I don't think my peers were aware that I was the source of the cold, but they must have picked up on the fact that whenever they stood close to me, they were uncomfortable.

"Go to the parties?" Quinn shrugs. "Maybe one. But Cat and Rafael weren't hanging out anymore, and I was always worried if I developed a crush on a guy that things might escalate—" she makes a motion with her hands as if they're little flames "—at a party."

The plane starts to move, slowly rolling toward the runway. Trying not to be too obvious, I eye Quinn to gauge if her nerves ratchet up at the knowledge we're about to take off. But she seems too tied up in our conversation to take any real notice.

"If you didn't party with them, when did you and Sammy start dating?" I ask.

"Oh goddess. Please don't call it dating." Quinn leaves me hanging on that, going quiet as the flight attendant talks through safety procedures. With my Pyro's focus back on the flight, I watch as her fingers curl into fists and her lips tighten in one straight line.

Not sure if the safety announcements just distracted Quinn from my distraction, or if she's actually intent on hearing everything said, I keep quiet until the woman in her navy uniform finishes pointing out all the exits.

The engines rumble, then roar, and we speed forward. Quinn grips the armrests, knuckles white and straining. I can't help myself. I place my hand over one of hers.

Her eyes fly to mine, wide and slightly panicked.

"If it wasn't dating, what would you call it?" Pitching my voice slightly louder to be heard over the engines, I continue as if nothing in our surroundings has changed.

She flinches at my question, but not as though she's offended or hurt by it. More like she's jerked back into our conversation without realizing she could be.

"Oh. Uh. Hooking up. Well, hook up. Just once."

"You didn't want to date him?"

Quinn shakes her head, red ponytail swishing with the movement.

"When I finished college, still a virgin, I decided a new tactic was needed. Specifically, finding a partner who could handle my needs. Sammy fit the bill, and he was single and willing."

I'm sure he was.

"You all kept in touch after high school?"

"Oh, no. It's not like we were friends or anything. But our crowd tends to cross paths. I was saying hi to Cat at one of her jobs and he happened to be there. We talked for a bit, it led to more, and the next morning I never felt any need to repeat the experience."

Is that a smugness I feel?

"Wow. Blow to Sammy's ego."

"Sorry." Her smile is rueful. "This must sound like I'm insulting your cousin. He can be cocky and annoying, but I don't actually dislike him or anything. He has his moments."

"Yeah. Sammy is a particular flavor everyone around him needs to get accustomed to. I look forward to the day when he grows up. At least a little bit."

"If only we had an idea of when that would be. I'd mark my calendar and throw a party."

We share a grin as the plane levels out. Quinn seems to have relaxed. I guess Sammy really is a mood dampener. I'll have to thank him when I see him next. Though I'd doubt he'd react well if I specified *why* I was thankful.

A shiver quakes through her, and I worry I've overdone it.

"Are you too cold?"

She blinks up at me, surprise coloring her hazel gaze. She lifts one arm, then her other, examining the raised hairs and goose bumps. I love how her freckles cover more than just her face, continuing their sprinkled pattern all over her body. The sight, and yearning to kiss each one, makes it easy to keep up a continuous chill.

"No." Quinn laughs, a thankfulness shining from her eyes and filling my chest with pride at my ability to keep her at ease. "I'm perfect. In fact—" A huge yawn takes over her face, practically cracking her jaw. She ends with an adorable smack of her lips, and I watch her eyelids droop. "I stressed myself out so much, now I'm exhausted."

"Here." I unbuckle my seatbelt and stand to rummage around in the overhead compartment, eventually finding the sweatshirt in my bag.

Back in my seat, I fold the soft cotton into a makeshift pillow.

"Lean on me," I murmur, placing the cushion on my shoulder.

Quinn slowly blinks, a small smile tugging at the corner of her mouth.

"I think you might be the perfect man," she whispers as her head comes to rest on me.

Chapter Thirty-One

QUINN

"Where's all the snow?" As we leave the airport, I gaze around at the bare concrete, damp from the rain falling in a light drizzle.

"Alaska gets summer like anywhere else. It's still August."

"You're still August," I grumble in response, disappointed that my great trek north hasn't resulted in a beautiful white tundra to ogle.

"Yes, I am." He grins down at me, but I can see the strain at the corner of his eyes, and I scold myself. This isn't some romantic getaway. August is here for his parents, and I'm here for August. None of this trip is about me. I already made the plane ride about me, and that's quite enough self-centeredness.

"You are. I guess this is now my favorite month." Pressing up on my toes, I give him a smacking kiss on his cheek. "Now let's grab a cab. Do you want to go straight to the hospital or drop our stuff off at your parents' place first?"

His arm wraps around my shoulders, drawing me to his side in a hug that also seems like a thank you.

We opt for a quick stop by the house, August reasoning he could grab his dad some essentials while there. I'm happy for the detour because I can change into something more presentable than my baggy, sexy-dampening flight outfit.

As we unload our bags from the cab, I stifle another exclamation of confusion. Turns out I'm naive, because I imagined that everyone in Alaska lived in a cabin. Really, it's August's fault with how he decorated Land of Ice Cream and Snow. How was I supposed to know that the Nords would live in a perfectly normal-looking house?

It's still a very nice house. The roof slopes dramatically, which gives the inside high ceilings. I bet August loves that. No bumping his head here.

Mrs. Nord is a big fan of quilts, and I've got to say, I like her style. I vow to one day sit in a window seat wrapped in a quilt as I sip from a steaming hot drink.

A girl has to have goals.

"Is this the house you grew up in?" I ask as August leads me through the front room toward a wide set of stairs.

"Yeah. We'll put our things in my old bedroom, change, then head out."

Both our things? In one room?

I want to ask if he thinks his parents would approve. I also want to point out that sleeping in the same bed isn't exactly smart. But I stop myself. Now is not the time to question or debate. Now is the time to support and make life easy on August.

Sleeping arrangement discussions can come later.

The bedroom we walk into is surprisingly sparse. Not to say there isn't anything in it. There's a bed, with another beautiful quilt, and all the basic furniture someone might need, which seems to have been carved out of rough wood. The place is a perfectly quaint guest room.

"Where are all the naked lady posters?"

August stumbles at my words, gripping a bedpost to steady himself before he turns to stare at me. "The what?"

"You know. The posters from a magazine's swimsuit edition. Or, like, a shot of a hot model on a sportscar or something. Normal teenage boy decor."

"You thought I'd have pictures of naked women all over my walls?" August's voice comes out strangled, but all I can do is shrug.

"I grew up with two sisters. I have no frame of reference other than movies. But I didn't envision this." I spread my arms to take in the charming but impersonal room.

The bedsprings squeak as August sits down heavily, his eyes on me with an odd expression, his teeth digging into his lower lip.

"What else did you expect?"

I pace to the window and peak through the curtains, finding a large backyard with a high fence surrounding it.

"You know. Sports stuff. Random clothes. Action figures. Car engine manuals."

"Car engine manuals?"

"Maybe! Teenage boys like cars. Right?"

"Some do, I'm sure. What else?"

When I realize August finds my guesses amusing, I keep going, happy to do anything that'll bring a smile to his face, even if I look silly in the process. Mentally browsing the teenage films I've seen, I throw out another option.

"Dirty magazines stashed under the bed!" Now that I think about it, those could still be there. I drop to my knees, searching for some sign of sixteen-year-old August. But there's only a plastic bin which looks to contain more quilts.

"Come here," August says, using a growly tone that's laced with laughter. I follow his command, pushing back against the warmth that sparked up at his voice.

When I'm around on his side of the bed, he reaches for my hand and laces our fingers together.

"A couple of years ago my mom redid this room. She said her baby bird had flown the nest, so she was going to make the nest look however she wanted."

I affect an over-the-top pout and enjoy his cheeky grin of a response.

"Here, I'll paint you a mental picture." August begins to describe the room, pointing as he speaks. "My bed was there, dresser there, desk by the window, usually covered in school papers and maybe a recipe or two. All my hockey gear ended up in a pile in that corner—"

"Sports stuff! I was right!" I pump a triumphant fist in the air. "You played ice hockey?"

He nods with a self-deprecating smile. "Yeah. I was okay, probably because I was bigger and good on my skates. But I was never aggressive enough."

That makes sense to me, remembering back to how sure of himself he was on our first date in that ice rink. How, even when I fell, I knew he'd be there to pick me up.

Yeah, August is not the kind of guy who would excel in a sport that so often breaks out in fights. In this moment, I vow to myself to fight for him. To be his rabid honey badger protector if he ever needs one.

"Okay, I have a mental vision of the stuff. Now, I'm guessing this wall," I point to the one he'd easily see while lying in his bed, "had the bootylicious babe."

August just chuckles, shaking his head. "No. No bootylicious decorations in here. You remember that I go into super freeze mode when I'm turned on right? My whole goal was to keep from getting horny so I didn't turn the house into an ice hotel."

"What are you saying? That you were celibate the entire time you were a teenager? Even with yourself?" I at least took care of things in the shower ever so often.

August shrugs, still giving me an adorable half-smile. "Most of the year it's around or below freezing outside. I'd just go off on my own for a while."

"You went on hikes so you could masturbate?" I stand in between his knees, cupping his cheeks with my hands. "You poor sexy ice god." His skin is cool when I press my lips to his forehead, but I don't mind. I never mind.

Normally, my heat feels comfortable, normal. But when I touch August, it's like my fire has grown stifling, and he's a cold glass of water after a long run or a dive into a pool after sitting in the sun for hours.

"Pretty sure it's blasphemous to keep calling me a god," he murmurs as his hands grip my thighs and pull me closer. Close enough to bury his face in my cleavage. His hum of satisfaction has me laughing and shoving him away.

Even though I want to hold him against me, maybe sink down on the bed with him and fulfill all his horny teenage fantasies, we have somewhere to be.

Plus, I don't want to set his parents' house on fire. Not a good first impression. Especially not when we have other serious shit to deal with.

I make another silent promise that once we make it through these next few hours, I will help August in whatever way he needs, including as a distraction from worry and grief.

"I think our gods are pretty forgiving." Stepping out of his hold, I offer my hand for him to take. "Now let's go see your mom."

The humor on his face drops away. I expect it to be replaced by solemn conviction or grim determination. Instead, he stares into my eyes, his own having faded to a pale icy blue that reveals a cavern of vulnerability.

"You'll come with me?"

His palms are rough in mine as I leverage him off the bed. With efficient determination, I don my honey badger cloak. If this world tries to mess with my man, I'll fuck it up.

Watch me.

But to him, I merely say, "Of course."

Chapter Thirty-Two

QUINN

I haven't been in a hospital since the day I was born. My Elemental blood probably has something to do with it. There's no definitive data on the topic, but Harley and Cat are as healthy as me, and I'm not aware of any others of our kind who've come down with anything even resembling a cold.

This building with sterile white walls and white floors, chairs with easy-to-disinfect upholstery, and troops of beeping, intense-looking machines comes off as foreign to me despite the handful of medical dramas I've watched.

As I let August lead, I maintain my protective aura, hovering just behind his shoulder.

A nurse with sharp eyes and a confident stance points us in the right direction once we tell her who we're visiting. My boyfriend powers down the hall, easily maneuvering his large body around beds and doctors in his way. Just as August steps into a doorway, a deep voice booms out.

"August! My boy. You're here." Like a kraken taking hold of an innocent sea vessel, massive arms snake out of the room and engulf my companion, pulling him out of sight. I jog after to make sure he doesn't need rescuing. But when I step into the room, I discover August has his arms in an equally tight hug around...*Bigfoot?* It's my best guest. Maybe Santa Clause. If the jolly gift-giver was a buff lumberjack.

To put it simply, the man is massive, with an impressive salt and pepper beard. I thought August was big, but this guy has a few inches on him.

"Hey, Dad," my man rumbles into the Bigfoot's flannel.

Whoa. August comes from mammoth stock.

Are all Ice Elementals this huge? Or did the Nords hoard all the tall genes for themselves?

An image pops into my mind of August's ancestors, Viking Ice Elementals, trekking across frozen plains until they stumble upon human villages where they seek out the tallest women to sleep with.

Of course, since these are August's ancestors, they're super polite, helpful Vikings that put a lot of effort into wooing their romantic interests. None of that pillaging nonsense.

Stop thinking about August's great great grandfather getting it on with tall women when you're seconds away from meeting his family, I scold myself.

After another round of backslapping and hugging, the two break apart, and I get a better view of the giant. Underneath the expertly sculpted beard, I catch the similarities between Mr. Nord and his son. They share cool blue eyes and strong cheekbones, along with the distinct mountain man build.

"I'm glad you made it," Mr. Nord says.

"Of course." August extends a hand in my direction, beckoning me forward. "This is Quinn. My girlfriend."

Suddenly, I'm aware of how awkward I've made this situation by insisting on coming. I'm not sure how I didn't think of it before. I guess I was too focused on figuring out how I could help my boyfriend, that I didn't consider how rude planting myself in the middle of their family crisis could be.

And would August have really told me no if he didn't want me here?

Goddess, I'm already messing this up.

Not for the first time, I'm wishing I had more girlfriend practice before finding the perfect guy. Seems like it's a matter of time before I lose him.

But then Mr. Nord's shaggy face breaks open into a wide grin as his blue eyes focus on me.

"Girlfriend, you said? You convinced her then?"

"What?" The one word is all I get out before I find myself in my very own Bigfoot bear hug.

"Dad, don't squish her."

The big man drops me back to my feet with a chuckle. "Sorry. I'm a hugger. Also wanted to check that you're real. Since you're basically a fairytale."

"I'm a what?" Hopefully, he doesn't mean everyone expects me to be sweet like a cartoon princess. I curse too much to be G-rated. Plus, I constantly want to lick his son like the Ice Elemental is my personal ice cream cone. Not really family-friendly content going on in my brain.

"Well, I've never met one of your kind before. Not many want to move up north I guess." Mr. Nord shrugs, staring at me with a joyful crinkle at the corner of his eyes.

My kind?

The confusion lasts for only a handful of seconds before his meaning clicks into place. "You mean Pyros?"

"Pyros? Is that what the kids are calling it these days?"

I smile at the exuberant man. "What were we called in the olden days?"

He guffaws, then strokes his hand over his mouth and beard as if to stifle a smile. "Cheeky. Now that I think of it, we didn't have special names. Makes sense though. Easier to talk about each other."

August's hands settle on my hips, pulling me back against his chest.

His father watches the gesture, delight sparking in his gaze. "And what fancy name do you have for us?"

"I..." My response trails off when I remember I have nothing to say. And to my surprise and embarrassment, I realize I really wish I had an answer. I don't like the fact that August and Mr. Nord don't have a special identifier while every other Elemental group does. Like we intentionally left them out of a club.

"Sammy calls me an iceberg sometimes," August offers, coming to my rescue.

"Hmm. That the same for you, Quinn?" Mr. Nord watches me, a teasing smile only partially hidden by his beard.

I'm betting the pale skin under my freckles is staining red. I'm not sure why I'm so mortified by this conversation. Harley has brought up a lot racier topics in much worse settings, and I've just rolled my eyes. But it's not so much the content that has me anxious.

It's more a sense of failure.

August should have an official insulting nickname like the rest of us. Because he belongs with us.

"I have to apologize, Mr. Nord. Until I met August, I thought your kind were extinct. So I never had a use for a nickname."

The man clutches his chest and stumbles back a step as if I've run a sword straight into his heart.

"Extinct? Like the dodo bird?"

I bite my lower lip, fighting almost childish giggles at his antics. When he offers me a cheeky smirk, I realize something.

Mr. Nord is a flirt. And not a *make women uncomfortable with unwelcome caresses and suggestive comments* flirt. August's dad is a goofy class clown flirt.

And I love him for it. Just like I'm starting to love—

No. No time for that train of thought right now.

Instead, I channel my own class clown flirting abilities.

"Oh no. Not like the dodo bird. Something much more majestic. Extinct like the wooly mammoth."

Chuckles rumble out from behind me, and I can feel the vibration in August's chest against my back as he laughs at how I tease his father.

The older man tugs on his very wooly beard as he grins at the two of us. "Well I hope my son has done his best to prove we still very much exist."

"Dad," August growls now, embarrassment clear in his tone. But I laugh and earn myself a wink from Mr. Nord.

This is going better than I could have ever hoped. In fact, this first meeting would be perfect if it weren't for the circumstances that brought us together.

The moment that thought arises, it's like I come back to the present.

Like I had a brief dip into an imaginary land where everything was okay in the world, but now I crash land in reality.

Mr. Nord must see the shift in my face, or maybe his son's, because he sobers up as well. His eyes get sharp, focusing over my shoulder on August.

"Your mother is going to be okay."

I knew that August was holding himself slightly stiff, but it's not until his father speaks those words, and my boyfriend's body relaxes against me, that I can acknowledge how tense he was.

"But she's still here?"

Mr. Nord nods. "When she fell she hit her head. Knocked herself out. I was a mess, but the doctors did all the scans and observed her overnight. She woke up, slightly confused, but that cleared up after an hour or so. She has a concussion, a broken ankle, and sprained both her wrists."

A sympathetic wince jerks through me, and August's arms tighten around my body. I'm not sure if he's comforting me or himself. Maybe both. I silently pray to the gods that Mrs. Nord isn't in too much pain and that my presence is somehow helping August deal with the fact that his mother is hurting.

Trying not to bring any attention to myself, I coax a small measure of heat from my veins, the maneuver easier with my blood so close to the surface of my skin after my earlier embarrassment. When I have a hold of the warmth, I push it toward August, envisioning rubbing my power all over his skin like a soothing lotion.

His grip tightens in what I take as a silent thank you.

"Concussions can be nasty," August says.

Mr. Nord grimaces. "Yes, but it could've been worse. They want to keep her for another day, just to be cautious, but when she comes home she's going to need to take it easy."

I glance behind me to see August nod, his face grim, but still with a hint of relief.

"Can we go see her?" he asks.

"Oh, no, August." I step away from his hold. "You should go in. I doubt your mom wants a stranger trying to introduce herself when she's laid up in a hospital bed." No matter how much I want to meet the woman who raised such an amazing man, I'm not completely insensitive.

August frowns, but before he can respond, Mr. Nord talks over him.

"I'm in need of a cup of coffee. Why don't Quinn and I go to the cafeteria while you visit?"

My boyfriend's eyes flick between me and his father before he sighs. "Okay."

I expect him to head straight into the room. Instead, he pulls me back into his arms, engulfing me in his own version of a mountain man hug. Mr. Nord is a good hugger, but he has nothing on his son.

Since I'm not wearing heels today, the top of my head reaches to just below August's chin. He tucks me there, with one hand on the back of my neck, the other arm encircling my waist. Meanwhile, I emulate an octopus, my arms twinning around his body and suctioning him close. The embrace lasts for only a few seconds, but the affection emanating from it is like restorative medicine. My exhaustion from the hours on a plane seeps away.

When we break apart, I feel healthier, and August gazes down at me with clear eyes before pressing a kiss to my forehead. Then, shocking me, he glares at his father.

"Don't scare her away. I barely convinced her to give me a chance."

I huff out a laugh, bringing both men's attention to me. Reaching up, I scratch my fingers in August's golden stubble and offer a comforting smile.

"If your mammoth of a father could scare me away, then I never deserved you in the first place."

As August blinks in surprise, the older Nord chuckles and offers his arm to me.

"Damn, am I glad I'm not extinct," he declares before leading me away.

Chapter Thirty-Three

QUINN

"You're alive!"

I roll my eyes as Harley's declaration screeches out of my laptop speakers.

"Of course I'm alive. What did you think was going to happen to me?"

"Anything! You've thrown yourself into the wilds of the north."

"It's Anchorage. Pretty populated here. I doubt some polar bear is going to wander into the Nord's bakery and chomp me." Not that I'm in the bakery at the moment. My first visit will happen bright and early tomorrow morning, and I'm a jittery version of joyful at the thought.

The world behind Harley tilts and blurs, and I try not to get seasick as she walks around with her laptop.

"A bakery is exactly where bears would go. So many delicious smells. And if they use honey on any of their pastries, you're done for. I'll start writing your eulogy now." My big sister clutches her boob and tries to look weepy. "My dear, dear Quinn. So brave. So foolish. Traveling to the dangerous tundra of Alaska, all in pursuit of an icy dick."

"You asshole!" I whisper-scream at her, my head whipping over my shoulder to make sure the bedroom door is closed. Last thing I want is for Mr. and Mrs. Nord to hear my filter-less family member talking about their son's package.

"I don't mean to imply an icy dick is a bad thing. Especially since I'm sure it's iceberg size. You'd tell me right? If he was so big that he could bust a hole in the Titanic?"

"No." I turn the volume down until there's only one bar remaining and I have to lean in close to hear. I should've known a chat with Harley would require headphones. "I would definitely *not* tell you that."

Harley sticks out her bottom lip in an over-exaggerated pout. So *that's* where I learned it from. "I thought you loved me."

"And I thought the older a person gets, the more mature they're supposed to be. How are you thirty? Seriously?"

"Whatever. Maturity is in the eye of the beholder. Until I start getting complaints from my clients, I see no reason to adjust the way I speak of the world and the delicious people that stroll around in it."

"I don't think your customers are the best measure to use."

The only response she gives me is a wicked grin paired with a blown kiss.

"How do you like his parents? Are they nice?" The perfectly reasonable questions come from off screen.

"Move the camera. I can't see Cat."

Harley does as she's told, a rarity, and soon I have an unobstructed view of both my sisters.

"They're really sweet. And August's mom is going to be okay. Eventually. Right now she's pretty battered and recovering from a concussion. But nothing is permanent."

"That's—" Cat starts but Harley cuts her off.

"Great. When are you coming home?"

"You're being super clingy," I point out, then grudgingly admit, "August got me a return ticket for Sunday." My Alaska visit will barely last a week.

"He got only you a ticket? Don't you mean he got *both* of you tickets? Isn't he coming back with you?" Harley raises one red brow at me.

A grimace threatens to contort my face, but I do my best to stifle it. From the concerned stare Cat adopts, my efforts were likely in vain.

"No. I mean, he's not coming back *yet*. I'm sure he'll get a ticket when his mother is feeling better."

Which the doctor said could be a couple weeks. Or a couple of months.

I don't offer up that info.

"Unacceptable."

"Harley!" *What gives her the right to be as upset about this as I am? And to then articulate it in a way I feel too guilty to even silently think in my own head?* "It's not unacceptable. His mother is hurt. You don't think we'd drop everything for Mom?"

"Of course we would. But once we knew, and she knew, that everything would be alright, our butts would be kicked to the curb. No one likes a hoverer."

"Is Mr. Nord not able to take care of her?" Cat asks her question in a tone that tells me she's trying to offer support and understanding.

Only, the answer doesn't help with my point at all.

"No. August's dad is very capable. But they have their bakery to worry about. Mrs. Nord can't work with sprained wrists and a broken ankle."

"Yeah, well, August can't work at his ice cream shop if he's outside of the continental US. What is he thinking?" Harley taps out an agitated rhythm on the keyboard with her acrylics.

Since when did my older sister start caring about my boyfriend's business?

"He's thinking like a good son."

"You know what's wrong with your man?" Harley asks.

I embody the honey badger, hackles raised in warning. "Nothing. Nothing at all."

Harley continues like she didn't hear the threat in my voice. "He's too helpful. I mean, I like it when I get free ice cream in the deal. But in this case, he's on track to fuck up his life."

"You're being dramatic." Only, this time I'm not sure she is.

I am intimately acquainted with the financial situation of Land of Ice Cream and Snow. The shop is doing well for a new business, but if the place has to close down for any length of time, I'm not sure August's dream will survive the neglect. Not unless he has some mysterious capital I don't know about. Some wealthy benefactor willing to shell out thousands of dollars to support their ice cream fix.

The image of a rich widow forms in my mind. She has a massive bank account thanks to her late husband, who she probably murdered but the police could never prove it. The black widow lays sprawled out on a chaise lounge in her ornate mansion as August serves her ice cream from a silver tray. Shirtless. In the scene, he's wearing pants, but only so she can shove hundred dollar bills into his waistband.

The fictional scenario enrages me until I replace the mystery woman with myself. Then my blood boils hot with lust.

Time to end the daydream!

Refocusing on my sisters, I realize they've been staring at me during my wandering mind session.

"Is he going to stay in Alaska?"

"Harley!" Cat scolds as I flinch back from the screen.

"What? No! He wants to live in Arizona. He has family there. And his shop."

Do I sound desperate?

Because I am.

"I think we can all agree that Sammy isn't the optimal family member. And what if his shop goes under?"

Does she have to be so morbid?

"It won't. And he has...me." Goddess, I hate how insecure that last word comes out.

He has me? So what? What are we even?

An experiment of a relationship. That cold truth snuffs out any fire that might've been brewing.

Luckily, neither of my sisters disagrees with my argument. They don't agree with it either though, so I can guess at the thoughts running through their minds.

"Maybe you should talk to him. Find out where his head is at." Cat makes her suggestions carefully, as if she expects me to start yelling.

But I don't feel explosive. The doubt about the future makes me feel small and insecure. Suddenly, I hate the fact that I'm in an unfamiliar room in an unfamiliar house. I want to be back in the heat of Phoenix. I want tiles under my feet and the sun stinging my eyes. When I look out the window here everything is lush and green. I want brown and burnt orange.

In the moment, I hate this beautiful land and how it's tempting August away from me.

"Yeah. I'll talk to him," I lie. Neither of them calls me out. Maybe because they can't tell. Or maybe they pity me. "Tell me about home."

For the next half hour, they do, and I try to let their words distract me from my melancholy.

I'm not going to talk to August about when he plans to return to Phoenix. The idea feels too much like me insisting he leave his injured mother behind, and I would never want him to do that before he thought he should. If my mom was hurt and needed me, I'd move the world for her. Of course, she only lives a short drive away, so the comparison doesn't truly equate.

No, I won't pester him with needy questions. I'll support him like a good girlfriend is supposed to do.

And I'll pray to the goddesses and the gods that he isn't done with Phoenix.

That he isn't done with me.

Chapter Thirty-Four

AUGUST

"You're being too tender with it. Did moving south turn you soft?"

I stifle a grin, attempting to look chastised.

"Don't you smirk at me. You think I can't see you?"

"Of course, Mama. I'm terribly sorry."

Only, I'm not really.

Well, I'm sorry that my mother is in pain and that the hurting is making her more snippy than she would normally be. But I'm not sorry to be on the receiving end of her scolding. Because as I deal with her continuous corrections, I can't help being grateful that she's still around to give them.

Not everyone walks away from a fifteen-foot fall. When I got my dad's call and heard the fear in his voice, I was terrified that my hurried trip back north would be some sort of goodbye.

But she's going to be okay.

"Sure you are," my mother grumbles from her wheelchair, hovering behind me. "You've got three times the muscle as your lady, but I bet she could knead that dough better than you if I called her in here."

Now I can't hide my smile. It's too good to hear my mom praise Quinn in the subtle way she does.

In the back kitchen of my parents' bakery, I'm surrounded but the smells of yeast and herbs. Leaning to the side slightly, I can peer through a small window to the front of the shop where a few square tables are arranged. Seated at one is my girlfriend.

Quinn has her crimson hair piled on top of her head and that adorable set of red-framed glasses perched on her nose. She's completely focused on the laptop in front of her, typing away, taking only short breaks to glance at printouts scattered across the table beside her.

How she's able to dive into someone else's finances at four in the morning is beyond me. I was barely able to roll myself out of bed when the alarm went off, and I'm relatively used to bakery hours. I told her she could sleep in.

Instead, she joined me in the shower, waking me up by kneeling down and wrapping her hot mouth around me.

I tuck the memory away as the tell-tale pinpricks of frost begin scattering over my skin.

If I freeze this dough, my mother will give me hell.

"Alright. That's good enough. Put it aside to rise and go give Quinn one of the cinnamon buns. Your father should be done frosting them by now."

While I use a wet cloth to wipe flour off my hands, I stare down at my mother.

"I would bet a good deal of money that this is not what the doctor meant when he told you to rest this next month."

One day out of the hospital and Samantha Nord demanded we reopen the bakery and that she be taken in to supervise, even if her two sprained wrists meant she could do nothing other than talk to us.

Or *at* us, more like.

"And haven't I always warned you against gambling? Now take me to your father and feed your woman before she finds some other handsome man who will. You know they're practically roaming the streets up here."

Chuckles sneak from my chest as I grip the handles of her wheelchair, carefully guiding her further into the kitchen. "You're having trouble with packs of single men nowadays? Are they getting into your garbage cans like the bears?"

She glares over her shoulder at me, but I spot the smile tugging at the corners of her mouth. Mama is normally more prone to smiling, but the problem is, she hates nothing more than feeling useless. Having to wait weeks to heal is going to destroy her nerves.

"Not that bad. But I had a young lady working the register, and you would've thought I'd started including free nude magazines with my pastries the way this place started filling with the single men. They only calmed down after she got a ring on her finger."

"You think she got engaged for some peace at work?"

Mama shakes her head. "Oh no. She's still unattached. She bought the ring for herself. I was going to introduce the two of you next time you visited. But I like your Quinn."

"You do?" I steer her around the bread slicer and come upon my dad decorating a cake. He's not great at the actual baking aspect of this job, but offer him a piping bag and his huge hands will sculpt the most delicate of designs.

"Do what?" Dad asks, straightening and pushing a set of reading glasses up to his forehead.

"I was just telling August, I've rethought my matchmaking scheme because I like his fire starter better."

"Mama," I chide, glancing over my shoulder to make sure Quinn hasn't wandered back here and overheard the descriptor.

"What? I wasn't insulting her."

"Still. She's working on her control. It's kind of a sensitive topic."

"Fine, fine. But I still like her."

"Me too." My dad gives me a huge grin, and my lips curve in response.

"Glad we all agree." I scratch the back of my neck, suddenly overwhelmed with a sense of self-consciousness. It's not that I doubted that my parents would like Quinn. She's sweet, and spicy, and makes me happy.

But seeing how easily they fall for the Pyro is more proof that she's my dream woman, and that losing her would be the biggest blunder in my life to date. Problem is, I have no relationship experience. I can't help an onset of anxiety and an evil little voice in my head claiming I'm going to screw this up.

"You're worrying. What are you worrying over?" My mother taps her cast against my leg to get my attention.

"Nothing," I mutter.

"It's not nothing. What has you frowning like that when we're saying how much we like your Quinn?"

I sigh, knowing my mom won't let this drop. "We haven't been together that long."

"So? She came all this way with you. That clearly means she's invested."

"Until I screw it up."

"Screw it up? How?"

"That's the thing. I have no practice. I don't know how to do a relationship the right way."

"The *right* way? Bah." My mom waves her hand in the air as if my words are annoying flies buzzing in her face. "There's no one, right way. And there's not a perfect way either. You'll make mistakes. So will she. You know a relationship is working when you move on from those mistakes."

"Listen to your mama." My dad adds his input as he returns his glasses to their spot on the tip of his nose. "Also, bring Quinn a cinnamon bun. Sugar lays the best foundation."

My mother smiles up at me as if to say *see?*

The two of them fit together in a way I hope Quinn and I do. Or will someday.

I'm willing to put in the time and effort to make that happen. I'm also willing to move past any mistakes, especially because I have trouble imagining Quinn doing anything that would upset me.

Without another word, I turn to the counter where a tray of warm cinnamon rolls awaits.

Carrying a plate with two treats, I head back toward the front of the restaurant, leaving my father to deal with Mama's loving dictatorship.

Only, when I get to the sitting area of the shop, I pause.

Quinn is so lost in her work, I don't think she hears me walk into the room. Her fingers dance rapidly over her keyboard, filling the quiet of the morning with soft tapping. I hover in the doorway, watching her. The whole scene is soothing, like the smell of hot chocolate. I want to drink her down in greedy gulps.

After a minute or two passes, I realize she is truly and deeply ingrained in her work.

What would a good boyfriend do?

Probably leave her to it, let her finish, since it's obviously very important.

But I have cinnamon rolls. A good boyfriend wouldn't walk away without offering her something to eat. Right?

I waver, finally deciding to approach as quietly as possible, set the pastries down, and then back away slowly in hopes that I go unnoticed. The maneuver would be easier if I wasn't so large. Halfway across the front room, my toe catches on a stool, sending the seat clattering and me wobbling, desperate to hold onto the rolls.

When I regain my balance, I find Quinn staring at me, a smirk on her face.

"I think I understand the layout of Lois even better now. You wanted all that space to accommodate Viking-sized bodies." She runs her gaze from my toes to my forehead.

Tension eases when I realize she's not mad about the interruption. I settle in a seat across from hers, laying the cinnamon buns I saved on the bit of table not covered in her work.

"You caught me. I've tripped over enough furniture in this place to leave me with permanent bruises."

My Pyro grins, then tilts one eyebrow up in question. "You sharing?" A red-painted nail taps the edge of the plate, and I eagerly nod.

"For you. Thought you'd be getting hungry."

"You thought right." Quinn picks up a pastry, the still warm icing dripping over her fingers. When she takes a bite, an erotic moan rumbles from her chest. "Did you make these?" She sucks on her sugar-coated thumb, making my dick twitch.

"The base. Yes. My dad did the icing. Group effort."

Quinn finishes after only two more bites, leaving me impressed and horny. My insides are solid ice.

"You all work well together."

"Years of practice." My answer sounds distracted to my own ears as I home in on a smear of frosting on her bottom lip.

"But they do okay without you?"

Since we're talking about my parents, I shove all sexy thoughts to the back of my mind.

"Normally. When my mom isn't out of the game. Dad has never really gotten the hang of bread. Pretty sure he still can't tell the difference between a teaspoon and a tablespoon."

Quinn nods, tapping a few keys on her laptop in an almost idle manner. "So you're probably sticking around until your mom is back in commission?"

My fingers reach to scratch the back of my neck without conscious thought. "Honestly, I haven't made any firm plans. But this is their source of income. They lose this, they lose everything. I can't let that happen."

"Of course not." Quinn reaches across the table to clasp my free hand, the warmth of her skin against mine automatically soothing me.

But I can't help thinking a good boyfriend would've said something else.

Chapter Thirty-Five

QUINN

I thought setting up in a cushy window seat would be a great place to get some work done.

Unfortunately, the view outside is utterly distracting.

Through the glass, I have a clear view of the Nords' backyard, and currently, there is a certain Ice Elemental down there who has decided to not only chop wood but to remove his shirt for the process. Heat thrums in my veins, warning me that I should relocate. If only my eyes would detach from the glorious view.

"That boy just can't stop." The gruff voice of August's father sucker punches my lust, as does the cooling presence of his power as he comes to stand next to me to peer out at his son.

"Does wood really need to be chopped in the summer?" Growing up in Arizona, I have absolutely no frame of reference.

"You do the work when the weather is good so you're ready for the cold season. Winter comes fast here."

Not fast enough for my taste. I've never seen snow other than in movies. I'm bummed that I've come to normally one of the coldest places in the United States, and I'm still going to leave without even getting a glimpse. I had this ridiculous fantasy of jumping into a giant pile of it to make a snow angel, then when August comes over to help me up, I'd tug him down with me, and we'd fool around surrounded by the perfect fire-power buffer.

Like an R-rated Hallmark movie.

Not a mental image that needs to be shared with his father.

"That makes sense. Of course, in Phoenix most people think our best weather is in December."

Mr. Nord grins at me over the lip of his steaming cup of tea. We all got back to their house an hour ago. I can't believe they haven't collapsed into bed, needing a nap. Mornings at a bakery are wild. Once customers started coming in, I'd tucked myself into a back corner, glancing up from my laptop periodically to ogle August as he worked the register and handed out pastries.

I can't decide if I like baker August or ice cream maker August better.

Probably the second because that means he's in Phoenix.

"We'll have to make a visit once Samantha is better. We've missed him something fierce. It's good to have him back home even if it's only for a short time."

Am I a horrible person for wanting it to be a super short time?

Yes. Yes I am.

I'm saved from having to answer when August walks into the room, shirt back in place, regretfully.

He grins at the two of us.

Mr. Nord lifts his mug in a silent toast. "Love it when my chores get done for me."

"Maybe I should back off. Don't want you to get lazy." August settles his hands on my shoulders, massaging a kink I hadn't realized formed in my neck. Guess that's what happens when I type on my laptop for hours straight.

"Please. I'm weak and old. I need my strong, strapping son to take care of me." The man pretends to whimper, which is hilarious paired with his muscular build and towering form.

I doubt Mr. Nord needs any help with physical tasks. My bet is that the problem arises from the amount of things needing to be done both around the house and at the bakery. That large load is what has August chipping in.

The son rolls his eyes before smiling down at me.

"Let's go for a drive."

Hmm, alone time with my guy? Sounds good to me.

"Where?"

His grin betrays his excitement. "You'll see."

Out in the driveway, I'm about to climb into the passenger seat when August stops me, his cool hand on my wrist.

"How would you feel about wearing this?" He holds out a black strip of fabric and gestures toward my eyes.

"A blindfold? Kinky. Are you taking me to your secret Alaskan sex dungeon?"

Icy air hits my skin, and I watch in fascination as August's fingers tighten on the cloth, little spirals of frost swirling over the fabric.

"You like that idea?" My smirk is wicked, and I know it. Little does he know, it wouldn't be my first time at a sex dungeon.

Of course, that was on a trip to visit Harley at work.

"Yeah, Quinn." He leans over to press an open-mouth kiss on the side of my neck. "I do."

Shivers cascade through me, and I think I might pass out from the pleasure of his breath against my skin.

"But it'll have to wait for another time," August says as he straightens with an all too satisfied smile. "Today's escapades are G-rated."

"Prude," I mutter.

He snorts as he ties the blindfold on. My vision effectively cut off, I need his help maneuvering into the car.

At first, the experience is strange. All my control of the situation is gone. The vehicle moves forward, and I'm at a loss. But after a few minutes of fighting off dizziness, I recline the seat and lay back, giving myself up to the Ice Elemental's surprise.

While on the road, August regales me with stories of bakery mishaps and wacky local customers, some of them reality show celebrities. Apparently, you can't throw a day-old pastry in Anchorage without hitting someone who's appeared on a reality TV show. The whole world wants to know how Alaskans live. Or at least a romanticized version of it.

But other than putting more thought and effort into how to stay warm for the upcoming season change, I wouldn't say the Nord's life is too different from my family's.

No living in a cabin without running water.

No wrestling wild animals for food.

Maybe I watched too many reality shows, too...

"Okay, my patient Pyro." August's grin is evident in his voice, and I love that I know how he'll look just from the way he sounds. Gravel crunches under tires as the car slows to a stop. "We're here."

"Do I take this off now?" My fingers fiddle with the knot at the back of my head.

"Just a second. Let's get you out of the truck first."

His door slams closed a moment before mine is pulled open. I slide from my seat, running my hands over his chest as if I need the wall of him to steady me. Maybe I do, maybe I don't. Tendrils of heat unravel in my veins at the soft texture of cotton over firm stomach.

"Quinn." August huffs my name, and the next second there's the hard metal of the truck against my back and August's mouth devouring mine.

I moan, silently hoping we're not parked in front of a preschool or something.

The strands of his hair slide smooth as silk through my fingers as I reach up to hold his face to mine. Points of pressure dig into my ass as August boosts me higher, making our make-out session easier.

He smells of sweat and the pine wood he was chopping earlier. I miss the sweetness of melted ice cream on his lips but still find myself drunk on the taste of him. I suck on his tongue, reveling in the way his hips jerk with each pull.

Heat pulses, smoldering coals searching for tinder to consume.

Without warning, August pulls back.

"G-rated." He pants as he scolds me, and I can't stifle a disappointed moan.

The bastard chuckles, his fingers trailing over my cheeks.

Then the world explodes into view.

"Gah! The light!"

He took off the blindfold without warning, and now the sun attempts to fry my corneas.

"Shit, sorry. I should've said." August presses my face against his chest, using his body to block the light.

After blinking for a minute or so, I finally can peer around me without flinching. We've parked on the bank of what looks to be a lake. We're not the only people here, other cars having pulled up alongside the water.

I wonder if any of them enjoyed the PG-13 show.

Thoughts of strangers watching me get down with my man evaporate as I pull away from August to stare out over the lake. The sight hits me hard, and before I make the decision, I'm jogging down to the water's edge for a better view of the opposite bank.

A gorgeous spill of white engulfs the scenery.

"A glacier." August steps up against my back, wrapping me in his arms. "You wanted some snow. I know it's not falling from the sky, but—"

"This is perfect." My fingers clasp his forearm where it crosses my chest. Where our skin touches, a chill creeps over me. The sensation is lovely, allowing me to believe I'm across the large expanse of water and digging my hands into the white mass.

August knows how to make my dreams a reality.

I hope this trip home hasn't changed what his dreams are.

"It looks so out of place though, like it hasn't gotten the memo that it's summer." The thought is out before I realize how forlorn my tone is.

August chuckles, his humor rumbling through me where we press together. "You're saying you want it to melt?"

"No! Of course not. I just...want it to feel like it belongs."

Is this what being in Phoenix is like for August? A giant, gorgeous frozen thing surrounded by perpetual summer? Has the heat started to wear on him? Slowly chipping away at his comfort like he's another casualty of global warming?

"It's beautiful here," I murmur, pushing down my depressing thoughts. Then I realize that I made one more argument for him to stay.

Goddess damn it, do I have to shoot myself in my own foot?

"It is. I'm not sure I always appreciated it when I was growing up."

August sighs and rests his chin on the top of my head. "Sometimes you have to leave a place for a little while to see all the amazing parts."

Something like a crack echoes in my ears. For a moment, I'm worried a chunk of the glacier has broken off and toppled into the water.

But then I realize I imagined the shattering.

My mind's way of pairing a noise with the pain in my heart.

Chapter Thirty-Six

QUINN

Somehow, I make it through my last full day in Alaska without moping. The schedule was the same as it's been the entire time here. Wake up at the ass crack of dawn, the four of us piling into Mr. Nord's SUV, and I work remotely while August and his dad bake under his mother's watchful guidance.

The early mornings and busy days aren't what has me scowling out the window. No, what I'm unhappy about is that I'm no longer going to be a member of the routine. Tomorrow, I fly back to Phoenix.

Alone.

He's not staying here forever, I silently tell myself. Or maybe I'm begging the gods for this to be true.

Either way, I do my best to believe that August hasn't fallen back in love with Alaska. That he'll still want to return to me in my desert hometown.

At the sound of heavy footsteps coming down the hall, I smooth all indications of discontent off my face, refocusing on rummaging through my suitcase for some clothes to sleep in. The baggage is a jumbled mess I'll have to put in order before heading out tomorrow.

August steps through the door, smiling when he sees me crouching on the floor. Am I imagining things, or did the happiness falter when his gaze passed over my suitcase?

Probably just seeing what I want to see.

"How do you feel about a bath?" he asks.

"A bath?" The question catches me off guard, and I move to stand. "Are you saying I need one?" Self-consciously, I tilt my chin down to attempt a subtle sniff of my armpit. From the crinkle of his eyes, I'm guessing my nonchalant gesture wasn't as smooth as I hoped.

"*I* need one." August steps further into the room, coming to lay his hands on my waist. "And I need to feel your naked body against mine in a safe space."

A gasp accompanies heat unfurling under my skin. Sucking in a bracing breath, I hold the fire back.

"You're suggesting a two-person bath?"

August nods before resting his chin on the top of my head.

"Mom and Dad have moved their stuff to the downstairs bedroom until she's on her feet again. We have this whole floor to ourselves."

Privacy. A bath with August. Him holding me, touching me intimately.

Suddenly, I'm desperate for the idea to be a reality. When I leave tomorrow, I don't know when I'll see him again. I don't know if I'll get to keep him.

"Well then, to answer your original question, I feel *very* good about a bath."

August steps back, but not before reaching down to give my butt a firm pat. "Follow me." He's grinning like a naughty teenager, which sends excitement flaring through my body.

As I follow him out of the room and down the hall, I can't help thinking back on the day we arrived, when August admitted he never jerked off in his own home during high school. Not a subject I thought I'd ever care about, but here I am, wishing I could travel back in time and give that sexually frustrated teenager a hug.

Tonight, though, he's the one with control, and I'm the one taking a risk. Still, I trust him.

The Nords have one of those luxurious claw-foot tubs in the upstairs bathroom. August sits on the edge, fiddling with the faucet.

"Only turn on the cold," I remind him.

He raises an eyebrow at me. "You sure?"

The idea of me needing a warm bath is laughable. Stepping up to him, I rest my hands on his shoulders, then slowly drag them down his front, enjoying the delicious ridges of his muscles underneath the cotton.

"Oh yeah," I murmur, my fiery pulse picking up strength. "I'm sure."

"Take your clothes off." August's demand comes out hoarse, which only gets me hotter.

With intentionally slow movements, I tug off my blouse, letting the material flutter to the floor. Next, I untie the little bow that holds up my linen shorts. Maybe others would find the Alaskan summer still too chilly to opt for sleeveless shirts and nothing covering their legs. But I have my never-extinguishing internal fire, plus the constant fuel that is August.

I could've walked around in a bikini and been perfectly comfortable.

Now, standing in the middle of the bathroom wearing only my red silky underthings, I give in to the urge to shiver. But not because I'm cold.

Hopefully I will be, though.

"Oh no," I murmur, my hands coming to my cheeks as if I've realized something disappointing.

When I meet August's eyes, his brow crinkles in concern, and he stands from the tub, approaching me with arms out. Preparing to comfort me. Because that's the amazing guy he is. Doesn't matter that he has a very clear oak tree in his pants. He's ready to set his lust aside if need be.

"What is it?" His grip comes to my shoulders, and I notice thin webs of ice have scattered over his forearms.

"It's only..." I stare up at him, making my eyes as wide and innocent as possible, even affecting a pouty lower lip. "I've forgotten how to take off my bra and panties." Clasping my hands under my chin, pleading with him by batting my eyelashes. "Do you think you could help me, kind sir?"

A trickle of cold air traces down the front of my body, like I'm getting felt up by Jack Frost.

August's forehead drops to mine, his eyes closed shut. "You're going to kill me," he mutters.

"I would never." My fingers circle his wrists, drawing his hands down to my chest. "I need you alive and well so you can touch me."

And he does, his thumbs tracing over my nipples through the material of my bra.

Heat pulses in time with his caresses, and I breathe in deep to maintain control.

Okay, my bad, this sexy time needs to be relocated. Now.

Grasping the bottom of his shirt, I pull the cotton barrier upward, forcing him to drop his touch and step away from me. Still, I maintain a hold on his shirt, and when it's off his head, I press the fabric to my face.

There's a trace of some piney soap and a hint of garlic from the pasta we had for dinner. Determined, I suck in an even deeper lungful. But it's the same as the first breath.

Now I'm pouting for real, even though I know it's juvenile. In fact, I'm so disappointed, I'm mortified to realize there's something like tears pushing at the back of my eyes.

Goddess, what is wrong with me?

August just finished pulling down his zipper when he picks up on my mood shift. "Quinn?"

I try for a sultry smile. It comes out flat, and August is back in my space.

"Are you teasing me again, or is something really upsetting you?"

Shaking my head, I push at the nagging thought. "Nothing. Don't worry about it. Get naked."

August snorts, a finger going under my chin, forcing me to meet his eyes. "I'm not taking my pants off until you tell me what's wrong."

Damn it. Damn him and his observant, caring nature.

"It's ridiculous," I say.

His thumb traces my bottom lip. "Let me be the judge."

With a sigh, I relent. "You don't smell like waffle cones anymore."

And gods, do I miss that smell. The scent I now so thoroughly associate with August. August in Phoenix.

The Ice Elemental grins down at me. "That makes you sad?"

"That you no longer smell like the most delicious, sweet dough in the world? Yeah, I'm a little bummed."

"Well," his touch falls away, "I can't have my woman upset." He moves to leave.

"Where are you going?"

"I'll be right back."

"You're going downstairs like that?" *Looking like the centerfold of my personalized porn magazine?*

August pauses in the doorway and takes a second to re-zip his pants. "Better?"

"Define *better*."

The man disappears, leaving the echo of a chuckle in his place.

Feeling lost, I glance over to the tub and realize the thing is almost full. With a quick turn of the faucet, the steady stream trickles off.

Dipping my fingers into the water, I instinctively know the temperature is cold. A little logical sliver in the back of my mind tells me others would shy away from the idea of fully immersing their naked body in a bath this temperature. But to me, it merely feels lukewarm.

Heavy footsteps in the hall herald August's return. He comes into the bathroom clutching a Tupperware container.

"Mom always has a few of these on hand in case she's craving ice cream."

He pops off the lid, and a familiar scent teases my nose.

"Are those..."

August passes the container to me. "Waffle cones."

This is one of the most innocent, yet at the same time most erotic, gifts I've ever received. I'm not sure what I even want to do with them. Rub them all over August's body until the smell melds with his cells? Or maybe I could crumble them on his chest and lick the broken pieces off.

That might get too messy.

Instead, I pluck one out and bite into the crisp treat.

Crunchy and buttery and sweet like syrup.

Once I swallow, I smile at my man. "While I eat this, I want you to take your clothes off. Slowly."

August smirks, even as the temperature in the bathroom drops. "I'm starting to think you only want me for my ice cream."

"I want you for a lot more than that."

My Viking ice cream god's cheeks go ruddy, and I love the bashful expression on his handsome face. Then his hands return to the fly of his pants, and I can't focus anywhere else. He follows my directions, every movement of his a slow tease. Hungry for him, I take another massive bite out of my waffle cone, pairing the sweet flavor on my tongue with the hot scene before my eyes.

August isn't wearing skinny jeans, but his thighs and calves are so muscular, he needs to give his pants an extra push to get them to fall to the ground. When he kicks them away, all that's left is a dramatically tented pair of red boxer briefs.

My eyes widen at the discovery. Then I giggle.

"You know"—he approaches me with measured steps—"I hoped that getting naked for you would elicit something other than laughter."

"I'm sorry!" *Great job at being a girlfriend...not.* I set aside my snack and step up to him. "I couldn't help it. We match." My sneaky fingers fiddle with the waist of his underwear, and I get to watch ice crystals scatter across his lower belly.

"We do, don't we? So I guess if I take these off," with a quick movement, he divests himself of the briefs, "you'll want to follow suit?"

All I can manage is a nod and a gentle shove, pushing him toward the tub. With August junior out, bobbing proudly, I need to submerge myself in water soon.

Understanding, August steps into the clawfoot tub, sinking into it until only above his pecks is visible. He stretches his arms along the rim and crooks a finger at me to join him.

If I were artistic in any way, I'd want to photograph or paint my man in this moment. I don't often treat myself to baths in Phoenix because of water shortages, so this one, filled with the eye-melting man of my dreams, seems like the ultimate form of self-indulgence. Time to revel in my own pleasure.

With a quick twist, I have my bra unhooked and on the ground, followed a moment after by my panties. August groans, his head falling backward, eyes shut as if in pain. When I step closer, I realize that tiny icebergs have formed on the surface of the water like little bath toys. Their innocuous bobbing has me grinning, and I carefully maneuver around lust-caused ice cubes. I slide into the water, which again feels perfectly warm to me, and I settle in between August's parted legs.

Skin on skin. The sensation is erotic and bone melting. Getting the urge to tease, I recline on his chest, pressing my lower back against the hard bar of steel between his legs.

August lets out another sound of tortured pleasure. Before I can start to work him, he's submerged his arms, wrapping me in a tight embrace. The hug starts out almost innocently affectionate. Simply a show of joy that the two of us are here, together, comfortable with one another.

But then his hands explore, sliding over my stomach and hips. A palm cups the lower swell of my breast, and I whimper. Though, that's nothing to when his fingers find the curls between my legs. Instead of passing right by them to get to the pleasure center, August pauses to do his own teasing. He gives gentle tugs that have my nipples puckering and my body twitching like he's found my puppet strings. For the first time in my life, I'm glad that my shying away from pain negated me from opting for a full Brazilian. I figured that most men wanted a woman bald downstairs, but if I wasn't going to get a chance to sleep with any of those men, why bother?

August is not one of those men.

As he continues to hover just outside of my folds, his other hand engulfs and fondles my boob. When his fingers flick against my nipple, my entire body jerks in response.

"You like that?" Even though he's behind me, I can hear the smile in his voice.

"Uh huh," is all I can manage in response.

August rolls my nipple between his thumb and forefinger, pinching with enough pressure to have my hips writhing in pleasure. Up until this point, I've been digging my nails into his thighs, but I can't take this edge of sensation anymore. Gripping his wrist, I push August's lower-sitting hand farther between my legs.

"Greedy," he murmurs, voice strained.

"Yes." *Yes, I'm greedy. Yes, I want you wrapped around me and exploring me always.*

As his cool touch circles my clit, and the second heated pulse under my skin beats in time with his movements, August releases my breast only to plunge his second hand under the water, between my legs.

There's a pressure at my entrance, his caress drawing my gasps. Then he's inside me. One finger. Two.

In my pleasure haze I clasp his wrists harder, holding them to my core, thrusting against his invasion. My mind is split between loving the sensation and wanting more. More of him. To spread my legs wide for the hard length of him that currently presses against my back.

"August." I groan his name, not sure how to ask for what I crave when my internal fire sets my words ablaze before breath even leaves my lungs. All I can do is let the ecstasy pull me toward the edge as nonsense sounds spill from my throat.

"That's it, my little Pyro. Get there for me. Gods, you're so hot against me. I want to feel your orgasm. Have your pussy squeeze my fingers tight." The dirty words brush against my ear, riding a chilled breath that has me shivering in bliss.

Then August licks my neck a second before pinching the skin with his teeth.

I boil over. Words cut off as my throat tightens with every other muscle in my body, then gasp out with the release of pressure. Water splashes over the edge of the tub in time with my waves of sensual rapture, the agitation caused by my mindless twisting.

When enough of the pleasure eases for me to think again, I realize that while I spilled the water, I didn't heat it. Not much anyway. There's not even steam rising from the top. The Ice Elemental balances me.

August holds me to him, stilling my body as he whispers praises in my ear. The man seems to enjoy the lustful puddle he's turned me into.

But who am I to complain?

My extremities are still tingling when he speaks.

"Ready for bed?"

That gets a laugh out of me. "Silly man." My voice is husky from my orgasm, my release empowering the sex goddess in me. "I'm ready for you."

Chapter Thirty-Seven

AUGUST

Ready for me?

"Do you mean...?" I leave the sentence unfinished, not wanting to presume.

When I suggested this bath, my intention was to do exactly as I did: touch Quinn until I got the chance to see her—feel her—orgasm again. Then hopefully she'd be more relaxed in preparation for her flight tomorrow. I've picked up on an underlying note of stress all day, and I can guess it has to do with getting on that plane without me.

She's leaving without me.

The thought threatens to drag me down to a dark place, but the descent is cut off by Quinn's hand circling my wrist again. She draws my palm out of the water, bringing the fingers that were inside her to her lips. Then she sucks them into her mouth.

The sensation of her tonguing the digits has my hips thrusting without thought.

After one last lick, the Pyro drops her head back on my shoulder, tilting her chin to stare up at me with a sultry gaze.

"I mean that you've gotten me all wet. Time to do something about that."

My insides freeze. Literally. I think if a doctor were to cut into me right now, they would discover that my guts have transformed into chunks of ice.

The chill must be seeping through my chest, but Quinn only presses herself closer with a purr.

"You feel so good," she murmurs as little whips of steam rise from between us. "I want you inside me."

A part of my brain is about to point out that I just was. But clearly she doesn't mean my fingers.

"We don't have to." I never want Quinn to feel pressured into sex with me, especially because she's constantly concerned about her powers.

But gods, I want to keep this going.

Instead of answering, Quinn moves out of my hold. I try not to let disappointment show on my face while I reach out to steady her as she climbs from the tub.

But other than shifting to her knees, Quinn doesn't attempt to stand. Instead, she scoops her damp hair off her neck, guiding the mass to fall forward over her shoulder. This leaves her back bare, and I'm fascinated with the constellation of freckles that continues even here.

Then my mind stutters as she bends at the waist, bracing her hands on the far side of the tub, and lets her knees widen a touch.

Her pussy is on gorgeous display, directly in front of my face. The folds have flushed dark from her orgasm. Droplets trickle over the dips of her core, and I wonder how much of the wetness is from the bath and how much I can claim credit for.

"August." Her voice is all teasing. "Do you like what you see?"

After swallowing multiple times, I am almost able to form a coherent answer. But then her hand appears, sneaking through her split legs and fingering that opening as if she's petting the petals of the most beautiful flower in the world.

All I can do is grunt, which earns me a husky chuckle.

When I shift forward, I realize I have to crack through a thin layer of ice that's formed on the surface of the water. Briefly, I revel in the fact that no shame arises when I see the physical effects of my power. I know Quin likes this part of me.

Hell, she might even love it.

Does she love me though?

Pushing the thought to the back of my mind, I rise to my knees, towering above my little Pyro. Quinn may be above average height compared to most women, but to me, she's perfect. The right size to cover her with my body but not to overwhelm her completely.

Which is what I do now.

My hands grip the sides of the tub, in front of hers, bracketing her naked curves. Quinn releases her hold only to grasp my wrists. I cage her with my body as our legs remain submerged in the water. Her back is hot against my front, and I press my nose into her neck, breathing in deep the scent of campfires and warm ovens.

"Take me hard," she whispers. "I want to feel you even when I'm back in Phoenix."

A groan wrenches from my throat as frost condenses in my gut and coats my skin. It only takes a moment to align my aching shaft with her warm pussy. The first slide into her supernatural heat is almost enough to have my eyes rolling back in my head.

The water sloshes as I thrust, and each time I bury deep in Quinn, I'm rewarded with a happy gasp from her lips. Keeping her demand in mind, I rut into her like a beast. Fuck her like the abominable snowman. The bathroom fills with the sound of water dripping on the floor and our skin slapping against each other. Every part of my body that touches hers burns. If only this blaze could stay forever, the shape of Quinn imprinted on me. All I want is more of the delicious sensation. Frustration at the thought that I'll have to give it up tomorrow makes the pounding of my hips almost angry.

Quinn groans low, and with the power surge the sound elicits, I direct my frost toward her clit, imagining what I would do if I could somehow be inside her but also tonging her.

My Fire Elemental gasps, her nails digging gouges into my wrists. Fire tears through my body, originating at the pressure points between us. Her molten essence is inside me, filling every inch of my being. Seeking to return the favor, I shout as my hips buck a final time before I spill into her, letting ice mingle with my cum.

With my remaining few brain cells, I clutch her around the waist and tilt us so we can sink back into the tub, barely noticing the vastly lower level of the water. As we lay wrapped up together, Quinn's body relaxes fully, as if all her bones melted with that internal heat of hers. After a moment, she lets out a small noise that I realize is a snore.

My Pyro has passed out.

As she sleeps, I gather her closer to my chest, wondering how I'll ever be able to let her board that plane without me tomorrow.

Chapter Thirty-Eight

AUGUST

"You can drop me off at the departure gate," Quinn says as I shift the car into the lane that leads to short-term parking.

"I can. But I'm not going to." *She flew all the way up here to support me, and she thinks I'm going to drop her on the curb with a quick wave goodbye?*

In truth, there were multiple times on this drive I considered getting "lost" until we're so late Quinn missed her flight and had to stay another day.

But that would be a shitty move, and I'm trying not to ruin this new, fragile thing between us. As it is, I don't know what distance will do to our relationship. I'd like to think we're strong enough not to let the time apart affect anything, but I'd feel more secure if we'd been together longer. If we had planted more roots. And if those roots twined together.

But she's leaving, and the ground is all loose dirt under my feet.

After grabbing a ticket at the entrance to the lot and finding an empty space, I put the car in park. Quinn meets me at the trunk, but I make sure to grab her bags before her reaching fingers can take hold of the handles.

"You don't—"

"I'm carrying your bags, Quinn. And I'm walking you to the security line. And I'm hanging out until you make it to your gate."

Something in my voice keeps her from arguing, and I'm glad. I don't want to bicker with her in these last minutes we have together.

I start to walk, the handle of her rolling suitcase in one hand and her small duffle bag clutched in the other.

"Wait." Quinn's touch on my shoulder has me pausing. "Here." She tugs on the bag, and I'm ready to scold her again when I realize she's just lengthening a strap.

Understanding her intention, I move to sling the strap over my shoulder.

The second my hand is free, Quinn laces our fingers together. She smiles up at me, and pairs it with an affectionate squeeze.

"You're going to make everyone in the airport think I'm high maintenance, carrying all my bags for me." She pokes me in the stomach playfully as we cross the parking lot.

I'm almost too distracted by the lovely heat of her skin to answer, but I manage a response. "Any man who sees us is going to wish he were the one carrying your bags."

Quinn snorts. "And all the straight women and gay men are going to be clamoring for your help the minute you step away from me."

Then I'll never leave your side. I keep the words to myself, knowing they're too heavy for this lighthearted goodbye banter.

"Maybe I'll make a few bucks before I head out then. Charge for my services."

Quinn lifts our joint hands to her mouth, and I wonder if she's going to kiss my skin. A moment later there's a slight, sharp pressure on my knuckle that has me stumbling before staring down at her, shock and arousal picking up my heartbeat.

"Did you bite me?"

Her smile is wicked and full of warning. "No one gets your services but me. Paid or otherwise."

"Yes, ma'am." I soothe the ice in my gut, the heavy weight of it an erotic pressure. I want to place Quinn's fingers on the bare skin of my stomach and have her warmth infuse every inch of me.

Instead, I pull our clasped hands to my mouth, pressing my lips to the inside of her wrist.

She shivers and smirks, all the while I'm basking in the steady waves of heat that pulse from her palm to mine.

I don't think she realizes the amount of control she's developed, and I doubt she'd believe me if I pointed it out. Quinn only sees her mistakes, not her triumphs. But I see them, and I catalogue each and every one in my mind. Right now, for instance. The only fire I feel is in her skin. Nothing spilling into the air around us. The same with our visit to the glacier.

Quinn Byrne still runs hot, but she's mastering how to keep her powers contained within the limits of her own body.

I'd like to think I'm the one she's trying so hard for, but that comes off as arrogant. Maybe I was the start of her growth, but no doubt she could continue to improve without me.

With someone else even.

My icy arousal thaws at the thought.

The airport is busy with people starting and ending their journeys. Quinn and I move through the crowds, finding the line for the airline ticket counter she's flying with. As we inch forward in the stream of customers, I experience the moment as if I'm in a dream. A bad one, where time is slipping away from me faster and faster no matter how hard I try to hold on to it. Our banter never started back up, and now I think frantically of something to say to make her smile again.

But the only words that come to me are heavy ones.

Don't leave.

I need you.

Stay with me.

I love you.

Massive weights that I worry could smother our new relationship. I'm putting so much on Quinn so fast already. Days after deciding to take this all slow, I was buying her a plane ticket to meet my parents. One of whom was in the hospital.

So I keep my mouth shut, locking down my panic.

"Sorry. I didn't realize it'd be so crowded. Guess we should have left earlier." Quinn murmurs this to me as we make another small shuffling step forward in line.

Little does she know I'd give most anything for the amount of people in here to double. To overwhelm the planes to the point that she couldn't board one. So she couldn't leave me.

Stop being selfish, I chide myself.

"Don't worry. You won't miss your flight."

The edges of her mouth curve down, and I give in to the urge to lean over and press a kiss to her forehead, hoping to ease her worry. Also trying to cover up how much I *want* her to miss her flight.

I love you, I silently add as I straighten up, praying to the gods that I can speak the words out loud one day soon.

And then hear them in return.

I do love Quinn.

It shouldn't have happened this fast, but I know I do.

This morning I came downstairs to see her at the kitchen table with my mother, playing Scrabble, and I fought against the sudden sensation of drowning. That's when I realized the reason I couldn't breathe was from an overwhelming surge of happiness and affection.

Oh gods, I thought. *I love her.*

Then my girlfriend glanced up from the board and caught me staring. She put on the most over-exaggerated, adorable pout.

"August! Tell your mom to stop being so hard on me."

Grinning to cover the chaos caused by my realization, I approached the table to offer my advice.

My mother scowled. "Don't help her. That's cheating."

"But I'm an accountant! I know numbers, not words," Quinn bemoaned, fiddling with her pieces, looking lost.

"You're speaking the English language right now, aren't you?" Mama's injuries made her feisty.

As the women continued their lighthearted bickering, I filled a mug with coffee from the still hot pot. Then I meandered back to the table.

"August." My mother's voice was full of warning. She took her Scrabble very seriously.

I held my free hand up in surrender. "I'm just looking. Swear on the gods."

Quinn's brow was furrowed in concentration as she studied her tiles. Then, with a sigh of acceptance, or maybe defeat, she plucked four of the little squares and carefully arrange them. I leaned forward to read the word, making the mistake of sipping some coffee as I did so.

Boobs.

Liquid scalded my windpipe as I sucked in a breath, and I spent the next few seconds coughing up a lung and trying to get a glimpse of my mother's expression even as my eyes watered.

All the while, Quinn watched me with pinched lips and dipped brows, no doubt waiting to see if I needed medical help. Once I was breathing normally again, she turned back to the game.

"Boobs. And I'm on a triple word score so that's twenty seven points."

"Your boobs are worth more than that." My comment slipped out before I could consider what I was saying.

Quinn grinned over her shoulder at me as Mama shook her head, all the while fighting a smile.

"You're damn right they are." The Pyro puffed out her chest, as if to put them on display. I had to grip the back of her chair to keep from sinking to the ground in front of her and burying my face in the tempting globes.

"Yes, and if you had spelled out *Quinn's Boobs,* that certainly would've been a higher point value. But it also would have been against the rules. You'll have to settle for the generic boob points."

I could hardly believe those words had come out of my mother's mouth. It's not that she's uptight, but we've never been the type of family to make sex jokes.

Apparently, Quinn was having an effect on us all.

At that moment, Dad had entered the kitchen through the door that led to the backyard. He brought the scent of freshly mown grass with him.

Sunday is the one day of the week the bakery is normally closed, which makes it household chore day. We still head into the shop later in the afternoon to prep for the rest of the week, but my dad is always busy in the morning with home-related tasks. I reminded myself to ask him for a list of things he wouldn't have time to get to.

My father smiled at each of us, ending on my girlfriend.

"You need me to drive you to the airport, Quinn?" he asked.

"I'll call a cab."

"I'll drive her."

Quinn and I spoke at the same time, and silence descended on the kitchen as a sick twisting filled my gut.

"Do you want to take a cab?" I asked quietly, not wanting to force her into a car with me if she didn't want to be.

"I don't want to be a burden." Her long fingers fiddled with another letter tile.

"You're not. I'm driving you."

Thankfully, Quinn didn't fight me on the proclamation, and I'm taking the fact that she's still holding my hand even as we step up to the ticket counter as a positive sign.

After checking her bags and getting her printed ticket, Quinn and I follow the signs directing us toward security. All the while, I try not to be obvious about how much I'm dragging my feet. We're about to pass a small convenience shop when I have an idea and pull her to a stop.

"Wait here a second. I want to grab something."

Leaving my girlfriend with a befuddled look on her face, I duck into the store and make a quick purchase. A minute later I'm back at her side, sliding my hand into hers.

"You going to tell me what that was about?"

"In a minute." Up ahead I spot the long, twisting security line, and I hate the sight of it. Glancing around, I eye a large column that could afford us a small amount of privacy. I tug Quinn toward it, tucking us into the corner.

"Here. Thought this might help entertain you on the flight." From my back pocket, I pull out a tiny booklet and hand it over.

She reads the cover and flips through the pages. "Sudoku?"

I nod and force my face into a smile. "Thought about a crossword puzzle book, but you're an accountant. You know numbers, not words."

That earns me a beautiful grin worth a lot more than the five bucks I paid for the little gift.

Damn, I'm going to miss that smile.

Not for long though, I remind myself. *Us being apart is only temporary.*

But for some reason, this separation gives me anxiety. As if our goodbye means more than goodbye-for-now.

And the fear that thought brings with it has me desperate for her.

"Can I kiss you?"

Quinn stares up at me, indecision clear on her face, especially when she glances around the crowded terminal.

I try not to push her, but as her mouth opens to give what I'm sure is a rejection, I add one last plea.

"I'll keep you cold."

Instead of speaking, she lets out a little huff as I notice her pupils dilating. Her widened eyes trace the shape of my lips, and before I can blink she has her hands fisted in my T-shirt.

"You better." The whisper is low and fierce and comes a moment before her mouth crashes into mine. She tastes like my toothpaste and hot cinnamon. I stifle my urge to groan, but can't keep my tongue to myself, dragging it across hers, diving deeper, as if I could consume her as easily as she has consumed me.

Letting my frost stifle her fire is easy with her soft body pressed against mine. I wrap us in an invisible barrier of chill, wondering if her hot touch against my cold will give off steam.

Quinn breaks away, panting. I find breathing equally as difficult, dragging in lungfuls through my nose. Luckily, there's no radius of destruction around us, and no one seems to have noticed or cared about our PDA.

My girlfriend presses her hands against flushed cheeks as her gaze connects with mine.

"I'll see you soon?" she asks.

"We can set up a video chat date." Talking to Quinn on a screen won't be near as good as being in the same room as her, but anything I can do to hear her voice, see her laugh, talk to her about my day and learn about hers is better than nothing. I need that connection, no matter how tenuous.

However, my response doesn't reward me with a smile. Instead, Quinn ducks her head, a second too late to hide the downward curve of her mouth. I'm on the verge of asking what went wrong when she steps away from me, taking all her glorious warmth with her.

"Goodbye, August."

The words are an ice cream scooper to my chest, digging out a painful chunk of my heart. Like she plans to take the piece of me with her, and the only way I can get it back is by returning to her side.

Of course, I will.

"I'll see you soon, Quinn."

Her head tilts back toward me at that, her mouth smiling again, but her eyes sad.

"I hope so."

Chapter Thirty-Nine

QUINN

This plane is at no risk of going down in flames, and it's probably an indication of mental instability that I'm depressed by that fact.

I had to leave.

I had to.

Did I though?

"Oh fuck you, heart." My mutter is low, full of self-directed venom. "I'm going to drown you in vodka."

I don't even like vodka, but it's something Russians would drink, and Russia is a giant icy tundra, and that reminds me of August.

Also, the ice cubes in my glass remind me of him. I poke one and then the other, watching them bob and float mournfully in my plastic cup. I had to pay seven bucks for this drink, and I'm going to make it an experience. Even if it's a lonely, depressing one.

"Why so down? Your drink no good?" This comment comes from my right side, and I'm slightly shocked there's a person next to me. Of course, I knew there was, in the general sense that this is a full flight. But I didn't truly acknowledge that there was a living breathing human inches—okay more like centimeters because this is coach—away from me.

"This drink is the only thing mildly good about this flight." I know I sound like a grumbly, pouty teenager. But what do I care? There's no one here I'm trying to impress. I'm not in a meeting with a client. And I'm not sitting in a delicious-smelling bakery or ice cream shop with the man of my dreams and sexual fantasies.

I'm surrounded by strangers, and I have zero motivation to pretend this is a fun time.

"The *only* good thing? You're a heartbreaker. Seriously, I'm in pain over here." The tone my seat neighbor uses reminds me of Sammy. Someone who's used to charming women right out of their panties.

Maybe if the person beside me *was* August's cousin, I'd attempt some banter. The Squid has his moments, and I know now that his flirting is mainly a ploy to make the people around him laugh.

But this guy isn't Sammy, so I don't bother to engage.

My mind sneaks immediately back to August. I mentally waver about heading down that trail, wondering about the safety of this flight if I were to become too immersed. But I reason that my failed desert excursion proved that just thoughts of him won't cause an inferno.

As long as I keep my hands out of my pants, the plane engines shouldn't erupt into fireballs.

I pluck an ice cube from my drink and hold it on my tongue, imagining I'm kissing my Ice Elemental. The sensation can't compare. His chill is lovely, but August is so much more than his power to me.

I'd want August even if he were human.

I mean, I did, obviously, at one point. I wanted his handsome face and muscular body and the rough feel of his beard on my thighs.

But now I know, I really want *him*. I may even...

I may even love him.

It's not just that he's the icy yin to my fiery yang. If all I was looking for from a guy was a dampening component, I could've knocked on a Squid's door.

August is more than the ice in his chest.

He's a man who will find me snow in the middle of the summer.

He's a man who will put his dreams on hold to help his parents keep theirs afloat.

He's a man who will give his friend's younger sister a job and a ride home without asking anything in return.

He takes a woman to an ice rink on a first date rather than a club looking to get her drunk and in his bed.

He's the type of person who's willing to go slow when fast is too dangerous.

He'll wear a ridiculous shirt to make me feel comfortable.

That's what he does. Almost every choice August makes is based on whether or not it will make the people around him happy.

I bet the most selfish thing he's ever done is choose to leave Alaska and start his own business.

I can't imagine how hard that was for him.

Was it too hard to do a second time? Will I get a call in a week or so from him, telling me he's not coming back?

The possibility isn't ludicrous. Just heartbreaking.

I take another hearty sip from my cup, half surprised to find the heat of my body hasn't melted the ice yet. That's when I realize my internal fire is barely one smoldering ember.

Looks like the best way to keep a plane full of people safe is to make sure I'm good and depressed before boarding.

"I like the way you drink. Don't even care what anyone thinks."

And put me in a seat next to a guy who likes to neg women.

I doubt he realizes how his douchery is aiding in our flight safety. The guy's brain is probably the physical manifestation of that horrendous shirt I asked August to wear.

I'm so tempted to tell my seat neighbor to fuck off, but I have another three hours strapped in next to him, so I pretend he's a white noise machine and reach into my bag for the pocket sudoku August bought me.

"Come on. We can make this a fun flight. You might feel better if you smiled."

Oh no he didn't. Hasn't the male population grasped yet the sheer horribleness of that statement?

Despite my resolution to ignore him, I can't help snapping back. "No. I think *you* would feel better if I smiled. But guess what? My facial muscles do not exist to give you pleasure."

"Hey, now." The asshole holds up his hands as if he thinks he needs to act out a surrender in order to calm me down. Because not wanting to smile for him is *so* hostile. "I'm just trying to be friendly."

"Feel free to stop putting in the effort. I'm not looking for any more friends." Not ones that spend more time looking at my chest than in my eyes anyway.

As if finally realizing his gaslighting tactics won't work on me, a frown creases his mouth.

Objectively, I can admit that he's a handsome guy. Dark eyes with thick lashes, paired with unruly black hair and a lean build give him an almost rock star vibe. And rock star arrogance too, I guess.

I prefer my men blonde with icy eyes and Thor's build.

No thanks, less-appealing Loki.

"Bitch," he mutters, loud enough for me, and maybe the woman in the window seat to his right to hear.

He's lucky my powers align with my lust. If I were wired like Cat, this whole plane would be a flaming comet plunging to the earth.

"There it is." I keep my voice at the same level he used, letting my disgust coat every word and the vodka fuel my rage. "There's your true colors. That toxic sludge bubbling just beneath the surface. You're such a *nice* guy, aren't you? So nice until a pretty girl doesn't want to hear your empty compliments. Then you shed your nice guy skin like the molting snake you are, and your fangs descend dripping poison, looking for my fleshy underbelly to tear into. Well, guess what, *nice* guy?" I lean in close, taking perverse pleasure in how wide his eyes grow at the menace in my voice. "I was raised in the desert. When I see a snake, I don't give it a chance to bite. I crush its skull under my heel."

He averts his gaze and removes his arm from the armrest he manspread onto the second he sat down.

The retreat should be a success.

But the righteous triumph dampens as quickly as it flared hot, leaving me dark and angry and on the verge of crying.

August isn't a nice guy.

Nice guys are a front.

August is kind. He's sweet. He'd never tell me to smile when I feel like frowning. Instead, he'd work himself ragged trying to find a way to make me happy again.

And now that I know how amazing of a man can exist, all others seem offensive in comparison.

Doesn't help that the asshole next to me is *actually* offensive.

The flight attendant approaches again with her cart, and I flag her down. With no idea what their schedule is, I want to make sure to grab a refill so I can make it through the flight without punching my seat neighbor in the face.

"What can I get you miss?"

"Another vodka with ice, please." Just because I'm miserable doesn't mean I don't have manners.

A throat clears loudly to my right, and my whole body tenses. Slowly, I turn, expecting the douche-y smile demander to start spouting a story about how I'm already tipsy and in no need of another drink. But I realize the person looking for attention is the middle-aged businesswoman in the window seat. She extends a hand to the flight attendant, credit card pinched in her fingers.

"I'll have the same and charge her drink to me." She flicks her beautiful blue eyes my way and offers a wink. "Craving some of that anti-venom myself."

The snake between us lets out an offended huff, then goes to recline his chair with an angry jerk. Of course, the gesture loses any type of power when he only goes back an inch.

A small amount of my unhappiness slips away when the woman and I share a commiserating smile. It's nice to have an ally against the jerks of the world.

With the second drink in my hand and a number puzzle in front of me, I do my best to block out the anxious, needy thoughts crowding my mind.

Not that it does much good.

Chapter Forty

QUINN

"You are strong. You are a badass. You have amazing control. You *will not* melt anything."

My reflection in the rearview mirror shows a determined glare without an ounce of doubt.

If only my insides agreed. Anxiety roils in my gut.

My plane landed fine late last night, and after waking up with a hangover, I decided to procrastinate on work and come here.

To August's pride and joy.

"Well, he's not inside," I reason out loud. As much as I hate that fact, I silently admit it means I'm likely safe to enter. No fuel for my fire waiting behind the counter in a shirt that hugs him tight.

After pulling the keys from the ignition, I shore up my gumption, leave my Jeep, and step through the doors.

A heavy, delicious scent surrounds me.

Waffle cones.

"Damn the gods." My muttered curse earns me a giggle from a little girl standing at the nearby trash can. When I catch her eye she sprints off, running up to another kid and whispering in their ear. The pair laugh again, and I know I've solidified my role as a corrupting force.

Oh well. It was bound to happen at some point. And keeping my language clean is not a priority at the moment.

With the sugary smell in my nose, I'm transported back to Alaska. To that claw foot bathtub. My internal fire responds to the direction of my thoughts. With a deep breath, I clear my mind and smother the heat. I need to focus on what's really important.

Balance once more restored, I walk further into the shop.

Land of Ice Cream and Snow is as busy as I've ever seen it, which makes my heart happy. I half expected to stroll into a ghost town.

I wait until Marisol gets done serving everyone in line before I approach the counter.

Before I can open my mouth, she's already glaring at me.

"What are you doing here? I thought you were in Alaska with August."

Grinding my teeth to keep a snarky retort at bay, I wonder if the young Squid will ever get over her dislike toward me.

Once I can relax my jaw, I answer. "I was, but I got back to town yesterday."

"August is back? Thank the gods. We're almost out." She sighs heavy as if unloading a large weight from her shoulders.

"You're almost out of what?"

Marisol waves behind her. "Everything. Is he on his way over? We need him to get to making more ice cream pronto. I doubt we'll last through half of tomorrow's shift if we don't restock."

Goddess damn it. Anxiety returns full force, buzzing like flies in my veins.

"Does August know about this?"

The teenager shrugs. "Denise—the weekend manager—has been keeping him updated when she comes. But he knew this would happen. He told us to close the shop if we ran out before he got back."

"Where is Denise now?"

"Probably at her other job. She's not full-time here."

I want to groan in frustration, but instead, I step to the side to let an elderly couple put in their ice cream order. As Marisol serves customers, I take the time to brainstorm what to do next.

Should I call August? Ask him if he knows how close his shop is to running out of product? Tell him to come back south or risk losing his business?

He's helping his injured mother.

And like Marisol said, he probably already knows. If I call him, no doubt I'll sound like I'm judging his choice. Making him feel guilty for whatever decision he makes. Despite my lack of experience as a girlfriend, I'm pretty sure I'm not supposed to make him feel even shittier about a bad situation.

Damn it. Damn this whole crappy turn of events. He shouldn't have to choose between his passion and helping his family.

After meeting the Nords, I can't even pretend that they're horrible parents demanding too much from their son. I know now that they're loving and supportive, and likely just as torn up about this as August is. As far as I'm aware, they didn't even ask him to help. He just did because that's the kind of man he is.

He's setting himself on fire to keep others warm.

But I *refuse* to let August's dream go up in smoke.

Admittedly, part of my conviction is based on my own self-interest. If August decides to move back to Alaska, then that's his choice. But I want it to be a *choice*. Not because his business failed and he has no other option.

My mind riffles through possible solutions until my eyes snag on Marisol, scooping a cone for the couple, a kind smile on the girl's face. The Squid can be sweet when she wants to be. And from what August has said, she's smart and determined despite her young age. Those sound like the perfect qualities in an ally.

When the customers have their treats and walk away, I step back up to the counter.

"August didn't come back with me. He's still in Alaska." No use in hiding the truth from her.

Marisol's eyes round with shock, and if I'm guessing right, a healthy bit of worry.

"He's not back? What—shit. We're going to have to close. Tomorrow." The Squid worries her bottom lip between her teeth.

"Maybe not."

Her stare focuses on me, sharp and suspicious. "What do you mean?"

"You love August."

The girl jerks back as if I slapped her. "Umm, you're crazy. I *never* said that." Then she plants her fists on the counter, leaning toward me with narrowed eyes as if contemplating going for my throat. "Don't even think of saying that to him, or I swear—"

"Goddess! Pause with the teenage drama for a second. I wasn't talking romantically, although maybe you love him that way, too. But that doesn't matter right now. What I'm trying to get at is that you care about August, right?"

"Of course I do. I did before you even knew him." She glares at me, arms crossed over her ice cream-smeared apron. "And he trusts me. August made me acting manager when he left."

She's so sassy when handing me that fact I'm tempted to smile. But that would likely just piss her off, and I need this conversation to be productive.

"This isn't a contest. It's a consensus."

"What?" The Squid is the living embodiment of distrust.

This is why I never in my life had any interest in being a teacher. Or a babysitter. Or any of the other multitude of jobs that require interacting with kids and teens. I can't talk to people under the age of eighteen. Plus, reining in my cursing is an impossible task.

"I'm starting this conversation over," I declare. "Okay. Here we go. Do you want to help August?"

She scowls, all suspicion. "You know I do."

"Okay. Good. So do I. Right now, we can't do anything about his mom. But, with him in Alaska, and the stock running out here, Land of Ice Cream and Snow is at risk. His shop. His dream." His reason to come back to our desert home.

"I know that. But what can we do?" Marisol fiddles with the ball cap she wears to keep her wavy hair tamped down. "This only works for so long without him."

"Normally, yes. But I think, together, and maybe with a little more help, we can give him another week. Possibly more."

After studying me for a long moment, Marisol offers a hesitant nod. "What did you have in mind?"

The next part of this plan all rides on one important hope. Needing to hear the right answer, I send a prayer to my patron Goddess of Fire, cc'ing the God of Ice in on the message.

"You don't only work the front counter, do you? August mentioned he's been teaching you how to make the ice cream, too." *Please tell me I didn't mishear him because I was too distracted by the sexy way his jaw tenses when he chews his food.*

"Well, yeah." The Squid shrugs. "But only the basics. I can't do anything fancy like he does. And I don't know all of his flavor combinations."

My heart rate speeds up, excitement and hope blending in a nerve-rattling mixture.

"That's all I'm asking for. What do you say? Want to save August's ass?" *That fine, delicious ass.*

There's only a moment of hesitation before the teenager gives me a conspiratorial smile.

Chapter Forty-One

AUGUST

It's four a.m. and I'm miserable.

Not because of the time. Well, not *only* because of the time.

Five days without Quinn, and I'm officially pining.

Also, I'm starting to feel cold. I've never felt cold. At least, I've never felt uncomfortable with the cold. But now the constant chill makes my joints ache and my muscles harden.

And it's still *summer*.

I can't imagine surviving an Alaskan winter with my immunity suddenly fading. It's as if finally experiencing heat has revealed the extent of my frigid existence up until this point.

As I slide another loaf of bread into the oven, a memory hits me. That day, all those years ago when I stuck my head in an oven similar to the one in front of me, desperately trying to experience the mysterious sensation.

Is that why I'm so hung up on Quinn? Is she just the final fulfillment of that tactile longing?

The idea has me pausing in the act of stacking dirty dishes. I examine the notion from all angles, poking and prodding at my motives.

But then I imagine finding out that Quinn had somehow lost her powers. If that were to happen, my main worry would be if her non-toasty skin would still find my touch appealing. All I would care about is if she would still want me.

Because I would most definitely still want her.

I crave every bit of her. Her disinterest in placating someone when they're clearly wrong. Her innocently joyful way of approaching new experiences. Her hidden need to protect those around her, even if it's from herself.

I want to watch her solve accounting problems, and I want to listen to her bicker with her sisters. I love how she takes no shit from my family and her willingness to burn off a gorgeous dress to get my attention.

I love her humor.

I love her fierceness.

I love her reluctant trust.

I love her.

And she's hundreds of miles away.

"Damn all the gods," I curse to myself.

Why didn't I tell her before she left? Who cares if the words are heavy?

I should have laid myself bare before her and shown that there was something worth waiting for. Something worth fighting for.

Instead, I told her we'd set up a video chat date.

A promise I haven't even been able to fulfill because my parents' Wi-Fi is as slow as a glacier moving over dry land.

We've talked on the phone, but our schedules don't align well with her taking on a suddenly huge workload and me having to get up so early each morning. The exact reason I'm standing alone in the Nord bakery at four a.m.

I told my parents not to come, just like I told Quinn to go home to Phoenix. Seems I'm great at asking for things I don't want.

A stab of guilt slices through me as I once again think about how much I don't want to be here. It's not that I'm eager to abandon my parents in their time of need. Only, every good thing I was building for myself back in Phoenix seems on the verge of disappearing.

Do my parents need me so badly that it's okay for me to give up all I worked for?

Again, I feel like a shitty son for letting the thought resonate in my mind. To work out my upset, I grab a section of raw dough and knead. The movement is almost meditative and gives me the time I need to think over the future.

One thing I know for sure, I won't be happy here. There were parts of Anchorage and being home that I missed, but after almost two weeks, I'm ready to leave.

I miss the low buildings and palm trees of Phoenix. I want a decent street taco and to see the wavy heat lines rolling off the blacktop when I step outside. The idea of stretching out in a lounge chair next to Damien's pool, holding a cold beer has my mouth watering.

And damn all the gods, I could be in his backyard oasis today if I was back home.

Home. Barely a year in the city, and it's already claimed that title.

It's the place. It's the people.

It's ice cream, and it's Quinn.

I need to go back.

But first, I need to run a bakery for another nine hours.

When I finally lock up at closing time, I'm exhausted. I barely remember driving to my childhood home, letting out a surprised huff as I park in my parent's driveway. My mind wants to shut down, but I pull in a few bracing breaths, pumping some oxygen to my brain, then jog through a dreary rain into the house and search for my mom and dad.

They're both in the kitchen, Dad fixing a sandwich, and Mama tapping the screen of her e-reader.

"Welcome home, honey! How was the business today?" My mother sits up eagerly in her seat, salivating for news. I wonder if this is how I look whenever I'm on the phone with my part-time manager, Denise. Her reports of Land of Ice Cream and Snow are what I expected, though not exactly heartening. I was only able to pre-stock so much product on such short notice. We spoke the day Quinn left, and the plan was to close the shop the next day when the ice cream would run out. That was the last check-in because I haven't had the heart to get back in touch and hear that the doors are locked and the lights are off and there's not an ounce of ice cream to serve.

I'm jittery with the need to return to Phoenix and find a way to recoup my losses. Losing a week of business won't be easy.

"Everything was fine." I give her a rundown of the day, settling my tired bones on the chair across from her and offering my dad a thank you smile when he sets the sandwich in front of me.

When I finish the update and my meal, I lean back in my chair, glancing between my parents and trying to figure out the best way to broach this topic.

"You know I love you both, right?"

My mother's eyebrows raise. "Of course, honey."

"Is something the matter?" Dad asks.

"Not exactly. It's just, I know you need my help here. But...I think I need to go back to Phoenix. Soon."

To my surprise, my dad whoops in joy, and my mom lets out a sigh as she smiles.

"We were wondering how long it'd take you to go," she announces.

"What?"

"If you didn't leave on your own, we were going to evict you," Dad adds.

"Evict me?"

"Yes, but a loving eviction." Mama reaches across the table to pat my hand. "With plenty of baked goods included to soften the blow."

"I'm not sure that makes me feel any better." The shock of their reaction has me too confused to process what this means.

"It should. You know we wanted you to stay close by. We love having you around. Seeing you every day." Now she cups my cheek. "But what kind of parents would we be if we chose what we wanted over you following your dream? And you're doing so well down in Phoenix. We're proud."

"You're not worried about the bakery if I leave?"

"Bones heal. Also," she glares over at my father, "I'm not an invalid."

"You're not going back to work," he grumbles.

"No. Not yet. But *you* are. I don't need you hovering over me every second of the day. And now is a good time to hire another set of hands like we've been talking about. I can train someone fine from this chair."

"I could help." The words are out of my mouth before I consider them.

Mama tilts her chin to stare at me, gazing deep into my eyes. "No.

What I want is for you to help *yourself*. Stick to your decision. Go back to your business. Go back to Quinn. If you stay here, worrying about us, you'll lose them both. And I would never want you to have the heartbreak of losing what you love."

Lose them both.

The idea has me wanting to drive to the airport without bothering to pack my bags. The urge to get to Phoenix as soon as possible is overwhelming. My shop is my dream, but if worse comes to worst, I'd close the place, deal with the debt, and a few years down the line try again. That outcome would be shitty, but manageable.

Quinn is not replaceable. She is one of a kind, and losing her would devastate me.

My Pyro is learning how to control her powers. I could see it, even if she couldn't. A scenario rises in my mind, of her arriving back in Phoenix only to discover how much progress she's made and deciding my icy ass is no longer worth the bother.

I need time to show her I'm more than a cooling agent for her haywire fire.

Does she know that she's more than her heat to me? Is she aware that I'll bend over backwards for the rest of my life just to see that snarky curl to her lips?

Probably not because I was too much of a coward to tell her. Too focused on fixing other people's problems to realize the ones I've caused myself.

If I've lost the cinnamon spiciness that is Quinn, I'm not sure I'll be able to forgive my knee-jerk reaction to help anyone I love who's struggling without thought or planning. When it comes to Quinn, I want to be selfish. I want to put my pursuit of her above everything else. Any guilt that arises at the thought is quickly snuffed out by the memory of her head on my shoulder, her soft snores in my ear, the complete trust she put in me to keep our plane from bursting into flames.

I want to be everything to her. Just like she's everything to me.

Chapter Forty-Two

AUGUST

The sign in the front door of my shop is flipped the wrong way, announcing to the world that Land of Ice Cream and Snow is open.

Things are off to a bad start.

I sigh, trying not to let annoyance and the workload waiting for me put me in too much of a mood. The estimated of lost earnings for this past week makes my skin itch. A whole week of profit gone, and that doesn't include the future ramifications.

Who knows how many people stopped by the shop only to find it closed and decided to get their ice cream at another place down the road? What if they never come back?

I'd like to think my product is good enough to inspire loyalty, but what good is a delicious scoop of ice cream if no one knows when they can get it?

As I climb out of my car, a woman holding the hand of a little kid approaches the front door. I'm about to jog up to meet them, hopefully convince them not to leave without first getting a coupon for a free cone in the future, but I stumble to a stop when she clasps the front handle and opens the door with ease.

The pair disappears inside, leaving me thunderstruck.

My brain tries to make sense of this situation.

I know how much ice cream was in the freezers when I left. Unless business took a massive nosedive, we should have run out a week ago, which is what Denise reported to me last we talked.

Land of Ice Cream and Snow is out of things to sell, yet somehow people are still strolling on in.

"Shit."

This is bad. Like, I'll probably need to fire someone bad. Leaving the shop unlocked? I'll be lucky if I haven't been cleaned out. And not just the money. My equipment is pricey on its own. Took all my savings to purchase it.

Dread scrapes against the inside of my chest. If my equipment is missing, this whole endeavor will be over. Land of Ice Cream and Snow will be done before it really got a chance to start.

I'm already mentally planning my call to the insurance company when I walk in the door, which is why it takes me a moment to acknowledge the sight before me.

My shop is full. And not full of angry, confused people searching for someone working the register. There are families and teenagers and couples filling up all the seats, chattering away to each other, and most importantly, *eating ice cream.*

This doesn't make sense.

The last time I talked to Denise we had maybe two days left of stock. But here I am, a week after that conversation, watching the proof she was wrong.

Could her estimate really have been that far off?

My attention shifts and my shock amplifies when I hear an overly charming, all too familiar voice at the front counter.

"This is our back to the basics week, lovely. Simplified flavors and extraordinary taste. What can I get you a scoop of? Or would you like me to choose for you?"

Sammy is at the register. Sammy is wearing an apron. Sammy is leaning on the counter, flirting with a woman who must be pushing eighty.

Why is Sammy working at my shop?

I hover by the entrance, watching as my cousin scoops what looks to be a cup of chocolate ice cream and hands it off to the woman with a wink, cheerfully accepting her dollar bills. With the way clear, I move forward until I'm standing across from him, still not fully comprehending what I'm seeing.

"August! You're back!" The Squid leans across the counter to clap me on the shoulder.

"What am I looking at right now?" I ask, drowning in confusion.

Maybe I fell asleep on the plane, and this is a weird dream.

My cousin hooks his thumbs in the straps of his apron, wearing his signature cocky grin. "You're looking at your handsomest cashier to date."

"My...what? What are you doing here?"

"Working, obviously." Sammy acts as if this is the most normal thing in the world.

I think my brain is about to explode.

"You're working in my shop? Behind my register?"

"Yeah, well, Marisol is too busy making ice cream to sell it. Plus, I think your customers like me more. Isn't that right ladies?" His eyes land over my shoulder, and I turn to see a group of girls gathered behind me, all wearing tank tops with what seem to be sorority letters. They're clearly waiting for their turn at the counter. At Sammy's question, a few of them flush, and there are giggles all around.

And I'm still trying to figure out what alternate universe I'm in.

"Marisol is—"

"In the back. Making ice cream, like I said. Go see for yourself and let me get back to work." He shakes his head as if disappointed in me. "So unprofessional, Auggie."

I don't know whether to freeze his shoes to the floor or give him a hug. Walking away is the best choice until I figure out what's going on.

When I enter the kitchen, I discover that Sammy wasn't pulling some strange prank on me. Marisol stands in front of the stovetop, stirring a steaming pot, adding ingredients into the mixture as Damien reads them from one of my handwritten recipes.

"There. I think those measurements are correct. Now it needs to get to the right temperature. Fingers crossed this tastes halfway decent."

The young Squid adjusts her hairnet and reaches for a thermometer, only then catching sight of me.

"August! Oh thank the gods." Marisol grins, but then the expression morphs into wariness as her eyes bounce to the stove then back to me. "So, I know this looks strange..."

"It looks like you've been making ice cream," I point out.

"She's been working her ass off, August." Damien comes to his sister's defense immediately, as if he thought I'd be mad about this discovery.

"I'm confused." My eyes feel raw as I rub a palm over them. "Can someone please tell me what's going on here?"

"We didn't want your shop to close down, but we were running out of ice cream. So when we got to the end of what you had made, I took over." Marisol gives me a hopeful smile. "I've been doing the basics. Ones you already showed me. Chocolate, vanilla, and coffee. Today, I thought I'd give mint chocolate chip a go." Her hand gestures to the cooking pot she's still stirring.

"That's..." No words can describe the rush of gratefulness that infuses my entire being at this discovery. I settle for the closest I can get. "Incredible. You're incredible."

Marisol and Damien smile, the expressions revealing how similar their faces are. A small family that I suddenly feel a part of. Still, as my mind struggles to comprehend this enormous feat of friendship, more questions arise.

"But...ingredients. Supplies. Where ...?"

"Go check your office." Marisol waves me away, her hesitation gone. Looks like I might have a regular partner in my kitchen.

Check my office? The mystery of this story grows.

I leave the Squids running my shop, showing more confidence in them than I ever expected to. Which is a reflection on me and how little I'm willing to trust my friends.

I'm getting a lesson today.

A beam of light spills out across the hallway from the cracked office door. For some reason, I slow down, stepping quietly and pushing the door open with a careful movement. I want to see what is happening inside before my presence disturbs the scene.

There's no wild mess waiting for me, as if someone tore through my records trying to find helpful information. Instead, I walk in on what is now becoming one of my favorite scenes.

Quinn at work.

She's behind my desk, and despite the fact that she's slimmer and shorter than I am, I doubt I've ever looked so in command of the surface. Her crimson hair sits piled on top of her head in a messy bun. Little wisps curl out around her ears and glow in the lamp light. Those sexy, red-rimmed glasses have slid down to the tip of her nose as she splits her attention between a pile of receipts and the computer monitor. The light from the screen illuminates her riot of freckles.

For a time, I watch her. When she originally came to my shop, back when all I could call her was a freelance employee, I wanted to sit in this room and admire her while she worked. But that would have been creepy and inappropriate. Now, finally, I get my wish, and I'm not ready to give it up.

But the decision isn't up to me.

Something must have alerted her to my presence. Maybe the sudden drop of temperature in the room. Whatever it was, her head jerks up, and she lets out a gasp of shock, clutching her chest as she does.

"Goddess! August? You're here?"

"I am."

On the flight home, I wondered at what kind of reception I might receive. I never expected to show up at my shop and find my family and friends hard at work. And nothing could have warned me that I'd find Quinn in my office, balancing my receipts.

But that's all business related. How will she greet me?

I don't have to wait long.

My lovely Pyro shoves herself up from her chair and sprints around the desk, all to crash into me. Like that day beside the pool, she jumps and wraps limbs around my torso, our bodies pressed tight together in a way I hope will never end. The main difference in this embrace is that she doesn't try to cover my eyes. Instead, she cups the back of my head and devours my mouth in a scalding kiss.

A groan spills from my chest without thought. My hands grab her ass, pulling her closer to me. I can't get enough. She's sweet and spicy and I want to lick every inch of her.

But just as my pants start getting tight, Quinn rips her mouth from mine.

"Put me down. I need to get down. Now."

Despite the intense urge to keep her close to me, I loosen my arms and let her go.

Quinn stumbles back until she collides with my heavy wooden desk. Her hands reach back to grip the oak, her knuckles turning white with the strength of her hold.

"Are you...is something wrong?" I plant my hands on my hips, trying to stop them from reaching for her.

Quinn's chest rises and falls in rapid pants, and she has her eyes shut tight as if guarding them against a glare.

"Too hot. You're too gods damned hot. This has only been working because you weren't here. And I missed—" She cuts herself off, with a shake of her head. "Give me a second."

"Whatever you need."

"No." Quinn's growled response surprises me, and I once again earn her fiery gaze. Only now I might go so far as to say she appears angry with me.

"I'm sorry?" Her sudden shifts are hard to keep up with, and I'm wondering how many more wrong steps I'll make.

"I said *no*. Not whatever *I* need. You're always doing what other people need." The anger leaves her eyes as her arms relax down to her sides. "What do *you* need August? That's why we're all here." She waves behind me as if to include the Squids in her point. "Because we want to help."

"Yeah. My shop. You're all helping run my shop." For some reason, I think speaking the words out loud will make sense of this situation I came home to. But I'm still lost. "How did I not know this was going on?"

Quinn cringes. "That's my fault. Or my decision. I asked Marisol and Denise not to tell you. I thought if you knew what we were trying then you'd feel obligated to manage remotely. Or that we'd make you feel guilty for being away. I wanted to see if we could keep things going here while you gave all your headspace to helping your parents."

"That's...but money. My bank accounts. You don't—"

"No! No, I have no idea how to get into your accounts." She turns, rifling through a few folders on the desk until she comes up with a blue one. From it, she slips a piece of paper. "I used my money. Like a loan. I wrote this up. A contract for you to pay me back, as long as we didn't ruin all the supplies we bought. But Marisol has been doing a kickass job."

Quinn extends the contract to me, and I already know I'm going to sign it even if I find out all the supplies they bought caught on fire.

"This is...too much." Now I'm positive this has to be a dream.

"Well, too bad. I already did it. And I'd do it again." The Pyro stands tall, hands on her hips, brows slanted in adorable determination. "As long as we're together, I'm going to take care of you as much as you take care of me. What you need matters. And if you won't ask for help, the people who care about you will still try to figure out a way to be there for you."

"Quinn." Her words have my chest clenching with an onslaught of emotions. "This is what I need. You. My shop. This life I've started building here. That's why I'm here now. My parents can manage. But if I lose all this, I'm not sure that I can. If I lose you..."

The idea has me panicking, and I step toward her.

She reaches a hand out to stop me. "Marisol has worked so hard. I don't want to melt it all."

"You won't though." Gods, she's so amazing and she doesn't know. "Haven't you realized yet?"

"Realized what?"

I take another deliberate step forward. "How much control you've gained."

Quinn's mouth pops open as if to deny my claim, but then her gaze turns inward. I can bet she's examining her power, trying to discover if I'm speaking the truth. After a moment, she frowns up at me.

"I still can't tell."

"That's okay." I shove my hands in my pockets and instruct myself to be satisfied with staring at her for the moment. "We can go somewhere else, and I'll show you. Or better yet"—my voice deepens—"you'll show me."

"August!" The pale skin under her freckles is fading into the same shade as her hair. "You have a business to run."

Damn it. She's right.

"Fine. For the next few hours, I'll be responsible. But the minute the shop closes, I want to take you somewhere you're comfortable getting naked."

Chapter Forty-Three

QUINN

"Oh, goddess!" The ice man of my dreams has his head between my legs, his tongue performing talented, wicked tricks. The sheets on my bed steam, but so far nothing has caught fire.

Does this mean August is right?

The memory of the confidence in his tone earlier helps ease my fears, and I can finally lose myself in the heady sensations of a man worshiping my clit. Tingles skitter over my sensitive skin to the point that I'm not sure I'll ever be able to put clothing on again. My back against the soft mattress overwhelms my nerve endings.

Suddenly, August wraps his cool strong arms around my thighs and flips onto his back. Now, I sit on top, straddling his glorious face, losing my mind at the drag of his scruff against my over-stimulated flesh.

His rough hand palms my ass, encouraging me to rock. With my fingers clawing at the sheets, I ride his face until I'm whimpering his name, on the verge of crying from the ecstasy of his tongue devouring me like I'm a decadent dessert.

My climax hits and words fail me. An inarticulate moan accompanies the pulsing of pleasure, and I barely register August sliding me off his face and moving to cradle me in his arms.

When the lusty fog clears from my mind, it's to find the Viking of a man gently kissing the thousands of freckles on my cheeks.

"You'll never get them all," I mumble, fighting a smile. "There's too many."

August runs his nose along my hairline, then nips my ear. "We've got time."

We do. I spread my hand over his peck, fascinated with the patches of frost that still remain on his skin.

"I missed you." Only a few days apart, and the one thing that kept me from spiraling was the mission of saving August's shop.

"I love you," he whispers against my hair. Despite the quiet way he speaks the words, I feel them hit my body harder than a lightning bolt, frying my insides. I'm a crispy Pyro, reeling from a confession of love.

"Because...I'm hot?" Anyone else would think I'm talking about my looks. But he knows.

August pulls me tight against him, running his cool hands over my back.

"Your heat lets me get close to you. But I love you because you're fierce and sweet and funny. When I'm around you, I get the sense that I've found my home." His nose brushes against mine. "I'd love you the same if you were a human, trust me."

Trust him?

Suddenly, I realize that's the easiest thing in the world to do.

"I believe you. Hell. I'm in love with you, too, you giant delicious ice cream god. I've never met someone as kind and strong as you. I know Phoenix isn't a beautiful winter wonderland like Alaska, but I want you to stay here more than anything."

"Quinn." The stern tone August uses has me tilting my head up so I can meet his eyes. "I never wanted to leave. This is where I belong."

Need erupts under my skin and next thing I know, I'm straddling his lap, sinking onto his perfect, hard cock, fucking the brains out of the man I love. August grunts with his thrusts, each guttural noise ratcheting up the fire in my veins until I'm sure if I were to cut myself, I'd bleed pure lava.

My orgasm rips through me and I scream, my back bowing, the icy man between my thighs cooling my feverish skin. The next second he's groaning deep, pressing his forehead against my collarbone as he pumps into me, the slickness of his pleasure spilling over.

The experience is decadent, and I can't wait to repeat every bit of it.

As we lay in the bed, tangled up together, panting like marathon runners, I grin so wide, my jaw cracks.

August loves me. I have an ice god all my own. A man who is a good person but also supernaturally good in bed.

My eyes drift around the room as I catch my breath.

And that's when I realize that nothing is on fire. There's not a single scorch mark.

The sheets are perfectly intact.

"I'm sorry," I say as I stand, not even taking a moment to revel in the slow slide of him leaving my body. "I need to check something." Without waiting for a response, I sprint to the main room where the thermostat hangs on the wall.

Seventy nine degrees.

We normally have it set to seventy eight. If I affected the climate at all, it was only by one degree. Still needing more evidence, I rush to the freezer and tug it open. A half-eaten carton of ice cream sits inside, and when I pull the lid off, I peer down at a solid mass of dessert.

"Maybe we should revisit the idea of fucking in my shop if you need ice cream this bad afterwards," a voice tinged with laughter suggests.

I whirl around to find that August has trailed after me. He stands in the middle of the room, completely naked, dick at half-mast.

"Look! It's still frozen!" I thrust the container into his chest, my excitement wild and uncaring at this point.

Comprehension dawns on August's face, and he gives me a sweet smile. "So it is."

"How much did you help?" My confidence from a second ago is wavering.

He tilts his head, watching me. "I didn't. I mean, I kept my mind on it when I was eating you out." His dirty words have me shivering. "But nothing happened. Then, admittedly, you saying you loved me and riding me like that ..." Frost spiderwebs over his skin. I want to lick it.

And I can.

With August, I don't have to be afraid.

An idea forms, and I shove the ice cream back in the freezer. "Would you mind helping me test this out? Right now?"

His grin is cocky, and I find I love the look of confidence on my man. "You want to go another round?"

I strut past him, clucking my tongue. "Not exactly. Put your briefs on. *Only* your briefs."

A few minutes later, I'm standing outside, dressed in a Land of Ice Cream and Snow T-Shirt I stole from his office. The closed sliding glass door separates me from August. He waits in my living room, watching me, a smile curving the corner of his mouth, strong hands resting on his hips. The fire smolders under my skin, but the chill of his power also brushes over me. Everything remains balanced.

I wave, and he takes a couple of steps back. The coolness dims, and my heat grows as my eyes linger on his bare chest. But the warmth doesn't spill out uncontrolled. So I take some time to play with the power. I open my palm and allow small flames to trickle over my fingers.

We repeat this, August moving backwards and me studying and manipulating the fire as his power's presence fades. Once he reaches the farthest point in the house where I can still see him, all chill is gone. The fire presses at my skin, wanting out.

But I don't let it.

When I beam at August through the glass, his lips twitch. It's the only warning I get before his thumbs slide into the waistband of his boxers and he drags them off.

I swallow, practically drooling at the sight.

With the view of a gloriously naked ice cream god stroking his quickly growing erection, the heat pulses in strong, heavy beats through my veins. Flames gather in my palms, bright and hot.

But my T-shirt doesn't catch fire. Neither does the stack of towels on the pool chair, nor the cloth umbrella standing a few feet away. Not even when I notice a bead of moisture at the tip of him, which he swipes with a thumb and rubs over his swollen head.

The sight has me panting. Burning.

But not out of control.

One more step, one more test, and I'll know I've mastered my Elemental heritage.

Slowly, flames still flickering between my fingers, I slide my hand under the hem of my shirt. August's stare follows my gesture, his heavy jaw tightening, ice blooming over his skin like winter flowers.

My curls tease my palm, sparking as if I were a live wire. When my touch makes contact with that perfect little bundle of nerves, my knees almost buckle, and I swear, I see August's lips form a curse.

Pleasure rolls through me in time with my strokes. My eyes flutter, my muscles quiver, my heat rises.

But my fire keeps close to my skin, listening when I kindly ask it to. As if I've finally learned the intricate language needed to converse with the magic of my soul.

I have it under control.

As I grin in triumph, a soothing coolness trickles over my senses in time with the slide of the glass door opening.

August stalks toward me, ravenous gaze focused on my playful hand as I continue to touch myself.

"My turn," he growls, sweeping my legs out from under me.

We end up sprawled on a poolside lounge chair, tangled together. As I straddle August's hips, he thrusts into me and sucks on one of my taut nipples through my shirt.

We fuck fast, hard, and full of joy. After we finish, both of us lie, panting, our heavy breathing mixing with the sounds of the cicadas that fill the evening air.

Then, before I've fully recovered, August lifts me up again. Only, this time, the bastard walks us straight into the pool.

I get out one surprised shriek before the water envelops my head. When I come up for breath, I discover a laughing August.

"You're dead!" I pounce, and a wrestling match ensues with ample dunking and splashing and giggling.

A piercing whistle has me pausing in the act of scaling August's back. When I glance to the side of the pool, I find both of my sisters watching us. Harley lowers her fingers from her lips, smirking all the while. Cat wears a more chagrined smile, making an effort to avert her eyes.

August's hands quickly dive beneath the surface to cover himself.

"So you finally got laid?" Harley asks.

I'm too happy to let my big sister's crassness bother me. Instead, I give her a middle-finger wave while wearing a self-satisfied grin.

"Damn right I did. And if you're hoping to see me erupt into unplanned fireballs in the future, you're going to be sorely disappointed."

My younger sister gives a supportive cheer as she tosses a towel our way. August does his best to wrap the soggy material around his waist as a deep chuckle rumbles through his back. The sound vibrates against my chest, and the water around us begins to steam.

Harley hooks a companionable arm around Cat's shoulders, guiding her toward the house. "Hear that? Now we can finally have half-naked men around the house. Thank the goddess."

Epilogue

AUGUST

One month later

"I can't believe Damien continues to invite back this many potentially cosmically destructive beings in his house at one time. Harley is lucky I even let her near where I live. Much less hold an entire kegger of Elementals." Quinn presses into my side as she stares out over the Sunday gathering.

Her concern is understandable. Now that I've joined the party, every sect of Elemental is present.

Squids, Petal Pushers, Air Heads, Stoners, Pyros and—

"Snow Cone!" Harley strolls up to us, expertly carrying multiple beers in her splayed fingers. "One of these is yours if you use your iciness to give 'em a good chill."

The eldest Byrne sister has declared that Ice Elementals shall henceforth be known as Snow Cones. At first I was put out. I make ice cream. A culinary art form. I don't peddle shaved ice out of a cart that you just dump flavored syrup on top of.

Quinn then pointed out that she didn't start fires for fun and my cousin doesn't spray ink out of his ass when he's irritated. All the code names are slightly insulting, and I got off pretty easy.

"She could've picked Snowflake or Santa Claus or something worse. Believe me, she has an evil, inventive mind."

I've decided to embrace the nickname. Especially because it means I'm part of this increasingly tightknit supernatural group. One more member of this massive family.

"Sure thing," I say to Harley, accepting a bottle for myself and one for Quinn, scoping out my girlfriend's ass to make the chill easy to manipulate. Frost speckles the glass of the bottles. Harley gives a finger wave of thanks as she saunters away.

As I sip on my beer, I catch sight of Damien flipping burgers on a grill on the opposite side of the yard. He's got a massive amount of meat cooking, ready to feed the entire gathering of close to thirty people.

"Damien's kind of paternal," I point out, nodding his way, and Quinn follows my eye line. "I think he likes giving our kind a safe place to just exist. I'm not sure we've ever had something like this before."

I found that out almost immediately upon moving here. In this backyard oasis, I'm safe. We're all safe.

"Hmm. I guess you're right. I never thought of these as more than parties, but I'm so used to hearing all the college-Damien stories. The guy's grown up." Quinn traces the fingers of her free hand over the back of mine where it rests on her hip. "That's really sweet. Him doing this for us all. Showing us we're not alone in the world. That we don't have to turn into secretive, magical hermits."

I grin at both her comment and the teasing way she strokes me.

"Don't let him hear you say he's sweet. Pretty sure he's still trying to cling to a little bit of his bad boy cred from the old days."

Quinn snorts before taking a long pull from her drink.

But a moment later, her relaxed demeanor stiffens.

"What's up?" I keep my voice low in case she doesn't want other people to know about whatever the issue is.

"What? Oh, just...I think things might get a little dramatic here in a moment. We have a new player on the field." With a hot hand pressed to my side, she shifts me to face the porch. "You see that? Over there?"

Quinn gestures toward the doorway that leads from Damien's kitchen to the backyard.

A man walks out, slim build, skin tanned by more than the sun, with brown hair lightened in places to an almost gold color. He looks familiar, and I realize I've seen him in a few pictures at Sammy's place. A childhood friend. Another Elemental.

"That? You mean the new Squid?"

"*That's* the reason Cat goes into a rage whenever she's around these guys."

"I thought it was because Sammy is always teasing her." I love my cousin, but he's far from perfect.

"Well, that doesn't help. But no. That," she jerks her chin toward the new guy, "is the only thing I've seen fully demolish Cat's sweet exterior."

"So we're supposed to hate him?"

Quinn taps her beer against her bottom lip, considering my question. "You know, I think I'm going to hold off on my judgment."

"Really? I have to admit, I thought you'd be more protective."

Quinn shrugs. "Sometimes people need protecting from themselves. Besides, we haven't seen the guy in years. People change."

"You mean, like becoming a badass at controlling their fire powers and falling madly in love with a Snow Cone? That kind of change?"

My girlfriend's lips pinch together, and she makes a big production of peering around the yard. "You think he fell in love with a Snow Cone? Where're they hiding?"

"Smartass," I mutter, leaning down to steal a kiss while palming said ass.

Quinn laughs against my lips, tasting better than the drink in my hand.

For the next few minutes, we banter with each other, flirt in our little bubble while the BBQ exists as a joyful whirlwind around us.

But after swallowing the last bit of her beer, Quinn abandons me for the bathroom. As I make my way around the pool, considering if I want to ask for a burger or hot dog off the grill, a small hot hand grabs my arm.

"I need you, August!" Cat's whisper is low and desperate. She presses her back to mine, and when I stare straight in front of me, I catch sight of the Squid Quinn pointed out earlier and realize I'm the only thing between the youngest Byrne sister and the guy from their past.

"Please, just be a wall," she begs.

"Um, sure. I can do that." There's not much I wouldn't do for Quinn's family, plus Cat has an air of innocence that hangs around her. Makes people want to keep her safe.

"Good. You're the best."

After a second of deliberation, I take a chance. "Can I ask why you need a wall?"

She keeps quiet, and I wonder if I'll get an answer. Now that I'm with Quinn, I find myself more and more interested in the little quirks of her family. Which means I'm fascinated by this unknown history between Cat and a mystery Squid.

"That guy over there." She tilts her head. "His name is Rafael. We don't get along."

Rafael. The name sparks a memory, and I remember Quinn's story on the flight to Alaska. About a Squid family they were neighbors with while growing up. A boy named Rafael who was friends with Cat.

I guess that didn't last.

"He's mean to you?" I ask.

"I have no idea how he'll be to me. But I know how *I'll* be to him. And if we throw Sammy into the mix, it's not out of the realm of possibility that I'll start a fire somewhere. Possibly on the roof of Damien's house."

"Really?" Pyros are fascinating.

"Not on purpose."

"Of course not."

"But it could get out of hand."

"Can't have that."

"No. We cannot."

"Do you want me to help you escape?" I glance over my shoulder in time to see Cat scowl. "Sorry, is that not what you want?"

"I want..." She trails off, and I watch in wonder as the normally cheerful, helpful, caring Cat grinds her teeth in anger as steam rises from her short red hair. "I want to not care."

Ah. Been there before.

"That's tougher than escaping."

She grimaces up at me, but then the expression morphs into something more rueful. "He makes me feel like a child. And now I'm acting like one, hiding behind you."

"You know"—I shift so I'm not craning my neck to look at her—"everyone gets pissed off sometimes. That doesn't make you immature. If you want me to keep an eye on your heat so there are no disastrous side effects, I can do that. Same as I did with Quinn in the beginning. Everyone should be allowed to feel how they feel."

Cat stares up at me, eyes wide. A slight shine overtakes her gaze before she blinks it away.

"You're a good guy, August. I'm glad you're part of our family."

Shit. Her words are a gut shot to my heart, and I get the sudden urge to heave this guy Rafael over the fence and out of Cat's life.

But she takes a bracing breath and squares her shoulders. "I think I've got this, but yeah. If you could be my backup, I'd appreciate that." And with a straight spine, Cat strolls away from me, not sparing a glance for the Squid from her past. Her entire focus is on a corn hole game happening in a sandy area up against the privacy fence. I silently cheer her on as she dons an almost visible cloak of confidence.

Unfortunately, it's at that moment that the asshole spots her.

I see it, the way the guy goes still, his mouth slack, eyes wide under the rim of his baseball hat. Rafael leans toward the little Pyro before his feet move, as if she's the sun and he's some dinky asteroid sucked into her orbit.

Damn it. It's pretty obvious the douche bag wants her.

This is going to make things complicated.

"Cat!" the Squid calls out, circling the pool to reach her.

Her confident stride from a second ago falters, and she whirls faster than a panicked rabbit.

The guy, Rafael, jogs toward her with a hopeful grin on his face. "Hey, Cat. I wanted—"

We don't get to find out what he wanted because the moment he's within reaching distance of her, the woman's arms shoot out. The movement is so fast, I doubt anyone could've stopped it. One second the

Squid is on dry land, expression all happy and hopeful, the next he's a messy splash in the pool.

"What the hell?" My girlfriend is back in time to catch the drama.

"Quinn!" Cat says her sister's name with a tinge of desperation coloring her voice.

Understanding flashes in her eyes. "Get out of here." Quinn is already palming a set of car keys. She tosses them, her sister snatching the keychain out of the air and jogging to the exit.

"Cat! Wait!" The Squid is at the edge of the pool, hoisting himself from the water, eyes locked on the retreating redhead. He might have been fast enough to catch her, too.

That is, if it weren't for Harley.

"Not gonna happen, fucker." The announcement comes as the oldest Byrne sister places her heeled sandal in the center of Rafael's chest and shoves him back into the pool before he's halfway out.

What shocks me the most is the glare on the woman's normally smiling face. I may not have known Harley long, but I've found she enjoys interacting with the world with a raunchy style of humor the majority of the time. I don't think I've ever seen her angry.

Right now, though, she's pissed off.

As Harley struts away, back toward the house, likely to make sure her sister's getaway is successful, the Pyro bends her arm behind her back, throwing Rafael the middle finger.

Quinn leans into my side, smirking as the Squid slaps the water and mutters a string of curses.

"What happened to protecting Cat from herself?" I ask out of curiosity more than judgment.

My girlfriend shrugs. "That doesn't mean forcing her to be around him. Especially because he has a lot of amends to make before he has a chance of deserving my little sister."

I nod, wondering how long I'll have to wait before I hear the story of their falling out.

But I don't push. We've got time.

"You ready to be a part of this?" Quinn wraps her arm around my waist, her touch warmer than the sun on my shoulders.

I'm not sure if she's asking about her fiery family or the no doubt drama-filled world of Elementals in Phoenix.

Either way, the answer is the same.

"Nowhere else I want to be."

Thank you for reading! Did you enjoy? Please add your review because nothing helps an author more and encourages readers to take a chance on a book than a review.

And don't miss book two of the *Casual Magic* series, EARTH MAGIC & HOT WATER, available now. Turn the page for a sneak peek!

You can also sign up for the City Owl Press newsletter to receive notice of all book releases!

Sneak Peek of Earth Magic & Hot Water

CAT

My wig itches, and once again I silently curse the man who made me wear it. The jellyfish exhibit at the local aquarium is supposed to be my happy place, but today the need to scratch thwarts the marine animals' relaxing powers. I sneak a finger under the false hairline, searching for the irritating spot.

I never used to wear a wig to the aquarium. This building was always my haven. Now, I'm forced to don a disguise if I want any chance of finding peace in the dim rooms lit only by the blue glow of fish tanks.

After my finger finds and scratches the itch, I sigh in relief, resettling into my casual stance in front of a round window that peers into the jellyfish enclosure. A mushroom-shaped head leisurely pulses, dragging spindly string legs in an arc through the water. I try to match my breathing to each of the movements, easing my anger to a simmer, hoping to extinguish the harsh emotion fully.

"Are they really made from jelly?"

The high-pitched voice at my elbow has me flinching back a step. I thought I was alone in this room in the early afternoon of a Tuesday, or at least alone in front of this display. But a little girl stares up at me, beads clacking together on the ends of her tight braids, as she watches my retreat.

She's a cute kid: gap where she's missing a front tooth, rounded cheeks, and curious brown eyes a few shades darker than her skin, except for where someone painted a mermaid on her face.

People always assume I'm good with children. I think it's the combination of being a short, soft-spoken—for the most part—woman in prime birthing years, but I know *zero* about what to do with them. Or how to talk to them. I was the youngest of my siblings, and neither of my sisters have any offspring that would force me to improve my skills.

If I had candy, I'd consider throwing some treats to distract her as I hustle away. But my pockets are empty.

At least this child isn't screaming, or crying, or trying to grab me with sticky fingers. She stands still, her eyes going back to the glass to watch the beautiful aquatic dance.

I could answer her question. There's no harm in that.

"Well, not exactly. Jellyfish have three layers. The epidermis, the mesoglea, and the gastrodermis. The mesoglea is jelly-like, but not the kind of jelly you eat," I say, using the same tone I'd tell a drunk customer at my job they're getting cut off. The tone says, *Look how nice I am! Please don't yell at me.*

"Wow." The girl steps closer, peering at the jellyfish from a different angle. "What do they eat?"

Again, it's a simple enough question to answer, so I list off a few items on a jellyfish's menu.

"Mommy says they sting, but it's all wet and squishy."

Not really a question. Still, I start to explain about venom, until a yelp cuts me off.

"Shay! There you are. Oh my god, I've been looking everywhere." A woman jogs across the room, going straight to the girl and scooping her up as if perching the kid on her hip is the most natural action in the world. Not sure I could manage that move, so it's a good thing I had no plans on trying.

"Aunty Mo, did you know jellyfish are made of jelly you can't eat?" The girl points to the creature.

"That's nice, baby, but you can't go running off on me like that. I didn't know where you were." While she scolds her niece, the breathless woman offers me a grateful smile, as if I helped her when, really, I just answered a few of the kid's questions. The fact that my first thought was to throw candy and run, rather than asking her about adult supervision, is one more indication babysitting is not the job for me.

"I didn't run. I walked. And I was here," the girl, Shay, says in a completely rational tone that has me fighting a snort of amusement. Even the woman, Aunty Mo, presses her lips together as if to suppress a laugh. I can see small traces of relation between the two in the shape of their noses and color of their eyes.

"Still, we need to stick together in here." The adult meets my eyes. "Thanks for looking after her." She doesn't give me time to point out that I didn't, really, before she's shifting to the side and talking to someone else. "And thank you for helping me look. Sorry I got so frazzled."

My instinct is to turn and find out who the fourth is in this sudden grouping, but my muscles weld into an immovable mass at the sound of a smooth, flirty voice.

"No problem at all. I'm happy to help."

Oh no.

He's here. Right here. A few inches behind me, here.

The reason for my wig.

Time to discover if my itchy disguise does the job I suffer constant scratching for.

Aunty Mo says something else to the man, but my mind is so focused on unlocking rigid joints and taking careful, casual steps to the side that I don't register a single word. His responding chuckle, though—that rolls through my body, touching each one of my nerve endings.

Don't shiver. Don't even breathe. Don't let a drop of blood fall in the water if you want to escape this shark.

Luckily, the room we're in is circular, with multiple halls branching off. I only need to shuffle a few more feet, and I can retreat like the coward I am.

No, I silently chastise myself. *I am not a coward. Anywhere else, I would be the shark, and tear his handsome head off. But I* cannot *get angry here.*

I'm only a couple steps from freedom when a shout fills the dimly lit space. "Lady! Your phone! You dropped it. Aunty Mo, she dropped it."

What hell dimension am I in!? I silently wail to myself.

Time to prioritize. Who even needs a phone anyway? We're all glued to a screen for most of our lives, the constantly glowing glass killing our eyes and our souls.

Let's everyone drop our phones and never, ever pick them up again.

But just as I've come to terms with my off-the-grid lifestyle and brace to sprint from the room, a body blocks my way.

Eyes on the tile floor, I take in his shoes first: brown, polished, laced and tied neatly. Not at all dangerous. The treachery comes when I drag my gaze upward. Muscular calves, wonderfully formed thighs, all shamelessly on display in a set of khakis that look painted on. Equally form-fitting is his white polo, with the stitched logo of Saltwater Oasis.

Is it even legal to wear such tight clothing? Is this how immaculate conception happens?

Everyone with functioning ovaries must merely look at him, and they're fertilized through the divine power of his sculpted body.

If I walk out of this aquarium pregnant, I will be *so* pissed.

I take juvenile pleasure in the fact that this sculpted specimen of a man fails to claim the coveted six-foot-and-over category most guys seem to desire. Unfortunately, because he stands at a respectable five-eight or so, my eyes reach his face faster.

Loose curls the color of cola brush skin tanned by genetics and the heat of the sun. Gray eyes—a hypnotizing shade I've never been capable of erasing from my memory, no matter how hard I try—burn through all my protective layers, despite having walls fashioned from firmer material than jelly.

Rafael Aguado gapes at me, recognition unhindered by my itchy faux hair.

Note to self: wear a masquerade mask next time.

A grin crashes across his face, so joyous I gasp in my next breath.

"Cat." He sighs my name, as if enjoying the taste of the letters on his lips.

My body has the opposite reaction. I'm wrenched back to fourteen, to another time he stared into my eyes and spoke my name—only then, my now ex-best friend wielded words against me like a weapon. Years have passed since that night, but still I feel the phantom of past tears running down my cheeks and shame flushing through me, heating the watery tracks until they dried in salty riverbeds across my skin.

The fire magic living in my veins rises in a dangerous pulse.

"No," I hiss, as I snatch my forgotten phone out of his loose fingers and shove him aside.

I need to get out of here.

Don't stop now. Keep reading with your copy of <u>EARTH MAGIC &</u>
<u>HOT WATER</u> available now.

And visit www.laurenconnollyromance.com to keep up with the latest
news where you can subscribe to the newsletter for contests, giveaways,
new releases, and more.

Don't miss book two of the *Casual Magic* series, EARTH MAGIC & HOT WATER, available now, and find more from Lauren Connolly at www.laurenconnollyromance.com

Her first hate and first love are back in town. Things are about to get heated...

Cat Byrne seems sweet, but she's hiding a volcanic temper. Her anger-fueled fire magic can melt tires off cars. Then her ex-best friend moves back to town, and the guy keeps popping up in inconvenient places, making sure she's running at a constant simmer.

Rafael Aguado hopes to calm the waters between him and Cat, but that's hard to do when she'd rather see him boil alive. Maybe the water elemental could cool her off with time, but he has romantic competition. Rafael lost Cat to a handsome earth elemental years ago, and he refuses to let his rival win again. Even if it means kissing the hell out of the magical man to throw him off balance.

Aspen Baumann's last relationship taught him an important lesson: never settle for less. Determined to have both the people he wants in his bed, the earth elemental attempts to regrow the bond between the estranged pair—with him rooted directly in the middle.

Hopefully, enough indecently steamy encounters can wash away past mistakes...

Please sign up for the City Owl Press newsletter for chances to win special subscriber-only contests and giveaways as well as receiving information on upcoming releases and special excerpts.

All reviews are **welcome** and **appreciated**. Please consider leaving one on your favorite social media and book buying sites.

For books in the world of romance and speculative fiction that embody Innovation, Creativity, and Affordability, check out City Owl Press at www.cityowlpress.com.

Acknowledgments

This story is years in the making, and I want to thank my beta readers, my agent Lesley, and the team at City Owl Press for all helping bring Quinn and August to the page. Thank you to my family for supporting me along the way. And most of all, thank you ice cream. You make everything, especially romance novels, better.

About the Author

LAUREN CONNOLLY is an author of romance stories set in the contemporary world. Some are grounded in reality, while others play with the mystical and magical. She has a day job as an academic librarian in southern Colorado, where she lives outnumbered by animals. Her furry family consists of a cocker spaniel who thinks he's a cave dwelling troll and two cats with a mission to raise hell and destroy all curtains. It should come as no surprise that each one is a rescue.

www.laurenconnollyromance.com

facebook.com/LaurenConnollyRomance

twitter.com/laurenaliciaCon

instagram.com/laurenconnollyromance

About the Publisher

City Owl Press is a cutting edge indie publishing company, bringing the world of romance and speculative fiction to discerning readers.

Escape Your World. Get Lost in Ours!

www.cityowlpress.com

facebook.com/CityOwlPress
twitter.com/cityowlpress
instagram.com/cityowlbooks
pinterest.com/cityowlpress
tiktok.com/@cityowlpress

Printed in Great Britain
by Amazon

28299576R00158